SKIN TRADE

REGGIE NADELSON

arrow books

Published in the United Kingdom by Arrow Books, 2006

1 3 5 7 9 10 8 6 4 2

First published under the title *Sex Dolls* in the United Kingdom in 2002 by Faber and Faber, London

Arrow Books
The Random House Group Limited
20 Vauxhall Bridge Road, London, SW1V 2SA

Random House Australia (Pty) Limited
20 Alfred Street, Milsons Point, Sydney
New South Wales 2061, Australia

Random House New Zealand Limited
18 Poland Road, Glenfield
Auckland 10, New Zealand

Random House (Pty) Limited
Isle of Houghton, Corner of Boundary Road & Carse O'Gowrie
Houghton 2198, South Africa

The Random House Group Limited Reg. No. 954009

www.randomhouse.co.uk

A CIP catalogue record for this book
is available from the British Library

Papers used by Random House
are natural, recyclable products made from wood grown in
sustainable forests. The manufacturing processes conform to
the environmental regulations of the country of origin

ISBN 0 0994 97840

Typeset by SX Composing DTP, Rayleigh, Essex
Printed and bound in Great Britain by
Cox & Wyman Ltd, Reading, Berkshire

SKIN TRADE

A journalist and documentary film maker, Reggie Nadelson is a New Yorker who also makes her home in London. She is the author of seven novels featuring the detective Artie Cohen ('the detective every woman would like to find in her bed' *Guardian*), most recently *Red Hook*. Her non-fiction book *Comrade Rockstar*, the story of the American who became the biggest rock star in the history of the Soviet Union, is to be made into a film starring Tom Hanks.

For
Alice, Fred and Justine,
with love

London
New Year's Eve

The fireworks light up Lily's face so bright she looks like a ghost. London crackles with the light and noise, the showers of gold, red, blue, white lights that spray from the cold black sky and tumble in waterfalls into the river. As we lift off, there's music from bands, some along the promenade by the river, some on barges or dinner boats named for exotic fish and jammed with people. Cubans somewhere play a lilting tune. The glass capsule we're in seems to sway in time to it and we gaze out at the lights, the city, our arms tight around each other, rising above the ground on the big wheel, dancing in the air to the Cuban music, me and Lily.

From above, London is a jewelled city. We're alone in our private sky-pod, this see-through spaceship that ascends slowly on the rim of the amazing wheel. I managed to pull some strings and reserve a capsule just for us. It cost me a bundle and, when we arrive, Lily says I'm nuts to have spent the dough, but I think she's pleased. Under my jacket is a bottle of Champagne; a couple of glasses are in my pocket.

An announcement over the intercom informs us that eating and drinking on board is forbidden, but I wink at Lily. What are they going to do? Haul us down from the top because we're sipping Champagne? Call the cops? I'm feeling great. I'm a little bit high. We've been drinking Champagne all night. Maybe when we get to the top I'll propose, try to get her to marry me. Ask her again. She always turns me down, but it's New Year's Eve.

Before we board the "flight", as they call it, we're hustled, all of us, the whole merry crowd, into a makeshift building where we get our pictures taken. They do it by computer, blue-screen the ferris wheel in later, so you appear to be on board. You can buy the pictures after the ride. Everyone poses and jokes and cheeses it up for the camera. A guy, he's wearing a silly Beatles wig, is getting his photo taken at the same time; he stares at Lily, then disappears. I don't blame him; she's looking gorgeous; I'd stare at her, too. I do.

We get lucky that night. Most of the capsules have official attendants, like aircraft, but not ours. The guy who should be on ours is late and we see him running towards us just as the wheel moves up. We're alone together. I smile at Lily like a lunatic.

The riverside promenade is spangled with white lights. All night long, everyone dances, strangers kiss, laugh, link arms, sing "Auld Lang Syne' before and after midnight, and anything else they can think of: "Rule Britannia"; "Yellow Submarine"; "The Star Spangled Banner"; "Satisfaction"; it doesn't matter. Happy New Year.

It's still early as the buildings below us along the river fall away. The hard drunks will come out later, but for now everything is sweet. Then I see Lily's face against an ecstatic waterfall of green-gold fireworks.

I can see her too clearly. The faint down on her upper lip seems to flutter nervously, the odd dots of dark color in her light blue-gray irises tremble, her eyelids snap open and shut too fast. Most of all, there's some kind of repressed terror on her face that's so pale it seems the noise, light, music, crowds, have drained the life out of her. Only the tiny diamonds I got her for Christmas sparkle in her ears. Lily has these little ears, too small for her head, very pink and polished. Her right earring catches the lights. In our glass cabin, I list in her direction, grinning. "What's wrong, sweetheart? What is it? Tell me."

"Nothing."

It's not the wheel she's scared of. Not the heights. Lily climbs mountains. Literally. It's me who hates high places normally, but it's New Year's and, until I see her terror, I'm happy – happy as I've ever been.

"Is it this?" I gesture at the wheel. "You're not scared, are you?" I tighten my arm around her waist.

"It's nothing."

Inside my arms, she's stiff with tension. Her body's rigid. Her eyes move in every direction. I think about that plane where the oxygen shut down. After that it flew for hours without a pilot, drifting, up, down, changing altitude, flopping over. When a couple of Air Force jets caught up with it, the pilots saw the windows were frosted over and they knew everyone inside had

5

frozen to death. Later, in South Dakota, the plane crashed. It was all on TV and the whole four hours, Lily had stayed glued to CNN. "Sometimes I feel like that plane," she'd said.

I said, "Frozen?"

"No.' She tried to laugh. "Adrift."

But that was years ago. Things are good. Ever since we met in New York on a hot summer night when we shared a smoke on the sidewalk like conspirators, she made me want to please her. I don't know, she just got to me, right away I felt it. She got under my skin from the beginning and I wanted to please her. In bed. Out. Maybe too much. She's self-contained and vulnerable, smart, sexy, curious. Lily's interested in the world, and she makes me better. She makes me laugh. Most of all what I fell for was her lack of guile.

I was born in Moscow and if, like me, you come from a place where everything is secret, masked, half-said, it takes years to shed the duplicity; it's bred in your fucking bones. Even after I got to feel American, even now after twenty-five years in New York, I can feel the corrosions of Russia and I hate it. With Lily there are never any smuggled messages. Until now. Something's happening now. I don't understand.

We got to London after Christmas. She was a little moody once or twice, preoccupied, but I figured it was a minor outbreak, like the flu. Lily keeps things under wraps. She gets scared sometimes, mostly by her own demons, then everything shifts back to normal. When I asked her, she'd shrugged it off. "Call it hormonal," she said. "I'm fine, OK?"

6

In her hand now, Lily clutches a Champagne glass hard enough to break it. I take it away from her, swallow the rest of her wine, but it's warm and flat. "Lily? Talk to me. Sweetheart? Please."

"Let's just watch.' She stares out of the window.

So I hold her and look down. I'm happy being back in London because it makes her happy and because now I have a smell for it. I never thought I could love any place except New York City. London ruffles my certainty. There are things here I love, the river most of all. I love the way they speak the language, ice maidens on the radio and TV who make the language spin like cut glass, cabbies with the ripe nasal whine. London is endless, huge, bigger than New York, open all night, gridlocked with traffic, buzzing, hungry, a city-state teeming with people from everywhere: Indians, Pakistanis, Chinese, Ethiopians with their exquisite carved faces, American tourists lumbering around in good-natured groups, the French looking svelte and shouting at each other, the Japanese scurrying behind a leader with an umbrella held over his head.

London is low-lying, so when you ride in a taxi you can look right into apartments and houses, some of them out of magazines with drop-dead chic stainless-steel kitchens., Others, with dusty plants on the window sills and sheer white curtains gray with age, could be set pieces out of my Moscow childhood. And all of it spread out below us now, the detail invisible, the outlines sharply etched – I can see the dome on St Paul's – as we rise into the night sky.

Almost at the top, four hundred and fifty feet up into the New Year's sky, the almost imperceptible motion of the wheel seems soothing, makes me feel secure. This is lovely, or should be.

Under my breath I hum "Moonlight in Vermont", a tune I'm crazy for. Sinatra's version. And Stan Getz. Most of all, Stan Getz. Sometimes I ask myself, usually around New Year's when I've had too much to drink, what I'd trade to be Stan Getz. Would I trade it all in? Lily? New York? How would it feel to be able to make his kind of a noise?

Lily wants me to love London so I'm loving it. I got a job working a paper chase for Keyes Security that would keep me in London for a couple of weeks. London and Paris. A missing persons deal, a bank account that had gone unclaimed, nothing special, but the job pays well. And it's in Europe.

The London she shows me is a boom town, streets crammed with people, bars full, restaurants packed, parties all the time. The hot young girls who crowd the sidewalks around Soho at night have bare legs and tiny skirts even in the middle of winter. There's money, but not much public violence, not like America, not yet. It's coming, though; you can smell it in the alleyways, under the bridges, the sleazier clubs. You can hear the rumble, the subterranean noise it makes before it surfaces full force, and there are the signs – the racist episodes, the bad cops, the hopeless refugees and the resentment towards them. Hospitals are short of beds and old people freeze to death in miserable apartments.

On the surface, though, it's fabulous, surprising, giddy-making. Crowds eddy up out of the ancient buildings, cling to the narrow sidewalks, drive fast cars down streets where there was only horseshit the day before yesterday, they jam into pubs and clubs in little buildings hundreds of years old. Thrilling. Over-ripe. Sometimes I wonder if it will burst suddenly. It almost happened a few years ago. I remember. I was here. The infection is spreading.

Looking down, I see the crowds like a single heaving body. Out of the dark mass of people, hands stick up with lighters, with sparklers, like a rock concert going on far below.

Somewhere I read even if the wheel fails, even if something goes wrong, the bubble is safe, the glass can't break. I'm not crazy about heights, but Lily wanted this, so I want it. A light buzz hits the back of my neck, anxiety opens a small cold pit in my stomach, but it's only Lily's nerves I'm catching. It's safe. We're safe.

She holds on to me so hard I can feel her straining through her thin silk shirt. She raises her arms to pull the heavy red hair off her pale, freckled neck the way she always does when she's nervous, scrapes it up, pushes it onto the top of her head, then lets it fall back. The pale-green silk on her arms looks almost white against the glass and the lights. She smells of Chanel and Swiss honey soap. Pressing against the glass wall, her face reflected in it, Lily blinks her eyes. "I want to go home."

"As soon as we're down. We can skip the party." I still have her Champagne glass in my hand. "Of course, sweetheart. We'll go right back to the apartment."

"I want to go home," she says again and I know she means New York.

9

As we reach the top of the wheel, the glass pod shifts up into place, stands proud of the wheel and I hold Lily as hard as I can. London spreads out for miles, the river a silver-black snake of water, the sky dappled with fireworks, the skyline, and beyond it the dark country-side, foreign places, alien places.

I say, "Happy New Year."

She leans against me and looks out.

Slowly, we begin the descent, the bubble slides down, hanging to the side of the wheel now. "Happy New Year, Lily."

Whispering, her voice so tense it makes the hairs on my neck prickle, she says, "I hope so."

Then the wheel stops moving.

Ten minutes later we're still hanging in the air on the rim of the white steel wheel. Lily's face is wet with cold sweat. She's shaking, the muscles working under the pale skin of her face, like frogs jumping. She whispers, "What's going to happen to Beth?"

It's the first time she's left Beth since the adoption, the first time she's been away. Beth is safe with friends in New York. "She's safe, sweetheart," I say, over and over. "Lily? You hear me? Listen to me!"

"She's only six, she'll be all alone, I want to get off this fucking thing." Lily's looking at the ceiling like she's caged.

"It's probably a power cut."

"There's an intercom." Frantically, she's pushing the button.

"Let me." I lean on the button and yell into the intercom, but it's dead.

10

It's only a power cut, I'm sure. I tell Lily it's a power cut. In the glass pods above and below us we see other people, waving, laughing, holding up Champagne bottles. Along the river, the lights from emergency vehicles flash. Nothing moves. Too many people, heaving bodies, drunks. A wind comes up, it makes us seem to sway. It's an illusion, but the thing feels as if it's swinging.

Distract her, I think. Keep talking, talk her down as if she's a woman on a ledge wanting to jump. Talk to her!

"Remember *The Third Man,*" I say, because it's Lily's favorite movie. She loves this movie, she wanted to come up here because of it. "Remember the scene in the big wheel in Vienna with Harry Lyme and, what was his name, the other guy, the naive American?"

She humors me, but her voice is numb. "I used to think you were the naive American. You were so in love with New York and America. Holly Martins. His name was Holly Martins, Joseph Cotton played him. Orson Welles was Harry Lyme."

"Yeah, and where Holly gets all sanctimonious and Harry Lyme says, look down at the people, they're just dots, would you really care if the dots down there stopped moving. Remember? What if I gave you twenty thousand for every dot that stopped moving, he says, how many could you afford? Tax-free, old man. Great scene. Right? Lily?"

Come on, I'm thinking. Please. Lily. Talk to me! Talk to me about this movie or about the fireworks or give me a kiss. She doesn't answer. Just stares out at the sky.

"That's one of the two or three million things you did for me, Lil, that movie, remember? You dragged me to

11

the Film Forum when they released a new print and I said, Oh, God, not another old movie, and you said, be quiet, this is great. It was great."

"How do you know when you meet a bad guy?" Lily said. "You think he looks like Harry Lyme?"

"Genghis Khan. Hannibal Lecter. Richard Nixon. Joe Stalin. I don't know." Just keep talking, I think. Come on. Yackety-yack, come on, Lily, please. Talk to me.

Without any warning, suddenly, like a plane losing altitude, the bubble bounces once. It stops. Bounces again. My heart pounds. We're four hundred feet up. I hold her and keep chattering.

"We're talking Dr Evil here?" I strike a pose, try to make her laugh. Make her pay attention. "We talking Henry Kissinger? Goldfinger? Mussolini? David Duke? Who? Come on, help me here, Lily, who's your number one bad guy, real, fictional, whatever."

"I think most of the bad guys look like everyone else. No horns, no tail." But she's not interested in the game; her speech is slow, frozen, dry.

"Forget the bad guys, then, OK Lily? Come on." I'm holding her as hard as I can.

The wheel seems to sigh in the wind now. Lily begins to weep. "I want to get off this fucking thing."

A few more minutes pass. Clouds are scudding across the sky, stars disappear, rain starts to fall. Little drops of rain, like wet marbles, tinkle against the exterior of the glass wall, pop open, run down its sides.

"It's a power cut, Lily. Look at me."

"How come the lights are on if it's just a power cut?" she says. "It's something bad, I've covered these stories,

12

I know how this works, you end up sprayed over London in a million pieces." She puts her hands against the door. It's sealed from outside. "Make them stop it," she begs. "There's a hatch somewhere, I read about it, for emergencies. Where's your phone?"

I try the phone, but the signal cuts out. It's New Year's Eve, people are calling each other, tying up the networks. Happy New Year.

There's a bench in the middle of the capsule, and I tug at her. "Let's sit for a minute."

The rain sluices down the side of the bubble. Lily, who won't sit, who stays glued against the glass, is silent. I try the phone again; there's no signal, or maybe the battery's dead.

"You don't know anything," Lily says. "Last year four people killed themselves jumping into the river New Year's Eve. Maybe others they didn't report. I swear to you, Artie. They set up a morgue last week. I know about this stuff. I hear about it. I saw the fucking morgue." Staring out, she clutches my arm hard enough to bruise.

She disappears into her own paranoia where I can't reach her. I'm stranded hundreds of feet over London in a ferris wheel that isn't working with someone I love who's maybe cracking up.

"My God."

"What?"

"My God."

"What is it?"

"Someone's falling. Look."

"No."

13

"Someone fell." Lily is yelling. "Someone. A woman. I saw her, Artie. I saw, out there, from the capsule below. A hatch opened, someone pushed her, it's why we stopped. This is why we stopped. Get me out of here."

But there's no one. I'm next to Lily, looking out, and there's no one falling. Lily is shouting. She's seen it, she says, a woman who tipped over and fell, into the river, into the dark heaving crowds, onto the road. She saw it in the light of a spill of fireworks that has already faded.

"There's nothing, sweetheart."

Lily resists; she pushes away from me, wants out, but I hold on to her. Over and over, she plays through the scene, repeating herself: a woman, she mumbles, falling. She's hallucinating and the rain falls and breaks on the glass. Crying, Lily shakes. I hold her.

For half an hour we float over London in our glass bubble. The rain comes down harder. I feel adrift, too, helpless, aimless, while Lily tries not to claw the walls. I can hear my own heart.

An hour later we're on the ground. A few emergency vehicles, a few medics, firemen. People are milling, laughing from relief. Some adventure! Some New Year's Eve! Never forget it. Cheers.

As each glass pod comes down, passengers climb out, some shaky, others full of bravado or excited because a television crew has arrived. There's no crime here, just the aftermath of a freak accident that left us stranded for an hour. No terrorism, either, not even a whisper. I can tell by the lack of special forces, or chaos or fear on the

14

faces of the cops. My arm around Lily, who's tense enough to explode, I find a cop and say, "What happened?"

"Nothing much," he says. "A power cut. A real bugger, though. Best go home now," he adds.

"Someone got pushed, isn't that it?" Lily says to him.

He thinks she's drunk. He humors her. "Those capsules are sealed, dear." He calls her "dear' as if she's a crazy old woman. I want to punch him in the nose because I'm worried for her.

Lily's voice is pleading. "Just take me home, Artie. Please."

"We're going."

She covers her face with her hands.

"Everything's going to be OK. It will. I promise."

"Artie?"

"Yes, sweetheart?"

"The woman who got pushed from the wheel, you don't believe me."

"Tell me what you think you saw."

"I think it was supposed to be me."

PART ONE

1

They found Lily two days later in an empty apartment in Paris. The apartment near the rue de Rivoli had high ceilings, gold-colored curtains streaked with filth, and a distant view of the Louvre Museum with the weird, alluring glass pyramid out front.

Before I got there, I didn't know if she was dead or alive. On the phone, they told me she was alive, she was critical. I didn't believe it. She was at a public hospital, Hotel Dieu; they couldn't move her. They seemed to know what the hell they were doing, or maybe they were lying, the way everybody lies when there's bad stuff. Keep the family calm. Keep them out. Let the pros do the job. I'd said and done it plenty when I was on the job, when I was a cop and a family would come to the hospital, pleading: How bad? And I'd say: We don't know yet.

We were supposed to go to Paris together that week, Lily and me. Out of the blue she said, I'll go on ahead of you, OK? She said it New Year's Day, the morning after the wheel. I'll go tomorrow, she said.

There was plenty on the news about the power cut; it was a freak accident. And Lily was fine, she was herself, she said she was sorry she had acted crazy as a bedbug the night before. She'd been feeling tired, paranoid, too much to drink, too many cold pills she took when she felt flu coming on. She was fine, great, she said. Then she told me she was going to Paris early. An old friend, she said. OK, Artie? You don't mind, do you?

"Some French guy with loads of dough and a funny accent?"

She laughed. "Don't be an asshole. There's only you."

It took me half the night to get there. In the borrowed apartment in London, I threw whatever I could put my hands on into a suitcase – my clothes, Lily's – and picked up her laptop. I barely knew what I took. The phone call from some Paris cop came after the trains and planes stopped, but I got a cab, found an all-night car rental and drove. I had to keep moving.

The car, which had a metallic odor of chrome, also stank of fake leather, cigarettes and the cherry air-freshener used to kill the stink of smoke. On the way to Paris, listening to someone babbling through the night on the radio, I smoked two packs.

The dark tangle of London roads took me across the Thames, where I passed the big wheel, a dark shape now against the wet sky. There were no boats on the river and it was raining. I got lost, chasing myself in circles until I found the motorway south to the coast. The rain froze and turned to sleet. It made the road hard to see, the distances between cars tough to judge. Hands sweating, I gripped the wheel tight and leaned forward, unable to lose the feeling someone was following me.

There wasn't any evidence; the night, the lights, the reflections on the road were playing tricks. In my rear-view mirror all I saw were the headlights of cars. But it wouldn't go away, this sense of someone there. The muscles in the back of my neck locked up. Then, in the distance, the tunnel itself.

Hard white overheads lit up the border like the railway spur into a concentration camp. The truck lanes were jammed with big rigs, the kind you see on interstates at home. The whole complex, roads, buildings, weigh stations, were drenched with that relentless light.

In the windows of the cars were the faces of drivers who looked beat, faces with a greenish cast from the lights. A woman, a red silk scarf on her head, leaned out of the car in front of me and emptied an ashtray into the road so the butts fell into a pool of diesel dripping from a truck.

It looked like some sci-fi construct at the edge of the world, the drivers heading across the border, traveling to some other planet. Planet Europe; it reminded me of New Jersey, its tangled borderlands, the smell of trucks.

Twenty minutes later, I drove into a two-story car train. It shunted forward into the tunnel. Someone came through, checked my passport, then we were in France. For a couple of minutes I got out of the car, stood in the train and stretched my legs, but it was cold and my gut turned over. I hate borders, even now. I never cross one without thinking of how we left Moscow by train when I was sixteen, heading for Rome first, then Israel.

After I got to New York a few years later, I felt I never wanted to leave again. For years, I never spoke Russian or saw the friends from home who called once in a while. I took my mother's name and Artemy Ostalsky became Artie Cohen. I never wanted to come back to Europe or Russia. I was an obsessive New Yorker. If I traveled, I went west if I could. I stayed in America. I got over it eventually, but now in the middle of the night, crossing the border into France, I felt for my passport over and over. For me, Europe was just a place where I had to keep moving.

2

Lily lay silently on the gurney, her face messed up bad. She was covered with a hospital sheet. Her eyes were shut, bruised and swollen. Her red hair showed at the rim of a plastic cap. Around her, doctors and nurses moved briskly. Rubber soles squealed on the hospital floor. People snapped out orders.

At the hospital, a hulking old building opposite Notre Dame, I lied and told them I was her husband and they let me stay with Lily before they took her into the operating room. Stabilize her, someone said. Someone beat her up bad, they wanted a look, internal injuries. I can speak some French, but I was lost in the rapid-fire talk, medical stuff, opinions, orders, information, even jokes. I resented the joking. Lily was sedated. She didn't know me. Her eyes were so swollen I could hardly look at her.

In the crowded corridor that smelled of antiseptic, I listened to the doctor who tried to explain, talking at me, telling me how bad she was. They wanted to put her shattered knee back together and set the fingers on her right hand. The fingers were smashed.

It came at me like gunshot, pieces of information peppered with advice, warnings, queries. When they wheeled her away down the corridor, I ran alongside until one of the nurses pushed open a swing door and they disappeared inside, Lily with them, leaving me alone.

My adrenalin gave out, then my legs. I sat down hard on a blue plastic chair. It was six in the morning. Someone gave me a cup of coffee.

They'd used some kind of a hammer on Lily, on the hard surfaces, her knee, an elbow, her fingers. They'd punched her in the face. They must have punched her over and over.

Her right hand they'd worked over with real attention, breaking every finger. Lily is vain about her hands, long, elegant hands with slim fingers. In New York, sometimes at night, I would stop by her place and find her with Charlene, the manicurist who makes house calls. They'd be crouched over the coffee table in the living room and Lily would look up at me and hold out the nail polish. Choose a color, Artie. Come on. Choose. Red. Pink. Black. Brown. Rouge Noir. I said Rouge Noir looked like blood, like a vampire had sucked your fingers. She laughed at me because I always chose bright red. She said it was the kind of color hookers like. I love watching her get her nails done.

The fingers were broken and I thought about the pain. My head was swimming, my back soaked in ice-cold sweat. I was cold. Sometime that morning, while she was in surgery, I must have dozed on the chair.

"Gourad." He held out his hand. "Maurice."

Lily was in a recovery room.

The French cop who saw me coming out of it was a tall ugly young guy with a sprawling body who spoke great English. He did eighteen months on the job in St Paul, Minnesota, he told me, and a year in New York. He loved New York. He had lived in Brooklyn, Park Slope, and he was crazy for the city.

He had a nose like a fingerling potato, small dark sharp eyes, springy black hair and shaggy eyebrows that met in the middle of his face. He was pretty dapper, though; the black jeans fit him perfectly, he had on black Nikes, a sheepskin jacket and a green sweatshirt from the Gap. A little gold cross hung on a chain around his neck.

Sleet was coming down outside. We got into Gourad's green VW Golf and he took me to the apartment where they found her. I told him I'd been a cop, I figured it might make him friendly. He let me look at the apartment. Five minutes, he said, no more. I asked who owned the place. He said it was held by a company, they were working on it.

All I got was the view of the dusty drapes, the marble fireplace, some blood on the parquet floors. Then Gourad hustled me out. He shook hands with the concierge, who had a dour, wrinkled face like a walnut. In the street, Gourad popped open a little red plaid umbrella and held it over us.

We both smoked while we talked. He told me what he knew, which wasn't much. He had arrived at the scene not long after the crime was reported. I asked him how he knew to call me, because the call came from him, not the hospital.

25

"It was written on her hand. She had a phone number written with a blue ballpoint on her palm. Her fingers were curled over it."

Oh, Lily, I thought.

Whenever I went on a job, she always wrote the number on her hand. A new job, a new number, a different cell phone, a strange hotel, she wrote it down so she wouldn't forget. The London number was on her hand, but she never called. It was this French cop who phoned me instead.

"Everyone calls me Momo," he said suddenly, like it would somehow cheer me up. He helped me unload the rental car and found me a cheap hotel room near the hospital. Up two flights. View of a bleak courtyard. Faded green bedspread, hard pillow, TV. I tried to sleep after Gourad left, but I kept seeing Lily's bruised, mute face.

She was so happy being in London. I liked it because London always had a pull on her, even after the case I worked there last year when the corruption leaked into the mainstream like sewage into floodwater.

Lily wants me safe, so I take safe jobs, even though I know I'm less exciting for her, that her old unease about me was always a kind of turn-on. She hates guns, but she's ambivalent about the excitement. Suddenly, I remembered something. That first summer. We were in Sag Harbor.

We went out to eat. I didn't have a jacket. Without asking, she took my gun and slipped it in her big straw bag. She knew it would be embarrassing if someone noticed. Lily hates guns as much as any other New York liberal. More. That was the point. She did it for me, put the gun in her bag. I think I really fell for her then.

In the drab room in Paris, my cell phone rang. I looked at my watch. It was six. It rang again. It was the hospital. Urgent, the voice said. Hurry. I bolted out of the hotel.

"Mr Cohen."

A black guy in a white coat, a stethoscope around his neck, shook my hand. His name tag said he was Dr Christian Lariot. He spoke good English and had a pudgy face. West African, I thought, but I was thinking in a fog of anxiety.

I crossed my arms over my chest to keep from shaking. "She's dead."

"No," he said. "No."

He talked to me about a sub-dural hematoma. In recovery earlier, while I was out with the cop, Lily complained of violent headaches. Terrible nausea. She vomited, then she passed out. They took her back into surgery again and drilled a two-inch hole in her head to drain out the blood that was pressing on her brain.

Lariot talked softly, precisely, carefully. I held on to the back of a plastic chair.

"Is she OK? Is she?"

"Give it a few days," he said.

"How many days?"

"I don't know."

"How many days?"

"Give it time."

"Will she die?"

27

He shook his head, but didn't answer.

Unconscious, Lily was in intensive care, and I watched while she lay there against the hospital bed, hooked up to machines, and seemed to slide deeper into the coma. Her fingers were in splints. Her leg was in a plaster cast. She was bruised and silent. She had closed her eyes and disappeared.

"Lily?"

There was no reply, no sound except the shattered breathing. She was in a coma, they said. Give it a few days, they said.

I couldn't reach her. Except for wanting her better, all I wanted was to kill whoever did this. I wanted to break their fingers and arms and legs and kill them. No one mentioned rape, I didn't ask, not yet, I couldn't. After, after it was over and she was better, I swore to myself, we were going away. Somewhere small and safe. Montana, maybe. To Chico. Nothing bad ever happens in Chico.

"Lily?"

I was tired. I wanted to lie down next to her now and go to sleep. One of the nurses came after a while and asked me to leave. Let her rest, she said. Rest from what? How can she be tired when she's not conscious, I said. The nurse told me to go. She was polite but irritated. There was nothing I could do. I kissed Lily and went back to the hotel. I called New York and left a message for the Millers, who were taking care of Beth. I sat on the bed. Before I got my clothes off, I fell asleep.

3

"Your first trip to Paris?" the manager of the hotel said the next morning, making conversation as if I were a tourist.

"Yes."

Cigarette hanging out of his mouth, he leaned over the desk and gave me a map. "You don't look so good," he said. "It's cold. I hate this weather," he added, then went back to his newspaper.

My first trip to Paris. It was wet and freezing cold, and the sky hung, the color of rotten oysters, low over the city. The grandiose buildings looked heavy, the monuments I knew by heart from a million pictures were grim and spectral, rain sluiced down the gutters of the stylish houses, and the parks were drenched. I tried the Metro; the platforms were wet with sludge.

The Seine flooded that week. Cars were banned from the roads along the river. It got colder, the roads turned to ice, tiny ice floes drifted on the river surface like pieces of white fat. People, their faces morose and weary, kept their heads down against the bitter wind; their umbrellas blew inside out.

After they put a hole in Lily's head and she fell into a coma, I moved between my hotel room, the hospital and Gourad's station house, stopping for food at whatever café I passed, not tasting anything, stoking up on the coffee, everything a blur. I didn't drink anything except coffee.

I needed to think, if I could. I was scared that Lily was still vulnerable. She was in a public hospital where anyone could walk in and out. Anyone. A guy with a hammer. A creep who didn't get his fill of her. Anyone. The cop I'd met, Gourad, was a kid. I wanted big-time brass on this, I wanted the best guys. I tried to call my sometime boss, Sonny Lippert, but he was in Washington and out of reach. During this time I never really slept, or if I did it was a light, anxious sleep.

Lying on the narrow hotel bed, prickly with anxiety, any noise woke me up and I never stopped thinking how helpless she was. Except for wanting Lily better, and wanting to kill whoever did it, all I wanted was to keep moving. If I kept moving, I could stand it. If I kept moving, I could shake the dread. I knew I was deep inside my own craziness now. Mostly what I did was stare at the green vines on the ugly hotel wallpaper and smoke.

My second day in Paris, I left the hospital and got the subway to Gourad's precinct. The train let me out in an underground shopping center. Forum des Halles. I tried to remember the street names wherever I could. I was an alien in Paris, didn't know my way around, but here, in this underground shopping mall, the smell of butter and sugar made me hungry. I bought an apple turnover and ate it while I watched two cops hassle a black guy who was hanging out near McDonald's. The pastry was flaky and the flakes littered my jacket.

There were plenty of black guys and plenty of cops. In uniform or in jeans and stuff from the Gap, there were cops all over the place. Two of them followed another black guy into McDonald's. I stood in the doorway and watched them tail him. On the music system, Miles Davis wailed out "So What?" from *Kind of Blue* while people scarfed their fries, gossiped, drank black coffee, examined purchases they'd made in the mall. Like a jingle on a loop, "So What?" stayed in my head the rest of the day.

I climbed the stairs out of the mall and crossed the ugly square to Gourad's station house. On the ground floor, a woman at the desk told me he was out, but I went up anyhow and ran into a cop I'd seen at the hospital with Gourad. She was a pretty woman with short brown hair and dimples. She was sitting at a gray metal desk, writing a report in longhand, drinking something that smelled of cinnamon.

Over her head was a poster from *The Big Easy* with Dennis Quaid on it. The cop stared up at it, glanced at me and, flirting, said, "You look something like him."

They ran Lily's case out of Gourad's precinct because it was the same area as the apartment where they found her. There was already talk about moving it to a special criminal brigade, but for now the paperwork was piling up on Momo Gourad's desk.

The station house had crumbling green walls, a holding cell with a plastic window in the gray metal door, typewriters, a few computers on the steel desks. In the kitchen was a microwave, a stained coffee pot, half a stale sandwich on wax paper – cheese – and a handmade sign that read: PUP FICTION.

"Police Urbain de la Proximité," Gourad spelled it out, laughing, as he suddenly came through the door. He gestured at the movie posters that were stuck up in the kitchen and the corridors. *The French Connection, Serpico, Lethal Weapon, Copland*. "Most of our guys is a bit, how do you say, film buff. Maybe a cliché, but who cares, right? You like Popeye Doyle, Artie? You enjoy Tarantino?" He grinned.

A joker, I thought. A kid. I said, "Who else is on this case?"

"Why, you don't trust me?"

I kept my mouth shut.

"I may look young," Gourad said. "But I'm very very good."

There was the smell of stale coffee and cigarettes. Everyone smoked. Everyone shook hands. The cops shook hands with each other, except for some of the females who sometimes kissed the men on the cheek twice. I almost expected them to shake hands with a sad-ass suspect I saw them drag in. She was a black woman with stiff blonde hair who wore a cheap down coat.

"What did she do?"

Gourad snorted. "She had a box cutter. Vicious little weapon. She was holding some meds for her boyfriend. The usual shit. Nothing." Except for a few weird locutions, Gourad spoke American like he was born there.

A detective in London once told me they were all racist bastards, the French police. They were a joke, he said, cops who couldn't cut it. But the guys at the Pup Fiction station house made me welcome, except for the chief, Gourad's boss, who had a balding sweaty head and a nervous twitch. He tapped his fingers on his desk like he couldn't wait for me to get the hell out.

He didn't part with any information. I asked him who owned the apartment where they found Lily but he couldn't say. I asked if I could see the file. He took a phone call. Like an amateur guitar player, his fingernails were too long.

And there was paper. I never saw so much paper in my life.

Gourad said to me, "Too much. We write everything down. You think Serpico was writing things so much like us?" He gave the thick files stuffed with paper a dirty look. Then he showed me Lily's file, offered me a chair and a cup of coffee.

Everything was written down in detail: the victim's history; the location; the cops on the case. It was all stuffed in a stiff, old-fashioned gray binder. Seeing the chief pass his office, Gourad waited until he was sure he'd left the station house, then said, "Come on." He took me into a property room. He tossed me a pair of latex gloves and left me alone inside with Lily's things. I knew what Gourad wanted from me: he wanted me to see what was missing, what the creeps took off her.

I put on the gloves and worked my way through the items, each bagged in plastic. There was Lily's suitcase and the shopping bags that the cops seized from her

33

hotel. One of the shopping bags was stuffed with gifts for Beth. The other had guide books to Paris for me. She knew I had never been to Paris. Lily had said, "You'll love it. I'll make it nice for you."

The suitcase contained a pair of black jeans, a narrow black skirt, a pale-gray suede jacket, an orange cashmere turtleneck, four white silk shirts, a green silk bathrobe I gave her one Christmas, underwear, some make-up, and three pairs of shoes. We were going to spend three days in Paris. Lily travels heavy. "What if it rains? What if I have to go somewhere big deal?" she always says, and it makes me laugh. Before she left for Paris, I'd said, "What if the President of France invites you to dinner? Maybe you should take an evening dress. What about a tiara?"

The clothes she was wearing were stored in a different bag. They found her at the apartment near the rue de Rivoli in her grey pants suit. Her black sheepskin jacket and her bag were on the floor next to her where she was left, beat up, like a rag doll. They took her good watch, the man's Rolex she'd bought herself once in Hong Kong, and a ring we bought on 47th Street from my friend Hillel. The earrings had been ripped out of her ears. I didn't think they were thieves, though. They took the jewelry for the hell of it, to cause her pain, make her hurt.

The creeps took her passport, but left her driver's license and her phone. They wanted her found. They wanted it known, what they'd done to her; this was a warning. She left London wearing the gray pants suit and a black turtleneck sweater, and that was how she was found, but the suit was torn, half ripped off her. I could see where someone yanked off her aunt's silver pin that Lily always wore on her lapel.

I held onto the jacket and I could smell Lily, her soap, her perfume, her own scent. The smell would stick to the bastard who beat her up, the individual human odor, the distinct smell of a particular human being.

The East German Secret Police used to keep your smell in a jar. Everyone they spied on, whenever they could, the Stasi got hold of your smell on a piece of cloth and put it in a glass jar. When you got out of line, they let the attack dogs sniff your jar so they could hunt you down. The dogs didn't have vocal chords. They removed the vocal chords so the dogs were on you before you knew it. They could smell you, but you could never hear them. I never found out how they got your smell, but it kept me awake for years, imagining the rows of glass jars, like jars for pickles or jam, but with your smell in them instead, the lids screwed shut.

I went through her clothes. I tried to pretend this wasn't Lily, that I was just on the job. I took a silk scarf. It was a small, sky-blue silk scarf she'd had around her neck and I stole it from the room. Lily's clothes smelled odd to me. Her own smell was on them, but there was something else: was it his stink? His stink would be on them. On her.

Gourad was banging on the door. He put his head into the room. "You found anything missing?"

I shook my head.

In the pictures, Lily's hair was different. Gourad showed me the Polaroids from the scene, pictures of Lily the way they found her at the apartment. We were at a bar, Gourad and me, where he took me. It was across the street from the station house, away from his chief.

Gourad was pretty forthcoming and it surprised me. I couldn't really place him. He seemed smart enough but he stumbled around with that little plaid umbrella like a jerk, so I wondered what his game was. He had on a good soft gray Italian shirt that looked like it cost plenty, a knitted tie and an expensive, battered tweed jacket. His face had a gray tinge like he drank too much. He looked in the mirror over the bar and fixed his collar every few minutes and I couldn't tell if he was nervous or vain. Probably both.

On the formica surface of the bar, he laid out the pictures one at a time: the apartment; Lily; two close-ups of her face. Her hair bothered me. I looked again and saw it was short. When she left London, it was to her shoulders; now it seemed short. The picture was lousy, though.

Sometimes when I look at pictures from a scene, I can put myself into it if I stare hard enough. I can imagine the room, the victim; sometimes I can get an idea of the assailant. Sometimes. So I stared and there was something about the angle, the way Lily lay on the floor, something apart from the bruises, the blood. It was the way her clothes had been torn, her naked legs half showing.

"Can I keep them?"

Gourad handed me a picture. "One. I can lose one of the pictures from the file."

I put it in my pocket to remind me, if I needed

reminding, what I wanted to do to the creeps who hurt her.

"You should eat something," Gourad said. He was holding back.

"I'm OK."

"Take a beer," he said.

"Give me her file."

"I can't do that."

"How come they left Lily's cell phone at the scene? What's your thought?"

"I thought about this, too."

"Maybe the turds are thinking of calling us."

Gourad grunted. "Maybe someone copied all the numbers, cloned the phone."

"You checked?"

"Sure we checked."

"Let me have it."

"Why should I do that?"

"Because I know Lily better than anyone in the world."

"I'll see what I can do." His face was closed and sad.

"What's the matter with you?"

He hunched his shoulders. "Nothing."

I said, "Who found her?"

He was silent.

"Who owns the apartment where you found her?"

"We're looking."

"Take me there again."

"I can't. I've already shown you too much. They've sealed it. I can't do that or my chief will be on me and on you like shit off a shovel. I'm sorry."

37

Shyly, Gourad invited me home for dinner. Any evening, he said. I got up to leave, zipped my leather jacket, then I turned back. He was watching me.

I said, "What else? What is it?"

He fumbled with his cigarettes. "You want some counseling? You want to talk to some shrink?"

"Don't be an asshole. I want information, not a shrink."

"It can help."

I grabbed Gourad's arm. "She was raped."

He put his hands out, palms up, a gesture of despair, and said, "Yes."

The hotel where Lily had checked in when she got to Paris had a pompous little manager who shook my hand as if there was something sticky on it. Very polite, but oily, he had a phalanx of lawyers in pinstripes by the time I got there from Gourad's station house. All the lawyers were clutching fancy briefcases, speaking French in modulated tones through pursed-up little lips, all of them peering out at me from behind their wire-rim glasses like I was some specimen. I should have left it to the French cops, maybe, but I couldn't sit still.

The manager showed me her room. It had heavy striped drapes on the windows and a king-size bed; Lily had planned on my being there the next day. The bed had been stripped. The police had taken away her suitcase, there was nothing left of her.

For a while I hung around the front door, watching people come and go, tourists, businessmen, ducking in and out of cabs and limos. It was freezing outside and a pretty, skinny woman in jeans and a mink coat, hurrying

38

through the door, caught my eye. "Brrr," she laughed, then added in English, "Too cold."

I got lucky when I heard the doorman speak Russian to a taxi driver. I made some conversation. He knew about Lily. He read the papers and he remembered her. "The tall redhead?"

"Yes."

"Sure I remember," he said. "She went out Tuesday evening. She didn't speak French. She asked me to get her a taxi and I said we had a car service we use and there was a driver available. So she took the car. You want me to get the driver?"

I gave him some money. He extracted a whistle from his overcoat, blew it, waved a car over. The driver got out and thumbed through his receipts.

"I can take you," he said.

Since I was a kid, I always wanted a look at Paris. Outside the car window, as the driver sped across town, it was white and chilly, the freezing rain still falling. I tried to lose the feeling that someone was following me, that I was like a rat in a lab cage and I didn't know what the test was.

On the other side of the river, in a nondescript area, the car pulled up in front of a modern five-story apartment building.

"I dropped her here," the driver said. "Your friend. This is where I left her. She was a nice lady. Shall I wait?"

"No," I said, paid him, got out and checked the street sign: Boulevard Pasteur.

On the building's intercom were numbers but no names. I didn't know who the hell I was looking for. I huddled under a bus shelter close by, away from the sleet that came down in sheets. I waited.

I was bone cold by the time a woman came down the street towards the building, carrying a bag of groceries in one hand and a pile of books in the other arm. She stopped at the building, fumbled with her keys, got the heavy door open, and held it with her foot. There was a picture of Lily in my wallet – Lily before she was beaten and bruised – and I ran at the woman with the groceries and stuck it in her face. I said I was looking for the woman in the picture. I was pretty incoherent and I figured she'd slam the door in my face. But she only put her bag down on the sidewalk and said in a southern drawl, "I know her. Yes. Who are you?"

In a café down the street from Martha Burnham's place, she ordered soup and chicken and a glass of red wine.

"I'm sorry. I missed lunch. I want to eat something before I go to work and I've only got an hour."

She had dark hair, a nice, placid face, wide hips, no makeup. About Lily's age. She was wearing a sleeveless down vest, a black turtleneck, black skirt and boots. She picked up the wine glass when the waiter brought it and drank the wine greedily. A red stain appeared on her mouth.

"Is she all right, Lily, I mean?" she said.

"How come you're asking? You've seen the papers?"

She shook her head. "I don't read the papers. I hate the news. I was so upset not to see her again, you know. I've waited twenty years to see Lily and we had a drink Tuesday and she told me about you, so I knew your name.

40

So we make another date, she never shows up. I didn't
know where she was staying. I tried a number I had in
New York and got a machine. So I figured something
happened." She put her wine glass down and cracked her
knuckles. "Then I decided she forgot. But something did
happen, right? You said the papers."

"She got hurt. You knew her in New York?"

"How?"

"What?"

Martha said, "Did she have an accident?"

"No. Someone attacked her."

"Who?"

"I don't know yet."

"Is she OK?"

"No." I told her what I could. "How did you know
her?"

"I want to see her."

"Not right now. We'll go together if you want, but
later."

"Is she conscious?"

"No. I need your help."

She said, "I knew her in college, then in New York.
I was from a little town in Tennessee so I was awed by
Lily who was from New York City and knew about jazz
and food and had met writers even when she was in high
school. For me she *was* New York City. We kept in
touch for a while, but I moved to France."

Her soup arrived and Martha spooned it up carefully.
Her honeyed voice still had vestiges of a southern childhood. "I always missed her," she said.

"I can understand that."

41 •

"You've been together a long time, you and Lily?"

"A while."

"Will you tell me what's wrong with her?"

"She's in a fucking coma in a hospital. Someone attacked her." I stopped myself yelling. "I'm sorry."

"Me too."

"I'm crazy with this. Someone beat her up." I showed Martha the police picture of Lily. She winced and I said, "Tell me what happened with the two of you."

"I don't know. Nothing happened. Lily called me from London."

"When?"

"Last week. She said she wanted to see me, she was coming to Paris and she wanted to meet up."

Lily had decided to come to Paris without me even before New Year's Eve. She didn't tell me until afterwards. Maybe something about the trip on the wheel convinced her.

I thought about Lily on the wheel, her terror, her flickering eyes, then shut it away and focused on Martha who was looking expectant, as if I could tell her why Lily canceled their date. But I had to know who this Martha was and what she meant to Lily.

I said softly, "So what do you do, Martha?"

She smiled. "I'm a social worker."

She ate in silence for a few minutes. She let me take my time and I was grateful. Martha Burnham was an intuitive woman.

Finally I said, "Look, Lily's hurt really bad, and I don't know why or who did this, or if they're coming back again, so I need to know everything you can tell me."

42

"You're a cop."

"Was."

"A good cop. Lily told me you were one of the good guys."

"I'm glad."

"Did she say anything about me?" Martha was eager.

"We were coming to Paris together this week and all of a sudden she says she's leaving ahead of me. She says she has a friend she wants to see. You were the friend, I guess. You don't remember the exact day she called you?"

Martha was disappointed Lily hadn't talked to me about her, but she ate some more soup. "The twenty-ninth," she said. "I'm pretty sure. Two days before New Year's Eve. I can check. She said she was thinking of coming. I was thrilled."

She looked at the picture again. "My God." She was upset but not shocked. She'd seen worse. She was holding out on me, but she was good at holding out.

I said, "Help me."

"How?"

"I can work this case. But I need you to tell me everything you know about Lily's visit to Paris, or anything you can think of. When's the last time you heard from her before the other week?"

"Years. I don't know. We exchanged Christmas cards, a phone call once in a while. That was it."

"You were close? Once?"

"Yeah, though I was too much of a hippie for Lily's taste." She ordered coffee. "I was heavily into wind-chimes back when. Communes. Sandals. Hairy women. You know."

"You have any idea why she suddenly called you?"

"I told you. She said she was coming to Paris. She said she wanted to meet for dinner. Like that, out of the blue. I said fine. I was so thrilled she called and I just said, sure, honey, of course."

"She called you when she got here?"

"Yes. She called me when she got off the train. She checked into some fancy hotel, I forget the name. Over by the rue Saint-Honoré, I think. She said come over. I said, too rich for my blood, honey, come to me. She said, let me take you out, Marti, she used to call me Marti, and I said, no, I want you to see my place, and I'll make my *blanquette de veau* for you. She sounded the same as always. She said I'll come for drinks. I'll bring wine. She didn't exactly trust my taste." Martha laughed. "She knew I was a lousy cook."

"She showed up?"

"She came by around seven and we had a bottle of wine and we talked a lot. I want to see her. Please. Can I go see her?"

"She's unconscious. She's in a coma. They hardly let me in."

"Which hospital is she in?"

I told her. The waiter brought her coffee and I got the check. I scribbled my cell phone number on a piece of paper. "If you think of anything?"

"Sure."

"So you don't have any idea why Lily suddenly called you?"

"You asked me before. She was coming to Paris. She said she called on an impulse. I had a feeling there was

44

something else." Martha pulled her fat silver-colored puffa vest tight around her body. "Poor Lily. You seem like a nice guy, honey, you do, but it was always so hard for her. It always made her guilty. She always had to save the world. It's why she became a journalist back when we all thought you could save the world by telling the truth."

"What was hard?"

"Being happy." She looked at her watch. "I ought to get going."

"You said you were a social worker."

"Yes."

"What kind of work do you do?"

"Mostly women."

"What kind of women?"

"It's not something I talk about much. It's not conversational."

"I'm not making conversation. I'm trying to figure out who hurt Lily so bad she almost died. So bad she doesn't know who I am. They broke her fingers, Martha. One at a time. They smashed them up slow, they hammered her so you'd hardly recognize her."

"I work with prostitutes."

"Is that what Lily wanted from you? Is that why she called?"

"I guess I wanted to think she called because she missed me." She drank the coffee. "Pretty insane, huh? I mean after twenty years. I mean, like, you don't call someone up after twenty years because you suddenly miss them, or you see a black and white cookie in a store and you go all Proustian and you think, my God, I wonder how Marti Bumham's doing, do you?"

45

"What?"

"They were our favorites. You know, the big cookies you get in New York, half vanilla frosting, half chocolate? Never mind. What about the attack? Anything else? Any marks?"

I told her as best I could. "You've seen this kind of thing?"

"Even if I have, the women I work with are prostitutes."

"Maybe Lily had an interest. Maybe she thought there was a good story in it."

"It's possible." Martha was rueful. "Lily could ignore people for years and then suddenly she'd turn up. Honey, she loved everyone."

"Except you."

"She needed a bigger canvas. A cause."

"What kind?"

"Whatever was going." She crossed her arms. "She was fabulous but she was a user. I remembered when I heard her voice. Out of the blue. She just assumed I'd be there for her after all these years."

Martha shifted her chair, turned her hands over and stared at them. There were no rings.

I looked at the big, capable American hands and wondered if she could beat Lily up, but it was only the paranoia eating at me.

I said, "I don't think that's really fair."

"I'm sorry. You don't have to defend her to me."

She pulled her heavy brown leather bag into her arms like a baby, dug around inside with one hand and took out a tooled-leather wallet. It was stuffed with cards, money, pictures. From it she extracted a plastic package of photographs. She took off the red rubber band that held the pictures together and, the bag dumped on the floor next to her chair, started playing the photographs out like a deck of cards.

I waited. Mouth sucked in, Martha concentrated on the pictures as, one at a time, she turned them up on the table in the middle of the wreckage of the meal. Finally, she pulled out a picture of her and Lily.

Two girls in Bermuda shorts and sandals, both laughing at the camera, their arms around each other. It was a bright summer's day; you could see the way the sun made them squint. Lily's red hair was long. It hung on her shoulders like a curtain.

"When was this?"

"Twenty-five ago maybe. We were at some kind of film festival, a woman's documentary film festival on Woman's Day, May that year, I think. East Berlin, if you can believe it. Fucking East Berlin what was." She snorted.

Without any make-up and the long hair, Lily looked incredibly young and very pretty. In the pink tank top, her shoulders were bony. Martha, who was wearing a green Dashiki over her Bermuda shorts, wasn't looking at the camera; she was looking at Lily.

Across the table from me, Martha gnawed the edge of her thumb. "OK, I had a thing for her, OK? I did. I didn't even know it. I mean it's not like I'm into women, exactly. I got married, I had kids, you know. Got divorced, too." She forced a smile. "It was just Lily. She was different. She was so alluring. You'd go to a restaurant or a rally, people would look at her. I mean she turned heads, you know? It's the way I always thought of it. She turned heads. Also, she'd do anything on a dare. She was physically fearless." Martha snatched the picture off the table and shoved it back into the pile of pictures, snapped the rubber band on, pushed it back in her bag. "I guess I was sort of in love with her."

I reached over and tugged her sleeve. "Aren't we all?"

"Thank you for that, honey."

"You call everyone honey?"

"Only people I like."

"It's OK, you know, about loving Lily. Just talk to me about the other night when you saw her, OK?"

Martha said, "I'm trying. So you think that's why she wanted to see me, Artie? It sounds right, doesn't it? one of her causes?"

"Did Lily know that's what you do?"

Martha said, "Sure she knew. She'd heard from a friend in London, a woman on the *Guardian* I know. She said she wanted to see the shelter I run. See what I was doing. Maybe meet some of the women. I wasn't at all sure it wasn't just her being nice about my work, the kind of thing you tell an old friend. I told her she better come wearing jeans or something, or they'd think she was awfully hotsy-totsy, you know?"

"You made the date?"

Martha nodded.

Battered women are one of Lily's causes. She puts a lot of time into an agency that runs shelters in New York, London, Third World countries. Her battered women are somebody's cast-offs, someone's human junk: a fourteen-year-old girl so badly burned by her boyfriend she stabs her own baby to death; a grandmother who puts up with a son-of-a-bitch husband who beats her to a pulp because it's all she knows and thinks she loves him anyhow. Hopeless, sad, ordinary women, but not whores.

"You think she got involved?" I said.

"How?"

"I don't know."

"What kind of prostitutes come to your shelter?"

"What kind are there?"

"Call-girls? Hookers? French? Foreign?"

"Mostly they come off the street. Kids, a lot of them. The pimps bring them into town, the girls hit the streets, I clean up the mess afterwards. Bitches, the French cops call them." She put on an accent. "Beech."

"It's big business?"

"Very big."

"Russians?" I knew it was Russians. Whenever I was involved, or anyone close to me, there was usually a Russian connection. I could never completely shake it.

"Some Russians. A lot of them have more ambition now, you know, get a husband, be a supermodel. There's Russian money around the Champs-Elysées. Clubs. Restaurants. Vuitton. Most of the rich Russians are in Biarritz or the South of France."

"How come?"

"What do I know? Maybe they don't like the cold. Maybe they don't like the Parisians."

"Who's running the show?"

"You think I know? If I knew who ran it, I'd do

something. I wouldn't sit here, would I? I'd do something." She was furious. "No one knows. No one talks. The girls are my job. Sometimes I get a look at the small-time pimps. They come in to pick up their girls. That's it. Nobody gives a shit so long as they stay out of the center of town, you know? They just shuffle them around. Get them out of the way of the tourists."

"The tourists don't go for hookers?"

"Depends which tourists. Sex shows in Pigalle, maybe. The more expensive tarts around the rue de Rivoli. There's this myth about Paris, the fancy brothels, what was it, Mme Claude's? We ain't talking Catherine Deneuve in *Belle de Jour* here, it's just girls getting raped for money in some crappy underpass at the edge of the city. What the fuck, it's a living, hon, and I'm a jaded old feminist cunt." She looked at her watch. "I have to get going."

"You work at the shelter all the time?"

"I teach English during the day."

"You like it here?"

"Sure," she said. "Paris is great."

"How come?"

"You trying to soften me up, honey?"

"Yeah."

"Paris is great because we're all expats here. All us foreigners. Unless you're French, you're never at home. I like it. I like the feeling of skimming the surface." She paused, then said, "I have to go."

"You work at your shelter every night?"

"Most nights."

"Show me."

Martha pulled her bag off the floor and got up. I followed her out of the restaurant and we stood on the sidewalk.

"Why?" she asked.

"Lily wanted to see your shelter. You said that."

"I said I'd take her right then, that night, Tuesday, but she said no, she had a date to meet someone at the Ritz bar, she'd come the next day. She never showed. I'll call you, OK, hon? I'm really late."

Martha held out her hand, shook mine quickly, walked to the curb, plucked a parking ticket from under the wiper of a beat-up yellow Renault, tossed it in the gutter and climbed in. I ran. I banged on the hood of the car, but she only looked up, waved, and turned the ignition.

I yelled, "Who was she meeting at the Ritz?"

Through the window of her car I could see Martha's mouth make the words, "I'll call you later."

I tried running, but Martha Burnham pulled into traffic and lost me.

At the bar of the Ritz I drank a Coke and talked to the manager. Who did Lily meet at the Ritz for a drink after she left Martha Burnham? I didn't believe it was the thug who attacked her, you didn't meet guys like that for drinks at the Ritz Hotel. It was someone else, someone who set her up, maybe, who got her to go to the empty apartment.

The manager was friendly enough, and he introduced me to the bartender who was on duty Tuesday night. I showed him the good picture of Lily. He remembered her.

"Who was she with?"

"I don't really look at the men." He laughed.

"But you remember her?"

"Yes. I remember the hair. I love redheads."

"How's that?"

"It was fantastic. Very red, very beautiful."

"Long?"

"Yes. To her shoulders. It was long."

I stared at the picture Gourad gave me. In the picture it was definitely short. When she left London it was down to her shoulders. At the train station she'd pulled it off her neck like she always does when she's edgy. At the Ritz it was still long. Martha Burnham had given me her cell phone number; I called her.

"I can't talk," she said. "I'm working."

"When you saw Lily, how was her hair?"

"What?"

"Her hair."

"Look, Artie, I'm in a meeting, I can't talk now. I don't remember anything special about Lily's hair. I'll call you," she said and hung up.

But I didn't believe her. Martha was crazy about Lily. She would have noticed her hair if it was chopped up ugly. I tried Martha again but the phone was switched off.

4

In the hospital waiting room a TV set droned on in French. What I could make out, there was an ice storm predicted, bad weather, a strike by French truckers. I couldn't sit still. The cop, Gourad, was probably doing what he could but he had a boss who didn't like me, and Martha Burnham had her own agenda.

I worked the phone as best I could. Tolya Sverdloff would come if I called him, but we'd had a fight and I couldn't ask. I felt I was hanging on to the surface of a frozen pond where the ice was cracking and if I didn't crawl forward, I'd fall through or freeze to death.

After a while, I went back to the hotel, got some sleep. I tried the phone again, looking for a contact in New York who had a line to the French police. I wanted someone with clout. The system here crackled with bureaucracy: there were heads and sub-heads and officials and sub-officials, and all of them had spokesmen and press officers, and I couldn't get anything at all.

The coffee in my hand was cold. I drank it anyway for the caffeine and sat on the edge of the chair looking at the wall where the wallpaper ended. There was a section of peeling paint. It made me think of Moscow. It made me think of our apartment. My father, when I was young, was in the KGB. He was a star. He was handsome and charming and very good at what he did. He believed; he was a true believer in the Soviet enterprise. His father had fought the Nazis.

My pop wasn't stupid. He knew there were problems, but for him the ideology was such a shining idea he clung to it. And we had privileges. A car. We had a decent apartment. We had some nice furniture. We got a paint job every few years. Then it changed. My mother, who's Jewish, turned angry. She saw the cracks in the Soviet fairy tale. She understood about the lies and the corruption, and she couldn't keep quiet. She knew we would have to leave some day; she made me learn English. She made me understand the West and gave me a craving for it with books like *Catcher in the Rye* and Louis Armstrong records. Then my father lost his job.

KGB creeps in bad raincoats watched our building. We moved to a smaller apartment and there was never any paint. I remembered. I remembered how the paint began to peel, the cracks grew in the plaster and my mother tried to paper them over with pages from a magazine. By the time we got out, by the time we left Moscow, half the paint on the kitchen wall had peeled off.

The phone beeped me now, but it was only a message from Keyes. I knew I better pay some attention to the case I was supposed to be working in the first place. I needed the money. I needed money if I was going to take care of Lily. It was a decent job and Keyes was a good firm. I liked the security work they put my way, it paid the rent.

After they threw me out of the hospital I went back to the hotel and sat up most of the night re-reading the case.

Keyes Security is based in New York, but it has branches in LA and in London, where they run the European business. They're always looking for ex-cops with some education who can do a couple of languages. Me, I do Russian, Hebrew, some French.

The private security business is big – it's been getting bigger ever since those freaks hit the World Trade Center last year. People are scared of everything and they're probably right. You can't go anywhere without people talking about bombs and nukes, terrorism, black-mail, money scams and the shit-for-brains thugs who'll do anyone for a quick buck. There's always a creep who just invented some new form of craziness.

Europe is easy pickings. With Nato getting bigger and borders down, you could travel from Vladivostok right over to London without anyone bothering you. And the more wired up we get, the less anyone pays attention to the little guys on the ground. You can stare at your computer and miss the point. Sometimes you have to get into the street. Anyhow, thugs like the creep who beat up Lily live under the radar.

When we were still at home, thinking of taking a vacation in London, I asked around if there was some-thing going where I could earn vacation money, buy me and Lily ten days away in Europe. All Keyes had was a paper case. A dead man's bank account. His name was Eric Levesque. The plan was, after New Year's in London we'd go to Paris together where Levesque's account was so I could finish the case. Lily would hang out and show me around.

But she left me in London and the next time I saw her she was in the hospital in Paris. I didn't care about the Levesque case now. I didn't care about anything except Lily. But I was in Paris and I needed the money Keyes was paying me.

The case involved a long-term high-interest account at a big New York bank that has branches all over the world, including Paris. A couple hundred thousand was in the account, a lot of money by my standards but nothing, as someone said, that would turn the head of a twenty-five-year-old dot.com exec, even one who crashed in the bear market last year. Two-hundred-forty thou, roughly, the account opened in 1994 and untouched after that. Three years later, Levesque was killed in an air crash off the coast of Santa Catalina Island. The plane went down, most of the bodies were trapped in the broken fuselage. Levesque was dead, divorced, no kids, no family. Poor bastard, I thought, when I originally put together the file in New York. There was no one who seemed to know him. All that remained was the bank account no one claimed.

The account could have gone unnoticed for a lot longer. If you have a couple of bucks in an account and it's costing the bank more to process it than you're worth, they might pay some attention. But a quarter mill? The interest piles up, the statements go out, no one

56

returns them, the bank assumes everything's fine. It could sit around growing interest for a long time. Which is what happened with Levesque.

His statements went to a PO box in LA, the box got paid for, the bank didn't even know Levesque was dead. No one at the bank was sitting around reading airline lists of dead passengers. Levesque wasn't famous. Who would care?

The trouble started a couple months back when someone tried to withdraw money from Levesque's account from a branch of the American bank in a Paris suburb. Someone went into the bank, wrote out one of Levesque's checks for the equivalent of twenty grand in French francs and forged the signature. Twenty grand was enough so that the teller went to her boss to verify the signature, but by the time she got back to the window, the customer had vanished. The signature looked OK at first, but the bank checked it. It was a forgery. The bank took a look into Levesque's business and found out he was dead.

So who the hell wrote the check? What kind of asshole goes around writing big checks on a dead man's account?

Someone called in Keyes – the bank I figured – and Keyes gave me the job. I ran the case in New York and LA, did the paperwork and followed up the trail as best I could. I tracked down a couple dozen possible but remote relatives; they were the wrong Levesques.

I filed a report. All that was left was running it in France where the check had been written. Sonny Lippert told me not to take the case. It was a dead end,

57

Sonny said. "Paperwork. And money," he said. "Just money. It's not for us, Art," he said. "It's bullshit this kind of work. Paper work. For girls. You'll hate yourself. You'll die of boredom." Then he tried to get me on a job involving a trip back to Moscow and I ran, so to speak, as fast as possible. I had been back to Moscow. Once was enough.

I didn't care what Sonny Lippert said. It was work. It paid OK, it kept them sweet at Keyes where they like me, my languages, that I have nice suits and I can hold a knife and fork right. Also, the job got me to Europe. It was what Lily wanted.

I fell asleep on top of the Levesque case file. When I woke up, it was Friday. I took a shower, put on clean clothes, picked up the folder and started walking. I walked across Paris where winter fog sat on the buildings and crept under your coat, but I walked anyway, found a café, ordered coffee and re-read the file.

I worked my phone, re-checked my machine and tried Sonny. I drank the creamy brew they brought me, tossed some change onto the table and walked away. I don't know what I was looking for. I couldn't sit still. I crossed the place de la Concorde.

There were homeless on the Paris streets, curled up against the buildings. I passed a long line, mostly men, outside a church with a soup-kitchen serving breakfast. On the rue de Rivoli a middle-aged hooker bargained with a Japanese tourist over a blow job. It was early, a pale film of snow was already on the streets, and from the time I left the café I felt someone on my tail, but this time I knew it was only the inside of my head. Everything spooked me here.

Paris. City of Light. Christ!

I was out of breath when I found myself in front of a bookstore with English books, maps, magazines. I recognized the name. It was the store where Lily bought the books Gourad found in her hotel room. I needed a map of Paris. I went in. If there was somebody following me, he'd disappear.

A few minutes later I was leaning against a table piled with books when I heard the voice.

"Artie Cohen?"

I backed away, hands in my pockets.

"Artie. My God, it is you, isn't it? That's what they still call you now, Artie?" He hesitated, looked at me as if he'd fumbled it, turned red. "Am I wrong? Oh, God. I'm so sorry, maybe I'm wrong. You don't recognize me."

I thought: who is this guy? What does he want with me? How the hell does he know who I am? I wanted to lash out at everyone. I had to stop; it was making me panicky and useless. He looked harmless, this guy who wandered into a bookstore early in the morning; it was someone I met at a party once, maybe, or worked a job with a million years ago.

I said, "Excuse me?"

"It's been a really long time. I figured you wouldn't recognize me." His accent was American. New York, I thought. Like mine. He grinned and held out his hand. "I'm Joe Fallon. Josef Fialkov, I mean."

"You're kidding."

He took off his glasses. When I looked at him hard, I could just make out the resemblance to the kid I once knew, a ghost of a memory. Fialkov was bigger, heavier, older. But it was him. Joey Fialkov.

He said, "Can we get a cup of coffee or something?"

There wasn't anything I could do for Lily except sit in the lousy hospital. So I said, "Sure. You really have fucking changed."

"You still living in New York, Artie?"

"How the hell did you recognize me?"

"I saw a picture of you somewhere. The *Post,* maybe? The *News?* You were some kind of hero cop, weren't you? I don't remember the case."

"It was the *News.*"

"I heard you were in New York. My mom heard. You know I tried to call you once years ago. I left a message."

"I never got it." It was a lie. One of those things you forget about. It was a long time back when I didn't want anything to do with Russia. I still don't.

"I looked through the window here, I saw you. Jeez, I can't tell you how happy I was to see you, Art, swear to God. How come you're in Paris? You have business here? You still living in New York?" Fallon talked a lot.

"Sure," I said again. "Yeah. You?"

"Son-of-a-bitch. Me, too." He looked out at the snow. "I wish I was home. New York, I mean."

I peered at him again. "You really are Fialkov, aren't you?"

He reached in his pocket and pulled out a wallet. Stuffed inside was a crumpled black and white photograph of him and his parents and sister.

He held it up to the light. "I was a cute kid," he laughed. "But small, and all the hair. I thought I was Paul McCartney. I always got shit for the hair, remember? How about breakfast? We could go somewhere."

We left the bookstore and went to a café two doors down. Fallon went up to the bar for cigarettes. He was a well-set-up guy, big – my height – and a couple of years younger. Fallon moved easily. He had on good black cords, a rumpled red pullover, leather jacket. He looked completely American.

I hadn't seen Joey for, what was it, almost thirty years. Josef Igorovich Fialkov. For a couple of years we overlapped at school. He was always ahead of his grade, and we hung out because he was the only kid I ever knew who really cared about jazz.

I taught him. I played him my *Hot Fives* album, then I discovered Stan Getz and he finagled *The Steamer* for me, God knows how. I still have it.

Joey fixed things, it was what I remembered most, Joey could fix anything, a radio, the purchase of a time-share in a Beatles publicity photo, chocolate, an excuse to cut school. Once he re-wired a lamp for my mother. He hung around our place all the time; my mother said he had charm which was not a Soviet quality, so she liked him for it. He was a freak to his own family; they were the kind of working-class family we all despised, good Party people, loyal, dogged.

Fialkov's family lived in a crummy apartment building on the outskirts of Moscow. The father was a Stalinist prick who named his kid Josef for his hero and beat the shit out of him. He was a maintenance man at a big newspaper, a drunk who came home, when he came home, filled with the righteous propaganda he read off the presses.

The mother worked in a meat factory; you could smell her when you went to their place. She kept icons in both rooms. The ancient photograph of Joey and his family was so potent it sucked me back so I could smell the past.

Over coffee I said to Fialkov, "You speak the lingo here?"

"My mother made me learn French. She was a meat packer but she had pretensions. She had relatives in Belgrade, it gave her an air. Somehow, in her mind having foreigners in the family elevated her, you know? Maybe she brought them home with the sausages."

"My mother made me do French too."

"Your family was different. I remember them. I thought you were a really lucky guy."

"Yeah."

"All I wanted was to get out, my first agenda. Your family left for Israel, that was it, there wasn't anyone I could talk to. I heard you went to America later. You didn't know how much your family meant to me then. But I was a kid. You were what? Fifteen, sixteen?"

"Something like that."

"I was thirteen years old. But I knew there was better than the big shit we called Communism. I knew because of you and your mother."

"We were real assholes back then."

"Not you," Fallon said. He picked up the coffee when it came and smiled. "Not Artemy Ostalsky. You were my hero."

"So where do you live now, in New York I mean?"

"Tribeca. You?"

"Broadway. Near White Street."

"A couple of blocks from me. Great. You travel a lot, Artie?"

"Some. You?"

"Business stuff. New media. I got in early. I got out in time."

"Smart."

"Luck, mostly. I got in on the ground floor, bought, sold. Silly money. Put the cash away. Somewhere, Artie, I got lucky."

"You were always smart."

"I could fix stuff. But you were the rebel. You were the kid who knew about rock and roll and jazz. You knew everything about the West. You could speak English before anyone. You had a godfather who could travel and bought you records, didn't you? You told me about Willis Connover's jazz hour on 'The Voice of America'. My father beat me so bad when he found me under the covers listening to it, I couldn't sit down. I didn't care. Remember outside GUM where there were older boys in big gaberdine raincoats with the collars turned up, like young old guys? And the terrible pubescent mustaches on their upper lips? And you could get some kind of disks off them, Chubby Checker singing 'Let's Twist Again'. Two rubles." He paused for breath. "I'm sorry. I know. I talk too much. Sometimes I think my head is so jammed with junk, it will explode."

He grinned. He had a stupendous recall for detail and one thing led to another, so as soon as he thought about

63

Chubby Checker he was talking about dance crazes. I could hardly keep up.

"You always had shoes that matched," he went on.

"Jesus, Joe, how can you remember all that shit?"

"You even made me Joe. You said Art was your Western name, and everyone thought this was the grooviest thing we ever heard. Anything that was West was, like, good. It was," he sighed deeply, "good! Then you said we should all have a Western name. Remember? The Borises even fought over who would be Bobby. Anatoly, you remember this guy, you made him Nat, like Nat King Cole. I think there was a Yevgeny who became Gino. So I'm Joe Fallon. Are you OK? You seem distracted."

I was thinking about Lily. "Yeah, sure, I'm sorry."

He crushed out the cigarette he was smoking and pulled another one out of the pack. "I tried to quit."

"Me too."

"You want to eat something? Have some breakfast or brunch or something? I'm starving. I've been up since six this morning." He hesitated. "It's OK. You probably have stuff to do."

"Let's eat something."

"Here?"

"Fine."

While we ate bacon and eggs and croissants, people looked at Fallon. He was a handsome man; the dark hair fell over his forehead. Behind a pair of stylish glasses with tortoiseshell frames, his eyes were friendly.

After we ate, he tossed the cigarettes on the table and we settled in with more coffee and smoked a half pack between us. We reminisced like guys do, half emotional, half joking, catching up. I was glad it was daylight. I was glad I wasn't alone. When I was alone and thought about Lily I was jumpy, febrile, nuts.

In 1978, Joe got out of Moscow. He spent a few months in Brighton Beach, earned some bucks, went to LA and got himself into college. He became an American citizen and went into the Air Force, where he had the run of the new computers just coming onto the market. By the time the PC thing was happening, he was on his way.

"Kids?"

He grinned. "Three."

"Wife?"

"Two. First a Russian girl because I was lonely, she was lonely, we were students. Our boy is twenty-two, if you can believe. Billy."

"Then?"

He flinched. "Her name was Dede. We had two kids. She was so great."

"Was?"

"She died three years ago."

"Christ. I'm sorry."

"Cancer. They got it late. I wanted to kill the son-of-a-bitch doctor who told us she had cancer, but she said to me, 'Darling, it's not his fault.'"

"I'm sorry."

"I left Scarsdale when Dede died. Our daughter Lisa's in her first year at Yale. Alex, he's seventeen, he's in prep school. I wanted him home, but it's what he needed. Before they went away, I was a regular suburban daddy."

"It sounds good."

"I loved it. I'm kind of at loose ends. I travel a lot now. Hey, sorry. This is gloomy stuff. You want more coffee?"

"Two Russian guys in Paris, you got to have some kind of gloom, right?"

"I don't feel Russian."

"Me either. I never did."

"I killed myself getting rid of the accent. When I heard my accent, it was like a bad smell, I wanted to be American."

"I know what you mean."

"You do?" He looked grateful.

I nodded.

"When Gorbachev got in and things changed, I realized there was this huge country and nothing in it and everybody wants something. I held off. I wouldn't do business with them, you know. For ages. Dede said this is nuts, I'll go with you. She even learned Russian. And I saw Russia through her eyes and it looked better. Sort of better. She could be in Moscow and look at the churches, the pictures, the museums, the subways, she could think about Chekhov, she could enjoy the Bolshoi. She made friends there. She made it OK for me again." He put his hand on my arm. "So what happened to you?"

"We left Moscow, we went to Israel. After the army, I beat it to New York. I became a cop. I liked it. I do private stuff now."

"You're married? Kids?"

"Not married."

"Happy, though?"

"I was."

"What do you mean?"

"Nothing. Forget it."

He saw I was restless. He said, "I should let you go," and reached for the check.

I wanted to say: don't go. I wanted to tell him about Lily, but I didn't. I didn't tell him because there was no point and I didn't really know him, didn't know what casual conversation he might have with someone who would talk too much. I had no leads on Lily's case. After twenty years on the job, even though I had quit the department, I was still a cop. I kept my mouth shut.

Joe said, "I really am going to let you go. I'm at the Raphael, and I have an office here. I'll write the numbers down." He pulled a business card out of his pants pocket and scribbled on it. "Listen, if you want to talk or anything, or get some food, I don't want to pry, but you look like a guy who's not feeling so great. Whatever it is, I could maybe help."

"You're still good at fixing things?"

"I try."

I got up. We shook hands, punched each other on the shoulder like American guys do. I said, "I'll call."

"You take care, Artie."

"Yeah."

Fallon zipped up his jacket. "Hey."

"What?"

"You still love Stan Getz?"

5

"Lily?"

There was a muscle that twitched in her cheek. Once I imagined I could see her left eye flicker. Later that morning, after I ate breakfast with Joe Fallon, I sat with Lily. She wanted something from me; I felt she wanted to tell me something. I sat by her bed and stared at her face, but it was blank and she was locked up inside her own body, plugged into life-supports, silent. When I leaned over her, the down on her eyelids seemed to flutter in my breath.

In a corridor near Lily's room, I found Dr Lariot. I couldn't meet his eyes, I was too scared of what I might see, so I kept my eyes fixed on the plastic name-tag on his coat and said, "I want to take her home. To New York."

She wants to go home I told him, but it was me who wanted it. I wanted my life back. Lariot put out his hand and I shook it, and finally I looked up at him, a mild-looking guy, going bald, dark-brown skin. Around us people rushed up and down the hospital corridor.

I dug in my pants for some cigarettes. "Can I take her home?"

"Absolutely not. You can't smoke in here either."

"Why not?"

"It's terribly risky, moving her. Please believe me, this is not a good idea."

Holding the unopened pack of cigarettes, I stood in the corridor and looked at him.

"Let's go outside," he said. "I could use one of those."

In the hospital courtyard, in a garden where there was frost on the grass, we smoked and walked. It was after eleven, but barely light; only a smudge of gray showed in the sky. Winter.

"What if it helps her? What if it helps to be at home?"

"I'm afraid you'll have to face it one way or another. I think it's going to be an enormous battle just to keep her alive. And even then it will be difficult."

"Even then what?"

"Even then there's a lot to cope with."

"You don't think she'll make it, you mean."

"I don't know."

"She'll make it." I wanted to grab his lapels and shake him and make him agree with me.

"There's a child? In America?"

"Yes."

"You'll need some help."

"I could use your help."

"We're doing everything we can," he said in an officious voice.

"How?"

69

He tossed the cigarette into a patch of snow. "I'm sorry you're unhappy."

"Everyone's just sitting around, and she's lying there."

"There's nothing we can do except wait."

"I can't do that. I can't do nothing. Maybe there's some other doctors I can talk to. There has to be someone."

He was offended. "If you like," he said. "That's fine. Do as you like, Mr Cohen, but it won't make any difference."

"That's pretty fucking harsh."

"Yes."

"How the hell do you know what's inside her head?"

Lariot stiffened. He crossed his arms over his white coat. "It's all about time, and to tell you the truth," he said, his voice edgy now, irritated, angry at me, "if she doesn't come out of the coma soon, she may not come out at all."

"Just another number to you guys, win some, lose some. Right?" I was mad at Lariot because I knew he was telling the truth.

I left the courtyard and went through the hospital to the street entrance. My phone rang. It was Carol Browne.

Christ, I thought. Just what I need. Carol fucking Browne, European chief for Keyes Security. She worked out of London, where I'd met her, and she was coming to Paris. She wanted a meeting.

She was a frosty little woman and she sounded pissed off. In the street I leaned against the hospital wall and listened to Browne and pictured her at the other end.

She was twenty-nine, small and efficient with big glasses and a faint, patronizing smile. Some of the guys at

70

the Keyes London office referred to her, behind her back, as the Garden Gnome. She talked the language of focus groups and marketing. She looked like a woman who went to the gym every day.

Carol Browne's smug voice dripped into my ear. Coming out of the hospital where I'd already offended the doctor, I thought: let it lie, man. It's a job. You need the money. You're freelance. Suck up a little.

"How are you, Carol?"

"Look, I'm not going to mince words. I'm coming over."

"That's nice."

"Don't bullshit with me, Artie. I'm terribly sorry about Lily. It's dreadful. The New York office is sorry. If there is anything we can do to help her, we will. So I thought I'd better say that first of all."

In my jacket pocket I found another cigarette, lit it with one hand, inhaled it like a drug while I listened to her and watched people mince past cautiously, trying not to slip. The pavement was slick as glass. It was Friday. I'd arrived in Paris early Wednesday morning. I was tired. I tried to focus on the conversation.

"Thank you," I said.

"We've got to close the Levesque case. I had a talk to New York. It's dragging on. It's open and shut, this one, isn't it, Artie? We know how he died, we've got his bank statements, all we need is to know who forged his bloody signature. We paid for your trip to Europe. It was a favor to the New York office, you know. We haven't got anything more than we did when you arrived in London."

71

I kept my mouth shut.

"I know it's not the best time for you, but it's a business. Our client hired us to check through all the records and find the forger. It's a simple paper trail, I'd have thought."

I listened to her, heard the whiney, arrogant British voice and I lost it. "Listen, Carol, just tell me what the hell you're saying."

"I'm saying if I don't get something from you in a week, which is more than reasonable, you're off this job. Not just here, either. I talked to New York. You can call them yourself if you like." In the background I could hear her tapping on her computer, hitting the keys hard. Tap tap tap. "I'm sorry," she added.

I pictured her mean small face again, the pointed chin, the frizzy hair, the supercilious look. But I needed the work to keep me in Paris. I needed the money to take care of Lily and Beth. I needed the company credit card to pay the hotel. For once in my life, I bit my tongue literally, bit it until it stung, tossed my half-smoked cigarette into the gutter.

"I'm on it today," I bluffed. "Look, I have a lead. I wasn't going to tell you until I ran it down, but I have a lead."

"What?"

"I have a lead."

"Come off it, Artie. You haven't a thing on Levesque, and I'm putting someone else on it as soon as someone comes free."

"Carol?"

"What?"

72

"Who hired Keyes? Who wanted the Levesque thing looked at?" I'd asked in New York, but no one was talking.

"Maybe the bank. Maybe someone private. There was a request for anonymity. We never ask. Anyway, it came through the New York office."

"So it could be some criminal who hired you, or some Nazi thug or any other kind of creep."

"Sure. Or some corporation. Or some crazy rich guy. We're not the police. We're in business."

"Sure you are," I said, but I was already walking to the Metro.

"I'm taking you off the bloody case, all right? I called to cut you some slack. You're not in any condition. I'll make it nice when I report to New York, but you know what, Artie?"

"What?"

"We've got to close this, and you're just not a closer." The contempt flowed through the phone.

"You'll have the goods later today," I said, switched off my phone and got the subway.

I got lost. I got the Metro to the suburb where the bank was. I got off at the wrong stop, then found myself heading across a small park where bare branches snapped in the wind and leaves crackled underfoot. I was in a hurry. Carol Browne was cutting me loose. Lily needed help; I had to get her home.

In Puteaux there was a hustle of activity: twenty-somethings in great outfits hurrying to modern buildings after lunch; fancy restaurants spilling confident, busy,

French people onto the sidewalk. They looked like advertising guys and women who worked at magazines, people with things on their mind and money in their pockets. The weekend was coming up. They had plans. Thin but sleek, they yelled into phones, laughed together, crossed the street against the light. A waiter outside a café stared at the bleak sky, sneaking a smoke. Lunch was over.

The bank I was looking for was in the middle of the shopping street. In the lull after lunch, only a few customers were doing business, writing deposit slips, waiting for a teller, women mostly, an old lady with her middle-aged daughter, a mother and twins, six or seven years old, all three in matching pink parkas.

The tellers worked behind a marble counter. The way the bank was set up, it would be easy to write the check, give it to a teller, then slip out before some manager arrived to ask any questions. I looked at the ceiling. There were no obvious surveillance cameras.

Someone with balls. You had to be pretty arrogant or really stupid to walk through the door, saunter in, write out a check on somebody's account, give it to the teller. I had already called the branch but no one was talking, so I figured it wasn't the bank who put Keyes on the job. At the bank, someone would remember. Hard to forget a guy who comes in and forges a check for twenty thousand on a dead man's account.

I got a deposit slip, filled it out and wrote a check to Eric Levesque. It was a pretty desperate idea, but I thought it might alert somebody high up or get them riled. At least I'd get a conversation.

I found a teller. The marble ledge where I leaned was cool and the girl behind the grille had her back to me, so I pushed the check through and waited. When she finally turned around, she was a tiny, pretty girl who smiled flirtatiously. Glancing at the check and the deposit slip, she punched a few keys into her computer. Her little face puffed out with stupidity as she fidgeted with her hair and fingered the collar of her blue blouse. She asked me to wait.

A few minutes later, a middle-aged man in a blue suit emerged through a door to the right of the tellers. His name was Stuart Larkin, he said in English with a Scottish accent. Branch manager. Shook my hand, then escorted me up a flight of stairs and into his office, industrial carpet on the floor, a tray of coffee on the desk and a TV and video player. For a few minutes we danced around each other.

Larkin, who was around fifty, had the good-natured face of a bureaucrat who looked open and gave away nothing at all.

I told him who I was and who I worked for. He was evasive. He poured the coffee, we exchanged useless information.

"You're from Keyes?"

"Yes."

"Do you want to tell me who hired Keyes?"

I was silent.

Larkin laughed. "No names?"

"Sorry. By the way, I didn't see any surveillance cameras downstairs."

"We have cameras."

75

"You have cameras, how about a tape with pictures on it?"

He said, "I have tapes."

"But you want to know who hired Keyes." I wasn't going to tell him I didn't know who hired Keyes, so I bluffed. "I can't tell you about the client. It's illegal." It was hot in the office. I needed answers. "Can I smoke?"

"Go ahead."

"Thanks."

"It was you who traced the address where Levesque's statements went? The post office box in California."

"Yes."

"Our security people are on it, of course," he said. "They're pretty damn good." He was faking. "We've had handwriting experts, we've determined the signature was a forgery. I'd like very much to help you, but it's just not in my gift."

I couldn't ruffle him. He had faced down a thousand angry customers, he could out-sit you, out-bore you, could drink coffee without answering anything until you were out of your mind and it was five o'clock and time for him to go home.

I had training, though. I grew up in the capital of bland bureaucracy. I could remember how to wait. In Moscow, even as a kid, you learned to wait. You waited in line, at shops, at school, for everything. In my family, after a while, you waited to leave the country. I could out-wait anyone if I had to. Larkin and me, we sat and drank the coffee and I kept my mouth shut.

He said, "I hate French coffee."

"You're Scottish?"

76

He nodded.

"They make good coffee there?"

"Worse than this."

"What town?"

"Glasgow."

"Nice?"

"That depends."

"What on?"

"Look, Mr Cohen, I know you don't want my advice on your next holiday destination." He pulled open a desk drawer, removed a brown envelope, slit it open, pulled out a video cassette, held it up.

"Surveillance tape?"

He nodded. "This bloody coffee's cold." He picked up his phone and asked for a fresh pot.

"Can I have the tape?"

"I doubt it."

"What would it take?"

"I imagine it might be possible to make you a copy at some point."

"What do you want?"

Larkin's secretary brought the coffee. He lifted the lid and smelled it. "It would take your telling me what you really know about Levesque."

I climbed out of the armchair and went to the window. It was snowing. When I turned around, Larkin was perched on the edge of his desk, leaning forward. He was going to confide.

"To tell the truth, we're fairly stumped here," he said.

"You haven't had your people on this long, have you?"

He didn't answer.

I said, "We, by we I mean Keyes, we've done the paper trail. His contacts, business associates, friends. There weren't many. He was some kind of freelance investment guy, lived out on the California coast most of the time, a loner." I paused. "But you knew all that because we shared it with you, and you didn't share anything back at all." I kept on bluffing. I didn't know what Larkin knew.

"I admire your ingenuity, Mr Cohen, writing out a check to M. Levesque. That way, rather than some low-level bank clerk, you knew the relevant executive would see you. You knew you'd get my attention."

"I tried the phone."

"I've been driven more than a wee bit mad by all this to tell you the truth. We can't have people coming in and trying to rip off twenty thousand dollars from one of our customers even if he is dead. I know Keyes are excellent. I'd be grateful for anything you have."

I yawned. I was drowning here in doublespeak and unless I put out, he wasn't going to give an inch. I wanted the video tape.

He looked up. "Am I boring you, then?"

"Yeah. You are. You're boring me with this cat and mouse stuff, and frankly, I came here to share some information, but you don't want to share, so I'll just say so long."

Slowly, I crushed out my smoke in the saucer of my coffee cup. Larkin took a call about a mortgage.

I excused myself, went to the bathroom, tried to call the hospital where there was no news, and Gourad, who

78

wasn't at his station house. There was a message from Carol Browne to call her hotel before six. I called the hotel and left her a message, I was making progress, I'd be with her. I knew I was going to have to give Larkin something.

I went back to his office. I smiled. He smiled. I put on my jacket.

He stood up. "You said you had information."

I nodded.

"Sit down, please." From his bottom drawer he took a bottle of single malt. "It's Friday, the end of the week, can I offer you a small drink?"

I sat down. "Make it a big one."

"With pleasure." Larkin sat down, found a couple of glasses, poured us both a hefty shot. I could see from the way he knocked it back that he was a drinker. Maybe even a drunk.

I said, "Why would anyone try to withdraw money on a dead man's account and think he was going to get away with it?"

"Because he wasn't aware the man was dead?" Larkin said.

"That's what I thought at first." The whisky was delicious. "But he had Levesque's check, he had some idea of the signature. He must have known Levesque to get as far as he did, why didn't he try faking it right? If he knew Levesque that well, wouldn't he know Levesque was dead, and he didn't stand a snowball's chance in hell of getting any of the dough?"

"I see what you mean."

"So maybe our forger didn't really want the money."

Larkin's bland façade broke. He refilled my glass, then his own. "That's bloody brilliant. But why?"

"You tell me."

"God, our own security people are all bloody worse than useless, desk men, they think you can do it with computers. If they have to get off their fat arses for half a day, it constitutes over-time." He tossed back his drink. "I'm sorry."

"I know how you feel."

"Who hired Keyes, then?"

"It really was on an anonymous basis. I don't know."

"Is that the truth?"

"Yeah."

Larkin ran his hand over the video tape. "If he didn't want the money . . ."

"Go on."

"He wanted to stir things up."

"Exactly what I'm thinking."

"But why on earth?" Larkin said.

"I'm working on it. You want to keep this a tiny bit quiet for a day or two, that I was here?"

"I can't do that," he said. "On the other hand, it's Friday and if I forget about it for a few hours, no one will be around until Monday morning."

"Thanks."

"You're welcome."

"What about the tape?"

"I might find a way to get a copy made."

"Make it fast," I said.

Larkin walked me to the door. "Where are you staying?"

6

In a dark parking lot outside the fair, I saw Mickey Mouse take off his head. The mouse head came off, the guy, in jeans and a sweatshirt, stuffed it in his little car – the Euros drive these cars that resemble toys – and put on a yellow ski jacket. He exchanged his mouse feet for boots and headed towards the fair itself, a makeshift amusement park, where there were still Christmas lights strung on wires. When I looked at the car close up, I saw a Euro Disney sticker on it.

I could hear the music from a couple of stalls; I could smell the sugar-coated peanuts they sold. To one side of the fair's entrance, I saw the bar.

I was here to meet Larkin. He'd called after I got back from the bank and asked me to meet him at a bar. "The bar is next to a fun-fair," he said. "Christmas fun-fair. Porte de Vanves. Take the Metro and I'll meet you."

A few people, dragging kids by the hand, hurried through the gate. Music played in the distance. Christmas was over; the weather was lousy. I went into the bar and looked around for Larkin. He wasn't there.

In the bar I ordered a beer, then a brandy. The guy with the Mickey head was moonlighting behind the bar, or maybe this was his real job and he did Mickey part-time. I was edgy. There were about half a dozen people in the bar, most of them watching soccer on a big TV. Most drinking beer. I drank the brandy, then another one. Larkin was late. I called the number he'd given me, but there was no answer. I waited another hour.

Finally, I asked Mickey if he knew Stuart Larkin and he said, sure, he was a regular. "Don't worry about him," he said in French. "Stuart is famous for losing track of time. It could be tomorrow night when he shows up."

"Someone mentioned my name?" Larkin was coming through the door. He wore a green fleece shirt and a thick tweed jacket. There was a video tape sticking out of the pocket and Larkin was drunk.

"You have something for me?" I gestured at the tape while Larkin ordered a double whisky and tossed it back.

"Sure." He plucked it out of his pocket and held it up for me. "Let's go for a walk," he said. "I need some air."

Somewhere inside the amusement park, "Yesterday' was playing from a boom-box. The snow fell in soft fat flakes as I followed Larkin through the park. Most of the rides were shut. A couple of men stretched tarps over the stalls.

The fair took up about five acres of ground. We walked until we came to a rickety roller-coaster, Larkin watching me warily the way a drunk watches you when he wants another drink and you have the bottle. I wanted the video tape.

I said, "Can we just do this? I'm in a hurry."

Larkin glanced at me then looked up at the roller-coaster. The wooden struts, painted white, looked like pick-up sticks in the dark. The guy who worked the thing wanted to go home, but Larkin stuffed some money in his hand.

"Give us a ride," he said. "Give us a roller-coaster ride."

"We're wasting time," I said, but Larkin patted the tape in his pocket and climbed into the front car of the roller-coaster.

The ground was slippery and as I followed him I tripped over an empty beer bottle, skidded to my knees, pushed myself up and kept going.

In the distance I could still hear the music, fainter now, "Michelle", with Paul McCartney singing the jingly music that could go around in your head until it drove you nuts. I was going nuts. I'd had some booze and nothing to eat and not much sleep. I was crammed into a roller-coaster on the edge of Paris with a drunk who had a tape I was desperate for.

I said to Larkin, "You're going to give me the tape when we get off this fucking thing?"

"Sure, Artie. Certainly I am. That's why I brought it."

I didn't see the guy on the ground pull the lever to start the roller-coaster. Somehow I knew, in that split second before it began, that there were two of them. Two men. I knew I wanted to get off, and I reached for the bar to pull myself up.

Something was wrong. I felt it the way you feel it when you board an airplane and you know something is wrong.

Something, someone, threw me back against the seat. At first I thought I was drunk. Then I heard it. The switch. The gears grinding, as the car bumped me down again, and shunted forward before I could get out. I jammed down the safety bar and gripped it hard. Larkin, who had pulled a can of beer out of his pocket, was laughing.

The car rattled up the first incline, the empty cars behind us shaking. Slowly, it climbed up until it reached the top and began to fall. Next to me in the dark, Larkin's face was pale, like a clown's, and he was laughing and laughing. There was snow on his head.

Then the cars rattled up again and fell. My hands were clenched over the cold metal bar. Finally we coasted down the last hill. I could see the ground a few yards away. But the roller-coaster didn't stop.

Again, it started to climb. It dropped, climbed again, faster now, or it seemed faster. It went on and on. In my head, I saw it break, saw the wood struts fall down like sticks, the car falling off the rails like a toy, crashing into the ground. I felt this thing would keep going until my head broke open and the brains flew out. When I looked at Stuart Larkin next to me, he was out cold.

Maybe I was dreaming. I looked out over the fair and there seemed to be more people in Mickey Mouse outfits and little Euro-cars in bright colors and I knew I was hallucinating. Cracking up. The roller-coaster started another ascent. Larkin's body rolled against me. We slammed down again.

Then it stopped.

The roller-coaster stopped so hard it threw me back

against the seat, against Larkin, and then came to a dead halt. I grabbed the tape out of his pocket. A small crowd had gathered on the ground. People were yelling. In the distance I heard a police car. I stuffed the tape inside my jacket, climbed out of the roller-coaster and ran. Looking over my shoulder, I ran until I couldn't breathe; the air in my lungs was frozen.

At the hotel the guy at the desk unplugged his video machine and dragged it up to my room. My head hurt. The roller-coaster ride scared me bad, but I had the tape.

I got a ham sandwich and some lukewarm beer. Next door someone was listening to a TV so loud I couldn't think. I banged on the wall. I put the tape into the TV and switched it on.

What was I looking for? I was looking for someone who could have forged Levesque's check, someone who could have had access to his checkbook, someone who was in the bank that day at the right time.

The teller had stamped the time on the check: 3.10 p.m. The tape ran from about 3 to 3.20. It was a lousy tape. After a few minutes, I slid onto the floor and put my face close to the TV. As if they were walking in water, customers moved languorously in and out of the bank, in and out of camera range. It was a quiet afternoon; there were only a few dozen people.

I played the tape again. There was only one interesting thing. During the period between 3 and 3.20 that day, there were no male customers, only women. It was a woman who knew Eric Levesque well enough to get his checkbook, to imitate his signature. It was a woman

85

who, if she knew he was dead, and she would have known, didn't want the money. She wanted to stir things up, make someone pay attention to Levesque, someone like me. I played the tape one more time. It was definitely a woman. There were only women.

7

The girl had been beaten to death then stuffed behind the billboard when they found her. On the billboard was a sunny landscape with a pair of teenagers in fifties beach clothes on bikes, toasting each other with orange soda, smiling cartoon smiles. There were blue cartoon waves, a yellow cartoon sun.

It was dark and the cops had rigged up temporary lights. People hurrying home turned their heads away. Others stopped to look. It had happened before. In Paris, people were blasé; in other words, they didn't give a shit, Momo told me. A foreign whore murdered and stuffed behind a billboard? They'd seen it before. The snow kept falling.

I'd spent part of the day looking for Stuart Larkin. It was Saturday and the bank was shut. I found an S. Larkin in Neuilly. I found his apartment; he was gone. The concierge told me he'd left that morning for a vacation and I knew they'd got to him. I knew someone didn't want me to have the surveillance tape, someone who got to Larkin, got him drunk, persuaded him to take me for a ride on the roller-coaster.

The billboard stood on a piece of waste ground in the middle of an intersection somewhere in the north of Paris. Snow fell on the garbage, empty McDonald's cartons, smashed cigarette packs, used needles, split condoms, dogshit.

The area, hard up against the ramps of an overpass, was cordoned off. Make-shift barricades were up. Police cars and vans, lights flashing, were parked everywhere and a clutch of men in overcoats and uniforms, heads bent, talked to each other and into phones. The body on the ground was covered with a gray plastic sheet; next to it was a bunch of carnations, hard, small, pink flowers on a gray crust of ice.

From behind the billboard, Gourad emerged sideways, dragging his big body out of the narrow space. His shirt was hanging out of his jeans, flapping in the wind. He shoved it back, lit a cigarette and saw me.

"Fuck. Fuck them, it's always the same," he said. "It's always the kids they go after."

"Who was she?"

"Some street girl. No one. They truck them in from the East. Fresh truckloads every week. Sometimes the pimps snatch them off the streets at home. Sometimes they leave them on the trucks, park a load of them under some overpass where people go to take a piss. The men pull up in their cars for a quick one. Sometimes they do it on the trucks. Jesus fucking Christ."

Gourad crouched down over the body like an animal tending its wounded young and pulled back the plastic sheet gently. I squatted beside him.

The girl looked about fourteen. She had been

88

murdered the night before, and all day, while traffic droned around her and people crossed the street, no one noticed. A homeless woman, scavenging for cans and loose change, saw something wrapped in a black plastic garbage bag. The girl was wearing a white raincoat and white jeans. Her blonde hair was chopped short and it was matted with blood. What you could see, she was beat up pretty bad. Her feet were bare and one was broken. He showed me her broken fingers gently, like precious evidence.

Momo Gourad covered the girl again, pushed himself off the ground and wiped his big hand across his face. He put some glasses on and peered at me. "You saw the fingers, you're thinking it's related to your friend, to Madame Hanes? Maybe, but I wouldn't bet on it. This is just about the poor fucking bitches. How is Lily Hanes?"

"The same."

"I'm sorry. Give it a little time."

"I don't think we have any time."

"Take it easy," Gourad said. "What the hell are you doing here anyway?"

"Looking for you."

"How did you know where to find me?"

"A cop at your station house. Pretty. Brown hair."

"Victoire?"

"Yes."

"You know your way around real good now, don't you, even the night shift. Where were you all day? I was looking for you."

I didn't tell him about the bank or the surveillance

89

video. It was mine and I needed something for Carol Browne. I wasn't ready to share with Momo Gourad.

"At the hospital," I said.

"Let's get the fuck out of here, Artie. There's nothing else I can do right now."

His car was across the street. We climbed in. He was already talking into his phone, looking out the window as more vans pulled up to the site. Gourad was nervous. Maybe the dead girl freaked him out, maybe he wanted to go home to his wife. He pulled the green Golf away from the curb, then drove like a crazy man until we got to a pub. "Le Frog et le Rosbif", the sign out front said.

It was hot, noisy, raucous, and Springsteen was on the jukebox. Guys Momo knew were at the bar. They shook hands with me. I ordered a beer, Momo a Coke – he was working that night, he said. He shucked his winter jacket, then peered in the mirror behind the bar and flicked his collar into place. I'd seen him do it before, twitch at it, then pick some imaginary lint off his lapel. Satisfied, he turned around and offered me his cigarettes.

"Momo, you ever come across an American woman name of Martha Burnham who works with prostitutes that get beat up, that kind of thing? Says she's a social worker."

Gourad looked up from his Coke. On his other side was a cop I'd met at the station house. I didn't catch his name but when he heard me mention Martha, he leaned over Momo and put his little pug-dog face close to mine.

"I heard of her," he said. "She sticks her nose in everywhere. She works around Pigalle a lot, which is my beat some of the time. She's a – how do you say in English? – a pain in the behind."

90

"Why's that?"

"Us, we try to clean up the streets. She's one of those bleeding-heart types who wants us to take everybody home and give them hot chocolate, you know? You understand?"

"Yes."

"There's plenty of girls, and I'm sorry for them, I really am, some of these are kids, twelve, thirteen years old, and they're foreigners, they're alone here. But our hands our tied by the special brigades who take over any of the big cases," Gourad said, then muttered, "Shit."

"What?"

"My chief. The boss."

Coming through the crowded room was the man with the sweaty head I'd met my first day in Paris. "We met," I said.

"I forgot. Lucky you, you get to meet him again." He stood up. "I shall salute like a good lieutenant."

Drumming his fingers on the bar, Gourad's boss asked for cigarettes. Then he shook my hand, but said nothing about Lily – she wasn't a priority. He was the kind of guy who probably thought if a woman got beat up, she asked for it, one way or the other. Anyhow, as he told me – he was talking, Gourad translating – there were truckers blocking every road into Paris protesting the import of British cakes and cookies. The French refused to eat eggs that came from British chickens because certain chickens had been diagnosed with a form of schizophrenia known to induce insanity in the human elderly. The French did not want diseased British pastry on their tables. He was serious.

I lit a cigarette to keep from laughing. I never thought I'd be lonely for Sonny Lippert, but compared to this joker he was a prince.

A few minutes later, we left. In the street, Gourad said, "You want to come with me?"

"Where?"

"My regular shift. Show you Paris by night. We got he/shes in the Bois de Boulogne where Maurice Chevalier sang 'Sank 'eaven for Leetle Girls', we got Albanian pimps, terrorists, human smuggling rings out of China, pickpockets on motorbikes. This is gay Paree, Artie. What's your pleasure? My car's across the street."

"Your boss doesn't like me."

"No."

"He wishes I'd beat it."

"He thinks, you being a cop, you're going to get involved with Lily's case."

"He's right."

"Don't do it."

"I'm not a cop."

"In your genes, you're a cop. He can tell. I'm hungry. You?"

"No."

He stopped for a Big Mac and fries, and offered me some. I shook my head. The fries smelled good. He leaned against his car, finishing the food.

"Help yourself, Artie."

"Thanks."

"Don't get me pushed off Lily Hanes' case, you understand? Don't make waves."

"How come it matters so much to you?"

"It's my fucking case is how come, you know? I said this to them when she got hurt, give me some time on this, OK, and I'll get it. I want it. Please. But, of course, I'm just what you call a detective, and they'll toss this upstairs to one of the big brigades where it will sit in a file and some commissaire will read it and then go for lunch for three hours. That's why I'm spending my free time on it. I hate the way the bastards are so callous. I hate the whole fucking system here. I hate the paperwork. You saw the chief. Yes sir, no sir, pretend we are playing soldiers, sir." He finished his food and tossed the container into a garbage can. "I saw your friend, Lily, and how hurt she was, and I thought, fuck them all. This is my case."

I passed him some cigarettes. He shook his head and looked for his own pack.

Face red with anger, Momo said, "I know stuff they'll never know but I don't write it all down. So, Artie, I'll give you whatever I can. You tell me what you want, OK? But do it quiet." Gourad was big, ugly and smart. He was much too good a cop for the shit he swallowed.

"On Lily, you did prints? DNA?"

"Of course. But these bastards who do this kind of stuff to women, I mean, no one has records on them. They appear from the East like from the slime and they disappear. No records. No nothing."

"Russian?"

"You got a special interest in the Russians?"

"Yeah."

Still leaning on the car, he looked across at me. "OK, I hear you. You want to tell me why?"

"I was born there."

Why did I say it? Maybe I figured if Momo was going to give me something, I'd have to share with him after all. He offered me his French fries; I offered him my past.

I said, "Also I've gone a few rounds with them. Not here, but they got connections and long memories. I fucked with them in New York, in London once. Low-life Russians. Rich Russians who are connected everywhere."

Momo nodded. "The muscle, the kind of thug that does women, they can be anything."

"The kid behind the billboard?"

"Who knows? There was one that was Albanian. This one tonight, who the fuck knows?" Gourad added, "Someone's been asking after Lily."

"What kind of someone?"

"Pompous little prick from your embassy."

"What the fuck for?"

"Lily's an American. An American gets beat up bad in Paris, the embassy takes an interest. Didn't they call you?"

"I don't know. I didn't get a message. You told them what, exactly?"

"It's freezing out here, let's get in the car," he said.

We got back in the green Golf. Momo slammed the door. "So you want to come along while I do my idiotic shift?"

"Sure. You told the embassy prick what?"

He drove into the night. "Me? I didn't tell them anything they didn't already know."

"The other guys working her case, you know them?"

"Sure I know them."

"What kind of cops are they?"

"They're OK. I mean they're what they are, some of them are smart cops, a couple are idiots. They'll do the case right if the boss leaves them be." He was defensive. "So what do you think Lily was doing in Paris in the first place? How come she gets to Paris and gets herself cracked up with a hammer the first night she's in town?"

"I don't know."

Momo was silent as he stepped on the gas. He adjusted his belly behind the steering wheel and squinted out the window, a cigarette hanging off his lip. On the dashboard was a photograph of a smiling man in a baseball cap.

"Who's that?"

"That is the most wanted man in France. A serial killer who murders women on the train between Marseille and Paris. We don't get a lot of serial killers in France. Not officially. We call them terrorists." He laughed. "Or foreigners."

"He looks harmless."

"Look, Art, I don't want to get brutal or nothing, but if you're going to work this, you need to get your brain in shape. You need to reconstruct the last days, you, Lily, what's been going on."

"Did the attack have a signature?"

"Maybe. You want to share anything with me that you found in Lily's stuff? She must have left things in London, papers, whatever."

"I got a quick look before I left London. There's nothing."

"Nothing?"

I said, "It's weird, she cleaned up her desk before she left like you do if you're leaving for a while, no credit-card receipts, nothing. I think she didn't want me to know what she was doing."

"You working some kind of case? Something that could concern people who don't want you nosing around and think Lily's in on it?"

"I don't think so. I'm mostly on a bank thing for a security outfit. Bullshit stuff, but I make a buck. Most of it's in America. There's a couple loose ends I have to pick up here."

He shifted uncomfortably in his seat. "Where were you last night, Artie? I tried to get hold of you. I came by the hotel."

"I don't know, out eating."

"The hotel clerk said you went over to the Portes de Vanves. You asked directions."

"I was meeting a guy."

"What guy?"

"Someone from the bank."

"About your case?"

"Yes."

"Anything else?"

If I told him about the roller-coaster, there would be questions, officials, forms to fill out, time wasted. I said, "No, really."

Gourad knew I was lying, but he let it go.

Outside, the city sped by in a wet blur. My hands shook when I lit a cigarette. "You said Lily was raped." The words came out flat, harsh.

96

"It looks that way. I'm sorry. You want the details?"

"No." Don't think about it, I said to myself. Just keep moving.

"What?"

I was talking to myself out loud. Momo looked at me sympathetically.

"Nothing," I said.

"Take it easy."

"Your guys are nowhere on Lily's case, isn't that right?

Gourad, angry, said, "You got it."

"Where we going?"

"My shift, like I said."

If I stayed with Gourad, he might open up. He wanted to talk. He was angry with the brass and I knew how that was, so I'd keep with him. "You from Paris, Momo?"

"Sure."

"Parents?"

"What's the difference?"

"Hey, I'm just making polite conversation. No one gives a shit where your parents came from."

"You think that?" he said. "You're from New York where no one gives a shit. It matters in France. You're not French unless you've been here five hundred years. I'm part Moroccan. My father's parents came over when he was a kid."

I kept my mouth shut.

"I wish to God I could spend all my time on Lily's case, but we waste our time on small shit. Last night we had to shake down some West African guys for swiping fake Vuitton handbags, then we picked up some Algerians for selling an ounce of hash. I could be working on the fucks who beat up Lily, who killed that little girl and stuffed her body behind the billboard. But we have to make Paris nice."

Gourad's fury spurted up out of him, it made him tick, it made him ambitious.

I said, "You got kids?"

"Sure. Nice wife, two nice kids, nice house in the suburbs. You'd like Monique. You'll come for dinner, she'll make her cheese soufflé. You like a cheese soufflé, Artie?"

"Sure. Thanks."

"One more thing."

"What's that?"

"You carrying, Artie? You have a weapon? It's not allowed in France. This is not the Wild West, OK? We're not in Texas."

I didn't answer. I didn't have a gun, not yet.

"Momo?"

"What?"

"Lily's hair. When you found her, how was her hair?"

"Short," he said. "Her hair was short."

"There was hair at the scene? Her hair?"

He didn't answer.

"Tell me."

"Yes. I don't know why. I don't know what the fuck this means, but something happened to her hair. We found chunks of her hair where they beat her up, like someone hacked it off."

★

98

Momo Gourad drove like a crazy man. He drove me around the parts of Paris he worked on his shift and kept up a stream of chatter. He was up-front about his own boss and the way, like most cops, he hated the system. He was also holding back, feeling me out, wary. He had some kind of personal investment in the case that I didn't understand. He had the gray binder with Lily's case file in his desk drawer and I wanted it bad enough to sit alongside him in the car and listen to him however long it took.

"It won't help, calling again," Gourad said as I started dialing the hospital for the third time. "Give it a break. Please."

I called anyway. There was no news.

Snow kept falling as Gourad drove. Everywhere, I clocked the streets, memorizing what I could, figuring out the city. Rue Saint-Denis where there were sex shops and peep shows and clubs marked *cuirs,* like they were selling leather goods. *"Salons de Lingeries", "Show Lesbiennes".* There were fast-food joints, fake English pubs, kebab stalls where huge lumps of meat turned on a spit.

A van pulled up next to Gourad's car. Through the windows I could see three cops in uniform, young guys in dark-blue jumpsuits. The driver had gelled hair and the focused prettiness of a storm-trooper in a Fascist recruiting poster. He saluted Gourad and pulled away. We turned into rue Blondel, where there were hookers old enough to be my mother.

We pulled up for a red light. Enormous breasts popping out of her white leather coat, one of them leaned against the car. She had on war-paint an inch thick.

In front of an ancient church, five or six guys loitered.

"Prescription drugs," Gourad said. "They get free meds on the national health service, sell them at three bucks a pop. Good business."

"It's organized?"

"No. This is small stuff."

I made conversation. "What about the big stuff? Heroin? Cocaine?"

"Other districts. Not so much on the street here. You see that McDonald's, man, the other side of the place Clichy?" He nodded in the direction of the restaurant. "It's a supermarket. You want to see? You can get anything. Dope. Ecstasy. Hash. What the kids call Mitsubishi."

He stepped on the gas, put on the siren, then drove me the wrong way around the square and pulled up in front of the lighted glass box that was McDonald's. Inside, people were slumped at tables, picking over their burgers, slurping up the Coke and coffee.

"You want something, Artie?"

"I'm not hungry."

"I wasn't talking about food."

I took it like a joke, but he was already out of the car into the street, looking through the window, working the pavement.

A couple of teenagers leaned against the window, cigarettes hanging out of their surly faces. One talked into a phone. The other watched him. Gourad came back to the car, mumbling about the Arabs.

100

"I thought you were Moroccan," I said and wished I'd kept my mouth shut.

"What's that got to do with it?" he said. "I'm not some fucking Arab."

"Lighten up."

"You know all us cops are racists, right, Artie? Everyone, good cops, bad cops, black, white, we're all fucking racist pigs, don't you agree? Isn't that the sociology? Isn't it?"

"Sure, Momo. Whatever."

I said, "Show me where the girls work off the trucks. The prostitutes. Show me where I can find the American. Burnham. Her shelter."

"Why?"

"I want to see."

"Whoever ordered the attack on Lily didn't come from around here."

"How do you know?"

"They don't mess with Americans. They don't go off-turf like that. It doesn't work that way."

"You must have some fucking idea who did Lily?"

He didn't answer. He drove on, out of the square, away from the neon lights and sex clubs and tourists traps. The streets were darker here, wherever the hell we were, and it was hilly. It was snowing harder. People slipped in and out of doorways like ghosts.

This wasn't Paris the way I had imagined it; dismal, hopeless, the ugly walls pitted with holes, scratched with graffiti, the streets slimy with garbage, this was another place. At the end of a narrow street, a ramshackle building was lit up by a couple of bare bulbs over the doorway.

"Burnham's shelter?"

"Yes."

"It was for the homeless. She took it over for the bitches. Sorry, prostitutes. I should be politically correct with you around."

I didn't answer. I needed some air.

"There's nothing here, Artie."

"Let me off, OK?" I put my hand on the car door. "I'll be fine. Drop me at the McDonald's. What the fuck can happen to you at a McDonald's, right?"

Gourad turned the car around.

"Burnham makes you plenty nervous, doesn't she?" I said. "Doesn't she?"

"I'll get you something tomorrow. I swear to God, Artie, I'll help you on this case." Momo sized me up, figuring if he should part with information. "I'm going to give you someone to meet. Somebody who might know about this type of beating, this signature." He scribbled a name and address on one of his cards. "Call her tomorrow. Say I told you."

"A cop?"

"No."

"Personal?"

"Yes."

"Show me Lily's paperwork."

"I can't."

"Then forget it."

Gourad was walking some kind of tightrope and it was stretched very thin.

"Listen, I appreciate your help, Momo. I really do. So we'll talk. OK?"

He maneuvered the car into an empty space outside McDonald's. I opened the car door. He put out his hand and I shook it. Something made him hesitate.

I said, "What is it?"

"There was someone."

"Who?"

"Someone who maybe had a piece of the action, or we heard anyhow, and maybe his outfit was a front. A model agency that was a front for whores. Part of a network. They moved girls that way, a lot of them, sometimes they could do it legally, get them visas. But we could never prove it. Maybe it's connected, the little girl that got murdered. Lily."

"What was his name?"

"It's classified information. The model agency looked legit on the surface. We're legally restrained from making it public. There's no decent evidence at all. You can't use what I'm telling you. Ever."

"Fine."

"I only mention it because he was American. He was part French, he had a French name, but he lived in America most of the time. It was a long-distance relationship."

"Where in America?"

"California," he said.

"Tell me his name."

"This is my ass, Artie, I mean we're talking my fat ass on the line if this gets out. You met my boss. He's a pompous putz, as you say in New York, who wants to hang me out to dry very very slow."

"It won't get out. Tell me his fucking name, please,

for Chrissake. Lily's lying there in that hospital. She could be dying."

He didn't answer and I got out of the car again. I was sick of the games. Gourad got out too, and leaned on the roof.

"His name," Gourad said slowly, "his name was Levesque."

I was halfway to McDonald's. As offhand as I could manage, I turned around and walked back to Gourad's car and leaned on it, facing him. I pretended my interest was casual.

"So where is this Levesque? It's a common name?"

He said, "What's that have to do with it?"

"Is it a common name?"

"He's dead. Levesque is dead. It's just a hunch."

"How long's he been dead?"

"That's where the problem is. He's been dead a long time. Around four years."

"He had a wife?"

"What?"

It was a woman who had tried to cash Levesque's check, so I asked Gourad, "Did Levesque have a wife?"

"How the fuck should I know if he had a wife?"

"Find out for me, OK? Just do it. Please. OK, Momo? Get me this information." I was leaning over the car roof. The snow made it cold and slick. "What was his first name?"

"Who?"

"Levesque."

"His first name was Eric. He was Eric Levesque," he said. "I have to go."

8

Trying to light a cigarette, I stood on the pavement where Gourad dropped me and he leaned out of the car and called, "Hey, Artie, you OK, man?" but I just waved and tossed the match into the gutter.

Eric Levesque. My head was pounding with the information. The attack on Lily had been my fault. Because of my case. Somehow, it was connected.

Outside McDonald's, a couple of kids waited. Black, Arab, I couldn't tell the difference. I was a fish out of water here, where tourists never came. You could buy dope at McDonald's and there were no monuments.

I went inside, ordered coffee and drank it from the paper carton. How was Levesque connected to Lily? Did something in the case get her interest? The model agency? Was that enough? Did she put two and two together and assume it was a front for prostitutes? There was a note about a model agency in Levesque's file. But when did Lily see the file? Why was she looking? Then I remembered.

It was London, in the apartment Lily's friend lent us.

★

We're kidding around in the London apartment, eating a huge chocolate cake, drinking Champagne and laughing, and Lily's telling me about Paris. She's going the next day.

I say, "It's a guy. Tell me. It's some debonair European guy with tight buns and loads of money."

She laughs. "Yeah, and who wears a gold chain around his neck and a diamond earring and keeps a yacht in Monte Carlo. Don't be a jerk," she adds, "though I think you're pretty cute for thinking everyone has the hots for me. It's friends, you know? Some research. No big deal, Artie. Swear to God."

"You feel OK?"

"Yeah, I do. I'm sorry about last night. I was crazy on that wheel. I got crazy."

"Sure?"

"Sure. So it's OK if I go to Paris ahead of you?"

"I can use a day to finish up some paperwork."

"OK, great." She always says this to close a conversation; when she figures something is concluded, a piece of work, a phone call, an argument, Lily says, "OK, great."

I look at her, her mouth smeared with chocolate. She looks happy enough, but her eyelids flutter double-time. A movie director we know at home once told Lily she blinks twice the rate of most people. Lily's brain is always busy.

I said, "You're restless."

"I'm always restless. I think there are people who are just travellers, who can't really settle, who never really belong any place."

"Like me."

"No, you're dying to be domesticated, you found New York, you settled. I like crossing the borders. I get a real buzz out of it, knowing I made it to the other side, you know? That I got there in time."

"What kind of borders?"

She said, "Whatever. I'd go climb Everest if I could."

"Push yourself, you mean."

"Yeah."

"Can we change the CD?" Elvis was on the CD player.

"Sure."

She takes it off and puts on some Erroll Garner we both like. *Concert by the Sea*. She gave it to me one Christmas.

"You know what?"

"What, sweetheart?"

"Sometimes when I'm with you, I don't feel anxious about the future anymore." She paused, then said, "Artie?"

"Mmm?"

"Can I ask you something?"

"Anything. Always." I start kissing her and she tastes of chocolate and she curls up in my lap.

"What's the job you're on?"

There's no guile at all in her face, not so far as I can tell, and all I say is, "You're interested?"

"Sure. Tell me about it."

"I want another glass of wine. Just one last one."

Lily giggles. "You always say that, just one more, and the waiter doesn't care, and I don't care if you have one

107

more or seventeen, you know that. So tell me." She reaches for the bottle.

Normally Lily stays clear of my stuff, so I'm pleased as a four-year-old she's so interested. "No big deal," I say. "An old bank account. No one's touched it, suddenly there's some activity. Someone writes a check. The signature looks phony. Maybe it was forged. Paper trails. The usual."

She says, "Is it a lot of money?"

"Some. A few hundred thousand. Enough to wake someone up."

"And there's some connection here, in London?"

"Keyes is running the case here. But it's a branch bank in the suburbs of Paris. It's how I worked the gig. Made them think it was important I came to Europe."

"You did it for me. The trip, I mean. Didn't you? You hate paperwork."

"I don't mind it."

"But you did it for me. Didn't you?"

"Yeah."

She winds her long arms around my neck and says in my ear, "You're a doll."

I grin at her like a fool. "I know."

"Let's go to bed."

Late at night, McDonald's smelled of rancid fat; the torpor of the druggy kids weighed on me too, and I drank coffee and thought about Lily. Something I told her in London, something she saw in the file, had made her interested in the Levesque case. Was that why she came to Paris ahead of me? So I wouldn't know, wouldn't stop her?

When I thought about her, I felt short on oxygen, like someone delivered a sucker punch. I'd been around hospitals plenty in the last few years. You learned to deal with the dead. Dealing with the coma victims, the half dead, the people out of reach, was harder. Like Lily, they were physically present; you could see them, even touch their flesh, but you couldn't make contact.

In McDonald's, watching some kids deal drugs, the others slumped over the tables, I felt if I let go for a second, if I stopped concentrating on Lily's case, she'd slip away. Just go. Never get back.

I've known Lily Hanes for almost six years, and she drives me crazy. She won't move in with me permanently, won't marry me. She's scared it will wreck things with us.

There have been great times. Not so great times when I pretty much gave up on her and went somewhere else, with someone else. I always came back.

I hate bullshit words like "brave' and "courageous", but Lily is both. She does nutty things; she takes jobs in some crap-hole because she thinks there's a good story. She goes out in the middle of the night because a friend is hurting or someone's kid is sick.

I've managed to pass forty without a wife or kids, my father's dead, my mother is in the nursing home in Haifa where she inhabits her Alzheimer's half life. I love Lily because she really is brave and she's straight with me. She knows who I am. In the middle of the night, it makes me less lonely. With Lily, it's been mostly good.

I drank the rest of my sour coffee. Her. New York.

The only place I can get my feet down, stop skimming the surface. If I could pull us out of this, I'd try again to get her to marry me.

At the table next to mine, a woman coughed until she spat up into a paper napkin. Her face was pasty. She stared straight ahead.

I leaned over and said in bad French, "You OK?"

"Fine."

"I'm looking for the American woman named Martha Burnham, you know who I mean?"

"No."

No one else in McDonald's knew, or wanted to, and I went outside and re-traced my way, remembering where Momo took me. Up the hill, I found the shelter with the bare white lights over the entrance. A heavy door led into a courtyard that stank of piss. The cobblestones were slick. I skidded, then turned left and banged on a door. Someone pulled it open from inside.

Framed in the lighted doorway was a girl with a thin, old face, though she wasn't more than eighteen. She had a cigarette in her hand. "What do you want?"

Again in my lousy French, I said, "I'm looking for a woman named Martha. An American."

"She's not here."

"Where is she?"

The girl turned away. I put my hand on her arm, she yanked it back as if I'd hit her. I said, "I'm sorry. I just need to see her."

"I don't know where she is, OK? She came earlier, then someone showed up and she left with him. That's all. I'm not her warden."

110

"Who's in charge here?"

"I am."

"Do you know where she went?"

"I wouldn't tell you if I did." She shut the door on me and I backed into the courtyard. I started walking towards McDonald's but I was lost.

I got my phone out and tried Martha Burnham's number; there was only a machine. There was no one on the street and I didn't know where I was. I walked faster.

Levesque, I thought. If Levesque ran the whores and gave the orders, then whoever beat Lily up was taking orders from a dead man.

Footsteps seemed to follow me, the hollow ring of heavy boots on the cobblestones, but when I turned there was no one. I was spooked. I started to trot. It was being in an alien place that scared me. I didn't know anyone. Jogging, I saw a lighted shop-front fifty yards away. As I got closer, like an oasis in a dark desert, the lights turned into a bar.

There were six tables and a bar and it was empty except for me and the bartender, who was listening to a Highlife track on a radio. I climbed on a stool and leaned on the bar.

"Bad weather," he said in French.

I nodded and asked for a beer. I was relieved to get indoors.

Over the bar was a long mirror and in it I saw my reflection. I looked lousy. The bartender put a cold bottle in front of me along with a glass, then disappeared behind a curtain next to the bar. I was by myself. I drank and watched the mirror. Behind me was the door.

I saw him in the mirror first. He filled it up. Behind him in the doorway were two other guys. I couldn't move forward because of the bar. I couldn't move back. The men in the doorway cut me off. I was trapped.

He wore sunglasses. The body was squat with sloping shoulders. The face was doughy and white and he had thin blonde hair that fell over his forehead. Around his neck was a gold cross on a chain and he had on a brown leather jacket. Black leather gloves.

I waited. I tensed up, waiting for them to attack. Nothing happened. The bartender didn't come back. The men barred the door. Blondie stared at me in the mirror. He took off his gloves.

Suddenly he grabbed my shoulder with the force of an ox and spun me around hard. Then he slapped my face with his open hand. The feel of flesh on flesh made him elated, I could tell; it revved him, humiliating me, and I thought: this is what he does to women. He would want them to know that, for him, they were only whores. He liked the feel.

Was this the creep who attacked Lily? Was his putrid stink of aftershave the odor I thought I smelled on Lily's clothes at the station house?

He'd hit me so hard, I stumbled and fell on the floor. Instinctively, my hand went to my face. Getting up, I slipped. By the time I was on my feet, the men were outside. They climbed into a car outside the bar. I saw it go. I ran into the street. The car turned a corner and disappeared. The street was deserted.

I was halfway down the hill. A hundred yards away, I could see a wide street. Traffic, lights, people walking fast, heads down against the wind and the snow. Somewhere I heard the wah-wah of a French cop car and maybe I should have waited, but I'd had enough of French cops.

I scrambled down to the main road. Outside McDonald's, I got a cab. I told the driver to take me to the hotel. He looked over his shoulder.

"Just take me, OK. I fell down," I said in French and he raised an eyebrow. He let me know he figured I was some hopeless American looking to buy cheap drugs. He offered advice on the subject. I closed my eyes.

When we pulled up in front of the hotel, there was a patrol car outside. Someone was looking for me, maybe Momo, maybe his chief. And Carol Browne might show. The last thing I wanted was an encounter with the garden gnome.

I crouched low in the backseat. The driver looked over his shoulder. I shoved some money in his face and told him to keep moving.

"Just go. Drive around for a while."

The driver went. We got to the Champs-Elysées which was still lit up for Christmas.

"Where to?"

I called Joe Fallon because I didn't know who else to call. I wanted to see someone from home. It was midnight, but he picked up. He was at the office, he said, working late, great to hear you, Artie. Come on over.

His office was off Avenue Montaigne. It was a cold impersonal suite of rooms, except for the family pictures and the loafers that lay on the bleached white wood floor

113

where he had stepped out of them. A pair of mis-matched socks were crumpled on top of the shoes. Behind the glass desk, Joe was massaging his bare feet.

"Hey, Artie, come on in. I'm sorry about this. I stubbed my toe so bad it's killing me." He reached over the desk, wincing with pain as he put his foot on the floor, shook my hand, sat down hard and groaned.

"I'm so glad you came. I could use the company. Let me just finish this one thing and we could go out and eat." He started typing something into a lap-top. "Take a look," he added, waving at piles of stuff in one corner of the room.

They were samples from companies Joe owned: vintage wine in bottles with art labels; foie gras and other fancy food in elaborate packaging; boxed sets of Champagne flutes; a rack with fur coats, at least one sable. There was luggage, silver, linen sheets, handbags, watches, there were models of cars and brochures for hotels where the rooms started at a grand a night. Aladdin's fucking Cave.

Toys, Joe said, and shut his computer. Most of the money came from the new media companies. "I bought and sold like baseball cards," he laughed. "'98, '99, you didn't need any brains, money just fell on your head. I had to put the money some place, I started buying fancy shit."

"Sounds like fun."

"I'm giving most of it to my oldest kid now. I'd love for you to meet Billy, he's a pistol with a really nice streak. He was doing great business, all of a sudden he tells me he wants to take time off to work with refugees.

I told him about you and he's crazy to get a look at someone from the old man's past."

Joe and me. Lily and Martha. The past never lets you go.

"What's going on, Artie? You sounded pretty cut up. You want to go out?"

I shook my head.

"That's OK. I've got some booze here if you want. Or coffee. I could make coffee?"

"No thanks."

"What's up?" He came around the glass table, still in bare feet and sat on a brown leather sofa with square edges. There was a chair next to it. I sat down and unzipped my jacket.

He said, "Maybe I can help."

But I didn't tell him much. I liked Joe Fallon. I could see him as a friend, but I was wary. I told him Lily was sick. I spun some half truths about a car accident.

"That's really bad. I'm sorry. What does Lily do?"

"She's a journalist."

"Artie?"

"What?"

"Would you let me get someone on it? I know good people. Doctors. The best."

"Not yet."

"Will you tell me when?"

"Thanks."

"But are you OK with the doctors here? Because we could get someone in from New York, you know, from Cornell or Sinai."

"You're still fixing things."

"I know how it is. I know how it was when Dede was sick, I was trying to fix it, cure her, find someone who knew something, and it didn't make any difference."

I was restless. I had to get out. I had wanted to see Joe, now I wanted to leave. I was drowning in my own craziness. It wasn't Joe Fallon's fault.

"Listen, Joe, thank you. For listening. This helped. Honest."

"You want to eat?"

"No. Not now. I'm going over to the hotel to try to catch some sleep."

"I could give you a ride."

"Don't bother. Your feet don't look so hot."

Hobbling, he walked me to the door of the building and let me out. "Call me."

"I'll call you," I said.

"Good. Just don't disappear on me again."

9

The sun was bright the next day, but when I got out of the taxi the wind was cold enough to blow the skin off your face. Digging the card Gourad had given me out of my pocket, I turned the corner of the Champs-Elysées and passed a group of Russians. The women, in fur, were chattering and showing off their purchases; the men stood by, alpaca overcoats with the collars turned up, smoking, talking. At the curb, a couple of drivers waited for them, leaning against big Mercedes. I caught snatches of conversation as I ran by. Should we go to Manray or Barfly, which restaurant, darling, they said to each other, and eyed a Vuitton shop.

I turned onto rue Pierre 1er de Serbie, a street with handsome houses and fancy stores. I looked for the house number Momo Gourad wrote on the card. It was important for him, I knew, giving me this address.

There was a silver Mercedes parked outside the house. I checked the apartment number and buzzed. Said my name into an intercom. Mentioned Momo Gourad. The front door clicked open. Inside, I climbed a flight of sleek marble stairs. On the first landing, a heavy door was ajar. I went in. The light in the hallway was soft.

From somewhere inside there were voices, chattering, someone laughing, a puppy barking. A voice called out, "Come in," and I followed the sound through the heavy door.

As soon as I went into the room, the lush smells washed over me. Two women were playing cards at a little gilt table in front of the fireplace where a fake fire blazed. Two more sat on a sofa yakking, one with a King Charles spaniel in her lap. The women were all young, in their late teens and twenties, all perfectly dressed in skirts and little sweaters, Gucci, Hermès – I sometimes read Lily's fashion magazines in the can so I know about this stuff. These were babes and they were expensive. Hair done, make-up perfect, nails manicured.

The bodies were also perfect, some natural, some surgical, take your pick. In a bar once I heard a guy say he liked fake tits better. I don't get it; they look and feel pumped up, hard and round, like sports equipment. But I don't like little girls, either.

Lily is always shifty about her age. She was past forty when I met her, but I think she's nuts to care and she knows it. I always tell her she's nuts. Who wants some dim model? It would be like doing it with an unformed child. I don't know, maybe I'm the one that's crazy.

The women looked up from their cards and smiled at me. I could shut my eyes and see the babes transformed into elderly women. Like the inmates of my mother's nursing home where they play cards all day, bent over the games, hairpins falling out of their thin white hair.

"I am Katya." She was older than the others, thirty, maybe, and as she strolled towards me, hand out, a big diamond glittered on her finger. Everything about her glittered, hair, eyes, diamonds. "Katya Strogonoff," she said in English with a Russian accent.

"Sure. And I'm Bobby Borscht."

"Very nice." She grinned. It was playful, this disarming grin, and seductive. She added, "Well, not precisely my real name, but is OK. Sometimes they are calling me Kate. Hello to you." The voice oozed attention. She wasn't tall, but the posture was perfect, as if she'd been to ballet class as a child.

I told her Momo Gourad gave me her address. She knew Momo, of course. He came to her parties, sometimes he took her to dinner, last time to Fouquet for oysters. It made me wonder where Momo got the kind of dough it would take for oysters at Fouquet, a restaurant I'd just passed on the Champs-Elysées. Where did he get the dough for Katya?

I took off my leather jacket and gave it to her, and she led me into an office, where she poured tea out of a samovar into glasses set in fancy silver holders. The office had black leather furniture and a black teak breakfront with smoked glass doors. Pastel silk flowers were arranged in Chinese vases.

Katya sat behind a large black glass desk. Under the desk lamp her hair was like hot copper, the eyes too green, the lashes too long. The pearls were real, though, and big as cherries. She looked me over tactfully. "Business," she said, "or pleasure?"

When the Soviet Union started breaking up and

119

Russian women began crossing borders for business, it was the Turks who labeled the hookers "Natashas". It was rough trade for these girls; they were the spill-out from the USSR, the debris.

The business exploded. The old Soviet Empire seemed to have an endless supply of gorgeous women. For the young ones with great looks – the mile-long legs, the Slavic cheekbones that could cut glass, the bee-stung lips – there were always guys, the men with money who wanted the right accessory. The Super Natashas, they were called, and they were thick on the ground wherever there was money; anywhere you could use a platinum credit card or buy a magnum of Cristal, these girls flocked, to New York, London, the Riviera, the Hamptons, like fabulous birds of prey.

They were seductive as hell, but not for me. I have a different fix on the Russkis given I grew up there. I was even offered a freebee one night in New York. The girl said I resembled a poet she once knew. Hip hop, she said, I resembled a hip-hop poet, a white guy, but cool. She was wired. I bought her a glass of Champagne and went home.

Clearly, Katya "Strogonoff" was one of them, a deluxe Super Natasha.

"Hello?" Katya was waiting.

"Sorry. I was thinking about something."

"Surely."

I offered her a pack of smokes. Instead, she picked up her own, shook the expensive box of exotic cigarettes lightly until one fell into her hand. I felt she could shake me down like one of her smokes if she wanted. She lit it with a Dunhill solid-gold quarter pounder, leaned back slightly, inhaled deep and smiled. The perfect tits tilted up nicely under the snug black cashmere sweater.

Katya had copied her performance from some movie. Maybe she went to the pictures with Momo. She knew the part, the modern Russian business broad, direct, confident, clinging, flirtatious, all at the same time. There was a Russian creep I once nailed who watched *The Godfather* like it was a training manual. It made him cry, he said. The Italians had more style than Russians; they had honor. I told him he was an asshole and got him locked up for a long time.

I drank my tea and played along with Katya Strogonoff.

"Business, pleasure, I don't know," I said. "What's going?"

"You are actual friend of Maurice Gourad?"

"You bet."

"Professional friend?"

"What other kind is there?"

"Momo likes party, maybe you are special party friend."

"Call it professional."

"I see." She straightened up. She understood I was a cop, and if I was, there was nothing in this meeting for her except maybe trouble. She closed her eyes and when she opened them again, they were hard and smooth like marbles, and very cold. She squashed the cigarette in an ashtray and waited. It was quiet now, both of us sitting out the silence.

I went first. "I'm looking for someone who did this.

Someone who hurt this friend of a friend." I tossed the picture of Lily onto her desk. "Momo says maybe you can help. Someone found her and hurt her very bad."

"Who is she?"

"Like I said, a friend of a friend."

"What makes you think I can help?"

"Momo Gourad thinks you know a lot of people."

"I don't know people who do these things."

"Would it help if my friend's friend had money?"

"It can always help, sure."

"So let's say my friend's friend has a lot of money."

"Is not real issue."

"This is your place, Katya? Your whorehouse?"

"I am not understanding," she said coolly, so I translated into Russian for her. She asked me my Russian name and I told her.

In Russian, she said sharply, "Don't be stupid, Artemy Maximovich Ostalsky. This is my flat. These are my friends. We have tea parties here, we play cards, we get together when we're not working. They each have their own flats also, you see?"

I looked at her.

"I'm telling you the truth." She leaned over the table. "It doesn't work like you think. People are stupid. They assume everything." Her Russian was educated.

"What were you?" I asked in English.

"What was I?" She spoke English in reply.

"In Russia?"

"I was doctor, pathologist. In Moscow. What do you care? You think it is only ignorant women, uneducated women do this thing, going with men?"

"I don't think about it."

"Doctors. Lawyers. Teachers. I knew brilliant girl who was nuclear physicist, but not paid for three years. She had two choices, sell nuclear materials to Iraq or work as whore in the West. She decides whore was more honorable. Also profitable. Which do you prefer? Her mom gave her life savings for face-lift. Also tits."

"Christ."

Katya laughed. "She did OK. She has nice husband in Silicon Valley, California, now. Two kids. Nice home. Her mom is living with them."

"So the girls are strictly on a take-out basis, is that it? They go with the men to their places."

"Something like that, but more complicated. Or not. Depends."

"What on?"

"Taste."

"So who owns this apartment?"

"I do. I told you. This is for parties."

"You don't live here?"

"No."

"You must make good money." I figured she took poor, vain Momo for some ride.

She said acidly, "The apartment is good investment."

"Who are your investors?"

She started blowing perfect smoke rings.

I picked up Lily's picture and held it out. "You don't know any men who beat up women this way?"

Katya picked up another cigarette and looked at it. She toyed with it, turned it around, examined the filter, then tossed it onto the desk, sipped her tea, put the cup down, picked up the picture and leaned back in the chair.

Suddenly I was so tired I couldn't play the game. "Never mind. I'll go."

"You swear this is Momo who sends you?"

"So you and Momo, you and my new good friend Momo Gourad, you're an item?"

As if she couldn't resist, she smiled. The hard features broke, the eyes warmed up; she blushed.

Katya got up and went into another room, where I heard her call Momo on the phone. Then she came back, pulled a cardigan off the back of her chair and put it on, buttoning it up to the collar. It made her look more like a schoolgirl than a high-priced hooker, except for the pearls. She fidgeted with her tea.

I said, "Memo's broke."

"I don't care. Money I can get. Momo gives me his soul."

"His soul?"

She looked up at me. "Yes. Why? You think I am only hooker for hire? You don't know anything, Mr Cohen. You forgot how it works over there, in Russia, at home. You do what you do for getting out. Like Americans say, you get a life."

"Momo helped you with your papers?"

"Momo, other people."

"How did you meet?"

She laughed. "I sometimes did forensics for police in Moscow. I am attached to police sometimes."

"You worked for the cops?"

"Sure. Momo was on conference long time ago. International police work. I keep his number."

"You thought it might come in handy?"

"Yes."

"What other people?"

"Not now." She looked at the ceiling. The old habits never really die.

"Someone's listening?"

"Is reflex."

"Why did Momo send me here, Katya?"

"Maybe he thinks I can help you with your sad friend of friend," she said. "Your lady was raped?"

I didn't answer.

"I'm sorry. I think about it because Momo wants me to. He asks me to. Do you want to walk with me, Artemy Maximovich? OK? Let's go walking. I love cold weather."

Bundled up in a tawny sable coat, yellow Timberland hiking boots on her feet, Katya followed me out her door.

We went to the river. It was cold and clear. At the Alma Bridge, Katya pointed out the tunnel where Princess Diana died. She walked me across the bridge and along the river. We walked for a long time.

Katya smoked and talked in Russian. She had pushed her orange mane off her face, tucked it up under a pale-blue knitted watch-cap. She walked hard, swinging her arms, pushing the pace. "I am sorry for you," she said. "About your wife. Her name is?"

"Lily. She's not my wife, but that doesn't matter. It's the same."

"I'm sorry."

"Thank you."

"The way they hurt her, it's known."

"How do you know?"

"I know."

"Who are they?"

"Pimps."

I waited. "They ran you?"

"They tried, but I got away. I think. You're never sure. I met a decent man who got me out of Russia, and then Momo got me papers. I never owed anything to pimps."

"But that's not how it is for most."

"No."

"Where do they work out of, these pimps?"

"Everywhere. Everywhere and nowhere. For pimps, Europe is just a clean plate, they can eat whatever they like, a snack here, a snack there. New York, of course, everything starts and ends in New York. This is where new Russians put down new roots. I would like to see New York City." She tossed her cigarette into the river. "You like winter? This is a healthy time."

"You're homesick?"

"Sometimes. You know why these girls are so popular with Western men – Russian, Ukrainian, Kosovan, Bosnian girls – you know why, Artemy?"

"Why?"

She stuffed her hands in her pockets. "Same reason you go to war for Kosovo, same reason French intellectuals are crazy for Sarajevo. They look Western. They look like you. They've got blonde hair, blue eyes. They speak of films and philosophy. You're cold?"

"Just tired."

She raised her hand as a taxi passed, we ran for it and climbed in. Katya gave the driver an address, then leaned back against the seat.

"Russians were bad guys before the end of Communism, bad guys after," she said. "Before, Communists. After, criminals. The whole country – one thousand years of hate, war, starvation, poetry, revolution, music, politics, art, literature, ideas, science, religion, killing, genius, people freezing in the snow, millions dying in wars – all reduced to this."

It was a speech she had made before, but she meant it, it was what fueled her. She went on. "This is what we are famous for now, you know? Not for Tolstoy or Chekhov, Gagarin, Bulgakov, Nureyev, Sakharov, not even Lenin, we are famous now for killers, greed, whores, shopping. All shit that is seeping out into world. You know what they do with girls they take to Israel? They take them to Egypt where border laws are easier, walk them across the border to Israel. Promised Land. Nothing changes, you know, Artemy." She took my arm and smiled. "OK, speech is now finished. You know Momo for long time?"

"No," I said. "Not long."

She smiled. "He is a very good guy. My mother would faint dead away if she saw me with Arab man." Katya giggled. "I think she would rather I am whore."

"You miss Russia?"

"I miss my mom. You are shivering."

"It's OK."

"You would like some hot tea?"

Not far from the hospital, the cab pulled up to an old gray building on the bank opposite Notre Dame. Katya got out and I followed her into a little courtyard and through a second door that she unlocked. She climbed the stairs and I followed. On the top floor she led me to a door and fumbled for the keys in her bag.

Inside, Katya pulled off the blue cap and her bright hair tumbled out. She held the door open. "I always wanted studio. I read about this studio thing in books on Paris," she said.

It was a small apartment, two rooms, the kitchen at the far end. The living room had white walls, a few pieces of modern furniture and, on a shelf, an exquisite little icon. There was a terrace covered in snow. I went to the sliding door and looked out. The view was wonderful. This was the Paris that was, on a brilliant winter day, so beautiful it could break your heart. Along the riverbank people strolled, tourists, students.

"What's your real name?"

She slipped off the rich fur coat and put it neatly on the sofa. "Ykaterina Vladimirovna Slobodkin. As you should say, big fat mouthful. Better Katya. Kate." She walked towards the bedroom. "Excuse me, please," she said.

A few minutes later she reappeared in faded jeans and a pink sweatshirt, her hair in a long orange braid down her back, face scrubbed, sheepskin slippers on her feet. From the kitchen she produced tea, cheese and crackers, a jar of cherry jam, a bottle of Cognac and two glasses.

Katya sat on the edge of the low sofa and served the

drinks and snacks. I sat beside her. Pouring out tea, smiling a little wistfully as she spooned jam into it, she looked like a young Russian housewife. Her face was bare and powdery, like a baby's.

"I want to help you, Artemy. Anything you can tell me about this beating?"

I drank some of the Cognac and the tea and said, "They really hurt her. They broke her fingers."

"On right hand?"

"Yes."

"Bastards."

"It means something to you?"

"I've heard of this, yes."

"Where?"

"I don't remember, but I hear. Some girl. They beat her the same way. They broke fingers on one hand, knees, ruin her face."

"Why did they do it?"

"Because she disobeys her pimp. Or gives money to her kids. I don't know. Shall I find her? Shall I look?"

"Yes. Look."

"There's some children? Your Lily, she has a child?"

"Yes."

She clutched my arm. "Make her safe."

"She is safe. Can I see you again?" I was clinging to the wisps of information.

"Of course. Whenever you would like. I'll make calls for you. I promise. For Momo I will do this. Anything you want."

"Thank you."

"It's OK." She poured more tea and for a few minutes

we sat silently drinking the hot liquid and smoking her exotic cigarettes.

"I'm grateful, really, I swear to God, I'm grateful as hell." I meant it. "I'll tell Momo."

"Don't be so grateful. I am not, how do they say it?" She paused, grinning like a pussycat. "I am not whore with heart of gold."

"No?" I smiled back.

She shook her head. "I don't have much heart left."

I tried not to smile.

"So, Artemy, I know this is cliché, but I cannot resist to make you laugh," she said and kissed me on the cheek.

10

The hotel phone woke me around six that evening. I'd left Katya Slobodkin earlier, gone back to the hotel, fallen asleep. When the phone rang it was dark. My head hurt from the Cognac.

Lily was dead. She was dead and my heart jumped around my chest in irregular patterns, the anxiety like a trapped animal running around, beating at the cage.

"Come immediately." Some nurse, doctor, functionary on the phone. Urgent. For a minute, not knowing if this was a nightmare or real, I couldn't move at all.

Come quickly. Please. As soon as you can. My heart went AWOL and missed a couple more beats. I dragged on some clothes, ran down the stairs and woke up the night guy on the desk who snarled at me. I kept going. Lily was dead. She was dead.

It was dark, I ran as fast as I could, head pounding, listening to the thud of my feet vibrating inside my head. The panic pulled me like gravity, made me feel I was falling, I could hear my feet, my own blood, moving me forward. I ran, crashing into a man who was out buying bread.

At the hospital, a guard tried to stop me, wanted ID. I pushed past him. Outside Lily's room, at the end of the corridor, a group of people stood, heads down, talking, and I knew: she was dead, it was why they had called, and I didn't know if I could live with it, if she was gone. How would I manage with the hole that opened up in my heart?

His huge face wrecked with fatigue and wet from weeping, Tolya Sverdloff sat in her room, bent over her, his hand around hers like a bear nursing a tiny bird. His huge black overcoat covered his body like a shroud. Lily's bruised arm sprouted tubes, her face seemed sunk into itself and there was a flat, damp quality to her skin that was the color of cement.

I came through the door. I said, "She's dead."

Tolya looked up. His face, like an Easter Island statue except for the dimples, brightened. "No, no, Artyom. She's better."

"How better?"

Speaking Russian very softly, he said, "She's conscious. She's been talking." He smiled. "A little talking. I think she's exhausted. She's asleep."

Lily was alive. I turned my head to the wall for a while.

Tolya stayed where he was, holding her hand.

"What happened?"

"I got in from New York, I came here. I'm sitting, keeping her hand warm, talking to her and feeling only despair, as if she was falling away, and suddenly I could feel her hand moving in mine. I said, 'Can you hear me, Lily?' and her eyes opened for a split second and I could see she was in there. It was Lily. I swear it to God. And she says, 'Tolya? Darling? Is this you?' It's going to be OK, Artyom."

He went on talking Russian to me, the purring, educated, actor's Russian Tolya speaks that always makes me feel I'm being had, that my soul is being fingered.

He hauled himself up off the chair so I could sit, then delicately passed me Lily's left hand. It was cool, soft, still limp, but there was movement; a pulse twitched, the fingers were alive.

"How do you feel?" I said.

She whispered, "Stay here."

"All you want."

"Good."

"Lily?"

"What?"

"Do you know who I am?"

"No," she said. "Stay." Her mouth was dry, she forced the words out.

For an hour, more, I sat with her. She opened her eyes again. Her breathing was steady. She recognized Dr Lariot when he looked in. She formed a few words, though I had to lean down, ear by her mouth, to hear her. Tolya stood behind me, watching.

Lily didn't know who I was.

"It's Artie, sweetheart," I said. "It's me."

Lariot, who stood at the door, asked us to leave. It was

enough for her for the first day, he said, with a tiny officious gesture of his pudgy hand.

"You see," he said to me, "it was right for her to stay here with us."

"What?"

"You might have trusted me all along," he mumbled under his breath, then added, "now, she needs rest. We must let her rest."

In the hall outside Lily's room, Lariot told me it was common, this memory loss.

"Will she get it back?"

"In time. Perhaps. Let her rest now."

For now, it was enough she was alive. I went out into the street with Tolya. He lit my cigarette because I couldn't keep my hands still.

"Let me help, Artyom. Please."

"I can do it. I'll take her home and I'll take care of her." I looked at Tolya. "What the hell are you doing here, anyhow?"

"I flew as soon as I heard. I wish you'd called me, I wish I didn't have to hear it from Sonny Lippert. I'm Lily's friend too."

I thought about the bitter argument we'd had, a stupid fight about money. Tolya didn't fight me fair, so we stopped talking, but I was glad to see the bastard. I was happy to see him. But I didn't want his money.

"I can manage. I can take care of her."

"Artyom, I love you for this, but you can't do it alone. She needs professional care. Also," he lowered his voice, leaning over me – I'm a big guy but Tolya's six-six at least – "also she needs to be safe. And Beth. It's better

134

you spend your time finding the creeps who did this to Lily." He tossed the butt he held into the gutter and moved aside while a trio of nurses passed. "Before they do it to anyone else."

Tolya has a paranoid streak. In his New York apartment once, he had a steel-lined room built, a "safety room". When the banker Edmund Safra died in a fire in his steel shelter in Monte Carlo, incinerated, literally, like a piece of meat, Tolya had his own room ripped out. "I'd rather have a good dog," he said.

I said to him now, "I'm taking her home. She'll be safe in New York."

"Don't be crazy, you can't move her yet, OK? We'll fix something for her. I talked to the doctor. I'll get her a private nurse. Also security. It's not good to move her now. This is a good hospital, I checked. Look, Artyom, they took a hammer to her. They smashed her knee, her elbow, fingers, they tried to smash her face." He was talking his own corrupt mixture of fast Russian and English, like he mostly does with me, and holding my shoulder hard. "You know what they are, people who do this. You know what they can do. Can your friends in New York keep Beth?"

"For a while. But not for ever. And I don't want your money."

"Good," he said. "Fine." He paused. "Who is she, this friend where Beth stays? She's OK?" Tolya doesn't trust anyone he doesn't know since a million years, or hasn't shared a sack of salt with as they say, some Russian bullshit proverb. I'm different. Tolya's cousin Svetlana had loved me. This made us related.

135

"She's Lily's oldest friend in New York, and her husband."

"I didn't ask about friendship. I asked do you trust her?"

"They're not the same?"

"No."

I met Anatoly Sverdloff maybe five, six years ago when he helped me out of a jam on a case in New York that eventually took me back to Moscow. I almost married his cousin, before she got blown up by a bomb intended for me. In Moscow, after my time, but still in the old days when they called rock music "musical AIDS", Tolya was a rock hero, a famous underground DJ.

Things changed; he became a businessman, he got rich fast. He buys and sells property, minerals, stocks, and, for all I know, people.

Tolya is divorced, his kids are grown up except for the little one who lives with his second ex-wife in Florida. Tolya likes strippers for company. He keeps a small apartment in Moscow and there's his parents' big dacha in the countryside where they still live; otherwise, he's pretty much quit Russia.

I don't look too close at Tolya's business. He got roughed up pretty bad, financially, physically, when he got out of line helping me. Sverdloff covers my ass when I'm in trouble. I step in it, he bails me out. He has the contacts and the dough. I was never sure who he was or how he moves so easily between what's legit and what's illegal. I never knew how he made the money and I don't care. He's crazy about Lily and Beth.

As we left the hospital, I could smell the brandy on his clothes. In spite of the black overcoat, his teeth chattered.

"You're cold? You want to rest?"

He said, "Shower first."

"How did you get here?"

"I got a ride." Tolya doesn't often fly commercial; he always knows someone with a plane. "I only heard last night."

We walked to my hotel, and I could see his mountain of a body slump.

"Lily will be fine," he said. "She will, you hear me, Artyom?"

"Yeah."

He clutched my jacket and said, "She'll be fine!"

I opened the door of my hotel.

Tolya looked at the lobby. "Jesus, Artie, I can't stay here. This place is a dump."

"Fine. Stay where you want."

"I ask you one more time, why you didn't call me?"

"I don't know."

"You don't know? You're still mad about that deal I did in Havana."

"No, I'm not mad. So, thanks for coming. Thanks." I switched to Russian. "Thank you." We got to my room and I went in. He followed and sat heavily on my bed. He dragged off his coat and then his jacket. The black silk shirt was creased. Automatically he emptied his jacket pockets onto the bedside table: wads of money held together with a platinum clip; keys; a lighter; a pack of little Havana cigars; cigarettes; a silver cell phone; a dog-eared paperback copy of *1984* that he always carries.

He once told me it was his first act of sedition as a kid, reading *1984*. The broken orange-and-white Penguin paperback, the same copy he had as a schoolboy, was held together with Scotch tape.

"What happened?" he said.

"Take a shower first."

"No, tell me what happened."

I told him. I told him about Lily's moods, about New Year's Eve, her trip to Paris, the beating, the fact she'd canceled out her life – no credit-card stuff, no phone bills. I told him about Levesque and Momo Gourad and the roller-coaster.

"Who was this guy you went to see?"

"Larkin? He was a guy at a bank. A case I've been working. He was a drunk."

"You never talked to him after?"

"I couldn't find him. His concierge said he went on vacation."

"So someone got to him."

"Yes."

"Someone who wanted to scare you."

"Yeah."

Tolya said, "What else?"

"A thug who threatened me in a bar."

"You left it alone?"

"For the time being."

"Good."

"Why?"

"You kill one of these guys out in the open, you bring a shit-storm on your head. This cop, this Gourad, you trust him? You believe him?"

I told him what I knew.

He said, "You think I'm going to believe a French cop?"

"You're saying he has his own agenda?"

"That's what I'm saying. What else?"

"He likes to eat a lot."

"Fantastic," Tolya's sarcasm was thick.

"Like you."

"Fuck you. You have a picture of Lily? From the scene?"

I went and got the picture of Lily and put it on the table. He stared at the police picture very hard and very, very softly said, "I'm going to kill them."

"Who the hell are you going to kill? We don't know who did this or why they did it, so calm the fuck down, will you and let's try to figure it out. OK? I'm sorry, I'm crazy, so go take a shower and we'll go get some food and talk. You look like shit." I smiled at him. "OK?"

Sverdloff nodded, picked up his overnight bag and went into the bathroom. I could hear the water run hard for a long time.

He reappeared in leather pants, a gray cashmere sweat-shirt and a brown suede jacket. On his feet were bright-green Gucci loafers; he gets them custom-made with solid gold buckles.

Tolya ran his fingers through his wet black hair and said, "You're right. I need food. First, we can visit your roller-coaster, also Mr Stuart Larkin."

The black Mercedes left us near the bar where I'd met Stuart Larkin. The bar was half empty. I didn't recognize the bartender. I asked the guy who was on if he knew Stuart Larkin.

"Who?"

I gave him the details.

"Never saw him," he said.

The amusement park, the little Christmas fair near the Porte de Vanves, was gone. There was no music, the sign was gone, the lights were gone, the stalls, rides, everything.

"Where is it?" Tolya was impatient.

"It's gone. Gimme a smoke if you have one, Toi, OK?"

Snow had been falling. I started walking, kicking at the snow and ice, but there was nothing, no tarps, no boards. It was as if I'd imagined the whole thing. It shook me. I felt I was hallucinating. I began to run, searching the empty lot.

"Stop it," Tolya called out to me. "Stop this."

"I don't understand."

"So maybe the season was over. Maybe the fair is finished," he said. "This happens. It's nothing," he added, but I could see he thought I was cracking up.

Panting for breath, I stopped, put my hands on my knees. "I'm glad you're here."

"Good."

"Don't worry. I don't want to fuck you or anything."

"Also good. You think maybe, Artyom, you think this whole business, this attack on Lily, everything, was a message to you? A warning?"

"That's what scares the shit out of me. This Levesque thing is connected and I don't know how or why. I go to talk to some jerk at a bank, some boring bank guy and I ask for a surveillance tape, and next thing I know someone wants to fucking scare me to death on a roller-coaster. It was a paper trail. Lily gets interested. She goes to Paris, the next thing I know she's on the floor of an apartment with her face smashed and her bones broken."

"Whose apartment?"

"I asked. No one knows. It's empty. The cops are trying to trace the landlord. I've been calling them every couple hours. Nothing. Nada."

"Why Paris?"

"She told me she was going to Paris to see a friend, do some shopping. I was going to meet her. Then I got the call. I told you."

"What kind of friend?"

"Martha Burnham. A woman she went to college with."

"Someone we ought to visit?"

"I visited her. She doesn't give much away. She works with prostitutes."

"So we'll visit her again." He peered into the dark, looking for the fun-fair.

"It's all gone," I said.

"Let's get out of here."

We got to the car and climbed in. "Where we going?"

"I'll get a room at the Raphael," he said. "You know this hotel?"

"I've heard of it."

"You want me to get you a room?"

"No."

"Listen, I'll check in and make some calls, then I want to see Lily again. OK? Meet me."

"Tolya?"

"What?"

"You ever heard of this thing with the hammer, the way they broke Lily's fingers? Someone told me it's a signature."

"I don't know. But there's plenty of whores in Paris, so you got to figure there's plenty of pimps to smash them up. Europe is jammed with whores; they're spilling out over the continent. Good business, Artyom. Guys are not satisfied with stocks, you can't fuck a stock, though they try. They want women, deserve women. Remember, it was Miliken, I think, who said after a hard day making money, it's company's job to see they get laid. You can't get a blow job from computer. You get me? This is bigger than drugs." He paused. "Who told you about the signature?"

I told him about Katya Slobodkin.

Tolya snorted. "You believe what you heard from a Russian hooker? What else you aren't telling me?"

"They raped Lily."

"My God," he said.

The car pulled up at his hotel and I followed him into the lobby.

"What?"

"I want to see these bastards with their brains on the floor."

142

11

Six days. It was six days since Lily was smashed up and I had pieces but no picture, no way to fit the puzzle together. Monday, when I woke up, I felt numb.

When Lily was unconscious, when I thought she was dying, I hurt all the time; it seemed that my skin would peel off and leave me without any protection. She woke up, I went numb.

I sat with her Monday morning. I was happy to hear her breath, happy when she opened her eyes. But I felt sedated, like the patients they rolled down the hall to the operating rooms.

Around eleven, there was a knock on her door, and an old man put his head in and introduced himself. I got up. Bernard Alpert, he said, how do you do, and put out his left hand for me to shake. The right hand was so crippled by arthritis it was clenched up like an animal's paw. He gestured to the empty chair near the bed where I'd been sitting.

"May I?" he said in English.

"Please."

He examined Lily. He spoke sweetly to her and she opened her eyes. I stood by the window watching them. After a while, leaning on his cane, Alpert got up. "I'll be in my office," he said and told me the room number.

I kissed Lily and followed Alpert. In his tiny office, where he sat dwarfed behind a desk piled with papers and books, he gestured for me to sit in the armchair. It was covered with an old bedspread.

"I had heard from Dr Lariot that you wanted another opinion. He asked me to look in on your wife."

"Thank you."

He was speaking English with a heavy French accent. "I do not know if you will thank me."

"Why?"

"In my opinion, it is not good. I must tell you." He was a handsome old man, but he had the lugubrious jowls of a hound dog. Maybe he got them from decades of delivering bad news. "I think her memory-loss is severe."

"Permanent?"

"It may be."

"Go on."

"I was told about the case and so I have looked in, and after I have examined her, I think I am right. It is quite a difficult situation."

I looked at the floor.

Tentatively, Alpert said, "I might have an idea."

"What? What is it?"

"It is not received wisdom, there are people who will tell you I am one old fanatical crackpot, possibly including Dr Lariot, but I have seen it before." His hesitation was driving me nuts.

144

"Please go on. Please!"

"Unless Madame Hanes, unless Lily confronts the reality of her attack, unless someone shows her exactly what happened, she will never recover her memory completely. There will be self-willed holes in it. There will be a void because her unconscious wants this void. Part of her doesn't want to know because it is too frightening. I believe that she was raped?"

"Yes."

"I've seen exactly this kind of case before."

"But if we find out what happened, and if I can make her understand, then she'll be OK. Is that right? She'll be OK if I can tell her?"

He said, "It's not always that easy, and the surgeons, the psychologists, the neurologists will tell you I'm crazy, but I've seen this."

"You said."

"I'm sorry. I'm repeating myself. I've seen it happen. You make the patient understand, you show them the truth, and they come back."

"The truth about the attack, you mean?" I said.

"Yes. There's one other problem."

"What's that?"

"We haven't got much time." Alpert looked at me.

"I don't understand."

"The longer this goes on, in my experience, the more reluctant she'll be. Physically she will get better. Her body can be repaired. The better she feels, the less need for remembering. The more she heals, the stronger she is, the more her brain will resist the painful information."

"How long?"

"A week. Two. I've never seen anyone come back in the way I mean unless they know the truth very quickly."

It was Monday. Lily had been attacked on Tuesday night. I was losing her. I was going to lose her.

"She doesn't know me."

"I am sorry about that."

"What if I tell her about me, about us, what if I fill in all the details?"

He shook his head. "It won't make any real difference and it might confuse her. Or she'll know you for a bit, then forget. Just sit by her for now, and if you can, find out what in God's name happened to her. She's an intelligent women. They make the best candidates for this therapy, and the most resistant. They're smart enough to know what they don't want to know."

"The police are working the case."

He snorted. "The police are working their case, not hers."

"Bernard Alpert? And his cockamamie theories of confrontation? You must be kidding," Patty Finkle said when I went into the hospital courtyard and called her. Patty's an old friend, a forensic shrink I've worked cases with in New York.

I looked at my watch. "What the fuck time is it over there, Patty?"

"Around five in the morning."

"I'm sorry."

"I don't fucking care about that, Art, but I'm scared shitless when you tell me you're doing business with that

146

asshole Alpert. Even that phoney accent like Maurice Chevalier or some shit. You expect him to burst into song."

Talking to Patty was like a wake-up call from a forgotten world. The brisk opinions of this decisive, opinionated, talented New York woman made me feel better.

"Everyone knows about Alpert," she said. "He's about a hundred and he's always looking for cases like Lily's to crank up his research. He's a very old man. He once had a reputation, and I think they still let him have an office over there, right?"

"Yeah."

"He worked up this theory treating GIs."

"In Vietnam?"

"During the Second World War, Artie. World War fucking Two. He went out on the front lines to treat them. Forget it. Bring Lily home as soon as you can and we'll get her the best fucking treatment on earth. And stop listening to Alpert. You'll make yourself crazy."

Patty was probably right and deep down I knew it, but I didn't care. We couldn't move Lily yet, I had to find the monster who hurt her. I believed Dr Alpert because I didn't have anyone else to believe.

"He seemed pretty smart to me," I said.

"I'm telling you, he once treated some soldiers with shell-shock after the Second World War, Artie. It's almost sixty years. He has theories about memory and confrontation. It is, if you'll excuse me, real crapola. I mean, you could lose your footing in it and slide right into the toilet. I'm sorry."

147

I kept my mouth shut.

"Lily will be all right. Just give it time. Hey, I saw Beth. I went over to the Millers. They love her staying there and I took Beth out to the movies with our kids. She ate the popcorn and the M&Ms. She likes to mix them together. She knows all the Disney tunes by heart. And then we took them all to Serendipity to eat those frozen chocolate things."

"Tell me the truth."

"She's marvelous. The kids adore her. We're all humongously grateful to you for letting us enjoy her."

"Thanks, Patty. Thank you."

"Listen, doll, Lily will be all right, Artie. Truly. She'll get better, you have to fucking believe that a hundred per cent."

As soon as I finished with Patty, I got a message. Carol Browne was in Paris. She wanted me at her hotel. It was a summons not a suggestion, but I had other business. I had to find the creeps fast. Whatever Browne needed would have to wait. I called Tolya, woke him up, asked him to sweet-talk Browne or bully her. I believed the old guy, Alpert; I had to believe him.

I also wanted a weapon. The next time I ran into someone like the bastard who slapped me in Pigalle, I wanted self-protection.

Momo Gourad told me Levesque was involved with prostitutes; I was working Levesque's case; because of it, Lily got hurt. I had to find out what happened and fast, fast, or I'd never get Lily back. Hurry, I thought.

★

"Lily?"

Her skin felt fragile, thin and cold. Her eyes were shut, but for the first time I knew she could feel my hand. Later, she reported to the English-speaking nurse that she liked me. She felt she had seen me somewhere before, this man with the brown hair, the blue eyes and the smell. It was the smell that attracted her, as if she knew me and my smell, but she didn't know my name or who I was. She didn't know how long she had been in the hospital or what happened. The first time she had opened her eyes, she saw Tolya Sverdloff in the chair, face like Mt Rushmore, holding her hand. She knew who he was. Later, she forgot.

"Lily?"

"Beth?"

I told her Beth was fine, staying with her best friends. She said, "Who are the Millers?"

I told her my name again after that, and kissed her head, but her eyes were closed. For a while I just listened to her breath.

12

"What do you need?"

There was a *Dirty Harry* poster on the wall over Gourad's desk at the precinct.

"What can I do for you, Artie?" He seemed troubled and remote.

"You know something about the creep who did Lily that you're not telling me."

"I'm telling you what I can."

"Tell me some more. He's a pimp? An enforcer?"

"Probably both."

"Where's he from?"

"I'm not sure. Maybe some kind of border thug."

"What's that?"

"They skirt the edges of established gangs, they like to work places you can disappear easy, the Czech–German border, Ukraine, Bosnia. All these places are good for whores."

"I met your friend."

He lit up. "Katya?"

"Yes."

"I'm doing what I can. I want him worse than you, I want these guys to stop dumping girls in Paris." He fiddled with a coffee mug. "We pick up the girls, we get blamed by the left, we don't, we get blamed by the right. You came by for something, Artie? I have to go arrest some boys for dealing Prozac. Important stuff, you know." He was sarcastic as he picked up his cigarettes.

"Let me put this theoretically, OK, Momo? Off the record. Can we do that?"

"I'll try."

"Suppose there was a guy in Europe, someone who knew how to handle it, and he knew it wasn't exactly kosher, but he wanted something so that he could take care of things."

Momo, who had worked in America, knew what I meant. "Go on."

"He wanted something that would help him work a case, especially if he was thinking of traveling some."

"I guess," said Momo, shaking a cigarette from the pack and tossing it to me, "I guess he'd go to the fringes of the flea market at the Porte Saint-Ouen. I guess he'd maybe look for one of the Russians who keep some shitty stores up there, or maybe one of the stalls where under the counter you could maybe get that kind of thing. For cash, of course."

"Thank you."

"It's nothing. I know you personally are not thinking of carrying a weapon in Paris, isn't that right, Artie? Because you know it's illegal."

"Absolutely right."

He changed the subject. "So Lily is better. I'm happy."

151

"She's awake, I guess that's better." I leaned over the desk. "I need this case solved, Momo. I need it for her. If I don't find out who did it, she won't get better. Talk to me. Who beat up on her?"

"If I knew, I couldn't necessarily tell you."

"Why the fuck not?"

"I want him to show me who's running the whores in and out of Paris."

"You said Levesque was involved."

"Was. Levesque's dead. You want to come home for supper tonight?"

"Monique's cheese soufflé?"

"Yeah, and the kids."

What about Katya? I wanted to say, but it was what a stupid prude bastard would say and I kept my mouth shut. "When it's over. Thanks."

"Artie?"

"Yeah?"

"The flea market operates weekends, mostly."

"Today's Monday."

"Monday's OK. Some stuff is open Monday."

"One other thing."

The phone rang; he picked it up and covered the mouthpiece. "What's that?"

"Katya. What's her real connection with all this?"

Momo didn't answer.

At the Porte Saint-Ouen I got out of the Metro. I had my briefcase, which I'd picked up at the hotel. For this job I needed a clean weapon from a guy who only wanted my money. I skirted the edges of the vast flea market. People emerged from the maze of stalls lugging crystal chandeliers and ancient suitcases.

Somewhere I could smell the potent grease of lamb cooking. I couldn't remember when I ate and I was hungry. Around the Metro were people selling mismatched shoes, old tin cans, war medals; there were stalls that cut keys and repaired TVs. Down one narrow alley, where the gutters overflowed with slush and garbage, the signs were in Russian. I tried a couple or three shops.

The fourth had a front window with a crack in it. Inside, the counter, the window sills, the chairs were piled with plastic boxes, chipped cups, styrofoam containers, and in them were findings; bits and pieces for broken jewelry could be purchased here — little stones, fittings, clasps. A sign in Russian announced it was also a pawn shop, and when a short guy emerged from a back room, I talked Russian to him. I told him exactly what I needed.

He said his name was Federov but everyone called him Ferdy. I showed him cash and the money made him eager, but I didn't want to make conversation, I didn't have time. Dr Alpert's words played over in my head — not much time, a week, a few more days.

Ferdy knew exactly what I wanted. There was no bullshit here, at least. He put his newspaper down and went into the back.

It was always risky. They could pick you up on weapons charges and toss you on a plane home, but I wasn't going anywhere without a gun. In France at least, unlike England, the cops carry.

Ferdy reappeared with a little .22, a piece of garbage. I waved it away, pulled out some more money. He

153

looked again and produced the weapon that I wanted: a Gluck in good condition that fit my hand. I paid, put it in my briefcase with the ammo he sold me, and left.

Up here in this crappy quarter of Paris, the Russians were obviously poor. Not like the bastards Momo mentioned, or Tolya's friends who lived in mansions in the 16th Arrondissement or the big hotels. People like Ferdy didn't take their vacations in St Barts, they didn't get their suitcases at Vuitton.

Tolya could have found me a gun, of course. Tolya would have contacts in Paris like he has everywhere, but I didn't want his people, not this time. His people were rich and polite, killers who skied in Gstaad. You had to play the part with them. You had to go begging. I didn't have time and I wasn't in the mood. I'd met some of them in London once. I wasn't exactly popular with the rich Russians in London and I figured they had friends in Paris and the friends would know who I was.

On my way to the Metro, I stopped and ate a steak and drank a glass of wine. In the mirror over the bar, I stared at myself. If Alpert was right, I had a few days to figure it out.

Was Alpert just a crazy old bastard like Patty Finkle said? I felt he was right. Lily is a woman who needs to look things in the face; she always says she hates not knowing. More than revenge, more than killing the prick who did it to her, I had to know. She had to know. On the train I sat and thought about it, but as soon as I got out and onto the street, the phone rang. It was Carol Browne. She was furious. I had been out of touch. I was off the case. I had promised her I'd close it, this Levesque thing, but I never called back. When Browne finished her rant, I buzzed Tolya and asked him to get on her.

He laughed. "Literally?"

"I wish."

Coming out of the hospital later, I bumped into Tolya going in. He had moved Lily to a room on the ground floor. It had two big windows facing the courtyard. She was sleeping. The nurse told me she had talked a little, then fallen asleep from the effort.

"I don't like the room," I said to Tolya.

"I fixed it. It's better. Light. Nicer room."

"It's too fucking exposed."

"No. This is better. I can keep a guy in the courtyard all the time. Also, if there's trouble we can get her out fast."

"Don't be so fucking melodramatic"

"How come you're mad at me all the time?"

"I'm just mad at everyone."

"I got three guys on this, around the clock. Trust me."

Tolya always has muscle on call, a network he taps into, most of them Russian guys, ex-weightlifters. Big ugly guys. Now I was grateful.

"By the way, I fixed your Ms Carol Browne," he said.

"How?"

He laughed. "Never mind how. I just fixed it. You'll be OK with her for a couple days."

"Come on."

"I hired her."

"Don't fuck with me."

155

"I told her. I say, Carol, I hear you are number one woman from Keyes Security, I don't want some underling, I want you, so I put her on big job and paid her double. I dropped few names, she was impressed. I even bought her lunch."

"You're nuts." Sometimes I loved this guy.

He laughed.

"What job?"

"I made up some crap about Russian gangsters."

"She'll buy it?"

"Sure, she'll have a check on her desk tomorrow morning."

"You'll stay with Lily a while?"

He nodded. "I'll stay."

"Until I get back?"

"Yes, Artyom. I will."

There were messages from Joe Fallon and Momo Gourad, but nothing from Martha Burnham. I left Tolya and went to her shelter, she wasn't there; I went to McDonald's. Through the window I saw her, head down, sitting opposite a young woman who looked rough.

I tapped on the glass and Martha looked up, her face blank. Maybe she needed glasses. Maybe she didn't recognize me. Again I tapped on the window, then I went inside. Martha saw me coming.

She got out of her seat, pulled the girl with her and disappeared into the back. For a few seconds I stood there. Martha was in the toilet downstairs.

I waited in McDonald's with a gun in my pocket. Eric Levesque, my dead guy with the bank account, had run

156

a model agency that was a front for whores. Lily found out and someone beat her up for it after she visited her old friend Martha Burnham, who was hiding from me in the toilet in a fast-food joint in Paris.

The junkies glanced at me sidelong from their coffee when I suddenly ran for the stairs. In the bathroom, a couple of girls, smoking weed, looked up, furious. They filled the doorway, they didn't let me through. I looked over them and saw that Martha was gone. There was a back way out where they put the garbage.

13

"Let me get you a room here."

"For Chrissake, Tolya, I have my own fucking room, OK?"

After I left McDonalds, I took a taxi back to the hospital, discovered he was gone, and followed him to his hotel. His suite had a parlor with a mural on the wall, a bar spread out on a white linen cloth and a bathroom as big as my apartment in New York.

"What the hell are you doing here?"

"It's OK," he said.

"You said you'd stay with Lily."

"I left Lily with twenty-four-hour private nursing, plus security on rotation. Around the clock. She's alright."

"Can you find out if there's anything on a cop named Gourad. Homicide guy, maybe. Vice. I'm not sure. He says he's working Lily's case. Maurice Gourad. They call him Momo. Get him. He has Lily's file and I want it."

"You look like crap."

"Thanks."

"I left my best guys with her."

"All right, OK. I fucking heard you the first six times."

Tolya looked surprised. I could hear how cold my voice was. I was tired. I had nothing to bring Lily, no story, no nothing. It was late. "Listen, I think I better go get some sleep."

"So how come you're here?" He reached over to the bar, picked up a pair of miniatures and with one hand, like a chef cracking a couple of eggs, emptied the Scotch into a glass. "Drink something. You're OK?"

"No."

"We'll eat." Tolya thinks if you don't eat you can't think.

I was too tired to argue.

"What do you feel like?"

"I want to work the case. I want Lily back."

"It's nine o'clock at night. You have to eat."

"Fine, we'll eat."

"Get yourself cleaned up and we'll get out of here," he said. He took the phone out of my hand. He pushed me towards the bathroom.

I had a shower, then we went downstairs to the bar and sat in red plush armchairs. Tolya ordered drinks and snacks and said, "So Lily. It was a way of warning you."

"Yes. You ever hear of a guy named Eric Levesque?"

He shook his head.

"You know people who run women. Come on, Tolya, you know all the creeps."

"This is not my area of expertise," he said, sipping a Bloody Mary. "What about this Gourad? The cop? Tell me what you already know."

"Like I told you, he's young, smart, he's married, he's in love with a Russian, a Natasha. Calls herself Katya Strogonoff. Real name's Slobodkin. You know her?"

"I met her. She looks good, but she's on the make. He's an idiot. You want to eat here?"

"Let's go out."

Tolya picked up his phone and made a call. "Come on," he said. "We'll go eat. It will clear our head. I swear to God, you'll love this place."

I was in jeans. "Let me stop and get some clothes."

"For this place you don't need to change. Later you'll change," he said, and I didn't ask what for.

The black Mercedes was waiting outside with a Russian driver. Tolya gave him directions, and we pulled away from the hotel. My glass was still in my hand.

"You have some business in Paris?" I said.

"Come off it, Artyom, you know what my real business is."

He opened a small bar in the back of the car, retrieved a can of cashews, unzipped it, took out a handful of nuts and ate them. "Better," he said.

"So what is it, your business?"

He licked the salt off his finger and laughed. "Keeping you alive."

The night was frozen, the stars very sharp in the clear, frigid sky. Paris was all lights as we crossed the city. The car finally turned into a narrow side street and pulled up in front of a restaurant.

"Not your usual thing," I said, glancing at the place.

Tolya likes his restaurants with a lot of gold; he likes them showy.

"This is better. Wait." His face lit up, expectant.

Inside, the headwaiter greeted Tolya like his long-lost brother. At the table reserved for us, automatically I took the chair with its back to the wall and Tolya sat down opposite me.

The waiter brought us a brick of warm, unctuous foie gras. There was fresh toast to go with it; the smell of the bread made me hungry. Tolya waved aside the menus and talked French to the headwaiter. Food arrived. It was like a drug. For an hour we ate.

It was pretty much the best food I ever ate in my whole life, the foie gras, the roast chicken, the shoulder of lamb with its crackling skin that slid off the meat, the potato cakes, and, after, crème caramel. We drank plenty of wine and ended up with old Armagnac; the fumes that came up from the glass were potent. If you drank enough, this stuff could make any problem disappear. I drank.

Tolya gestured for the bottle and the waiter put it on the table. "Better?"

"Much better."

"They do it different from anyone else," Tolya said. "The French, when they cook it right, the food is different. Better. Before they gave most of the country away to McDonald's and Pizza Hut." He looked at the remains of his dessert. "I always want to eat this food. You want anything else?"

"You must be kidding."

"I'm going in the kitchen to tell them, OK?"

"Sure. You got a number for your guy, the one you left with Lily?"

He took out his cell phone, punched some buttons and handed it to me. I went outside the door and skidded where snow had frozen. The trees were festooned with little icicles.

Tolya's guy said Lily was sleeping. I told him to get the nurse, who also said Lily was asleep. I wanted to be there. I was like a kid with an obsession. I wanted to be there and I wanted to be away so I couldn't see her bruised face and broken hand. For the first time since I got to Paris, I was mildly drunk.

I went back into the restaurant, sat at the table and picked up the Armagnac. Tolya pulled a gold case out of his jacket and extracted two Havanas. "You want?"

"Sure."

We sat late. We sat until the last customer left. Tolya made me take him through the case one step at a time. We finished the Armagnac.

"I don't know what I'm doing here, I should be working the case," I said, but I was too stewed to get up. Stewed was how I felt. Stewed like fruit in brandy. Not drunk, mellow. Mindless.

"We have to figure this thing out with logic," Tolya said.

"You think you can get logic on a case like this off a bottle of Armagnac and a plate of foie gras?"

He was a little drunk, too. The heavy, aromatic booze made his big face pink. "Is about keeping you alive, Artyom. Drink. Food. About keeping you alive." He smiled. "Also, me."

162

There was nothing much I could do this time of night except keep calling Martha Burnham, so I got back in the car with Tolya. It took us to my hotel where I changed, then Tolya's hotel, where he put on a tux, which made him look very big, very regal.

"You like it?"

"I feel under-dressed." I had on my best Hugo Boss suit that I bought at Century 21.

"I don't blame you."

"Thanks."

"You're welcome." I followed him back into the car.

"This is wonderful place, Artyom. Paris. Wonderful. You can find anything here." He waved his hand in the general direction of the city. "Anything."

Tolya moves around, he makes money, he minds other people's business. Sometimes it takes a while. It usually involves prowling some city, New York, Hong Kong, Moscow, in the middle of the night.

I said, "Listen, Tolya, are we going somewhere that's going to help me on Lily? Because I'm not really up for hanging out. I'm in a hurry."

"Maybe this will help, and anyway, what else are you going to do at midnight, Monday, in Paris? What?" Then he said suddenly, "So the guy is dead and alive at the same time."

"What guy?"

"Your Mr Levesque," he said as we turned a corner and pulled up in front of a club.

I checked the street sign. Sixteenth Arrondissement. The street looked rich, cold, sleek and sober. A man in a quilted jacket walked a couple of expensive poodles; a woman, heavy fur coat hanging open, pearls showing, ducked into a taxi.

"I'll tell you what I think, Toi, OK?"

"Tell me."

"I think it's all bullshit, you know. I think someone's putting me on is what I think. Someone who knows the case I'm working and wants to fake me out."

"Maybe." Tolya climbed out of the car and I followed.

There was a wrought-iron grille in which stylized black birds and flowers were trapped in gilded iron leaves. From inside, subtle lights shone through the opaque glass doors that were etched with Art Deco patterns.

The doorman recognized Tolya and pulled open the gates for us. Inside, the smell of rich people enveloped me; there was chatter in French, English, Russian, Japanese.

"What the hell are we doing here?"

Tolya smiled. "Looking for Monsieur Levesque."

The emerald in Tolya's ear flashed. We sat at a table in a corner. People, men mostly, sauntered up to him, shook his hand, hugged him, addressed him in French, English, Russian, even once in Chinese. He beamed. The diamonds in his cufflinks were big as marbles. He pulled out the cigarette case so people could admire the ruby on it. He ordered magnums of Cristal. I held one of his Havanas in my hand, sat and watched. The women were spectacular.

It was like something out of a James Bond movie. From the next room, I could hear the sounds of gambling, the click of the roulette ball, the dice, the chips. I looked up. There was a painted ceiling; the moldings were covered in gold leaf. The high French windows were draped with white brocade. The waiters, in white tie and tail, moved between the tables with bottles of wine and trays of caviar. Maybe because I was still a little boozed up, I wanted to laugh out loud.

The women were young and there were dozens of them, some at the tables, some on a tiny dance floor at the far end of the room. All of them wore evening clothes, and when my eyes adjusted to the low light and the flicker of candles, I thought they seemed to be acting.

This was a set. The director would appear any minute and call for a cut, and the extras would squat by the wall for a smoke and a cup of coffee.

A second wave of guys came at Tolya, again hugging him, exchanging business cards, whispering in his ear and when this wave ebbed and we were alone for a minute, I said, "So tell me."

"What's that, Artyom?"

"What is this place? It's fucking ridiculous."

"Sure."

"You know it's ridiculous."

"Sure, I know."

"You putting me on, man?" I was getting restless. "What are we doing here?"

"I'm looking for information."

"Come off it, Toi. I'm going back to the hotel. I got stuff to do."

"You think I don't want for Lily an answer to the shit they did? I also got stuff. Same stuff as you."

He tossed back a glass of Champagne. His eyes suddenly swam with excitement, lids flickering. I followed his gaze. He was watching two women make their way towards us, one black, one white. There were beads of sweat on his forehead now.

The girls arrived at our table. He introduced them as Ivoire and Ebene, and I thought: gimme a fucking break here. But they sat down, one on each of Tolya's knees, and he poured Champagne for them. The white one was Russian, a Super Natasha with greedy eyes. The black girl had a lilting Caribbean accent. Martinique, she said in French. "Je suis Martiniquaise."

He held on to them. He looked at the cleavages, first one, then the other. He put his hand delicately on the white girl's breasts and smiled. The black girl took his other hand and put it on her breast. He was like a giant baby.

It's Tolya's weakness. He's crazy about strip clubs, lap dancing, all kinds of titty shows. I tell him all the time it's only pussy for hire, no matter how fancy, but he gets red in the face; it makes him furious. He likes to think it's the real goods.

"You want to dance with one of the girls, Artyom?" he said.

I shook my head and he took both women onto the dance floor, where the girls knew the moves and Tolya wiggled his fat ass a lot to "Brown Sugar".

"May I sit down?" The voice came from behind me. "Your friend asked me to keep you company."

I got up.

She was very pretty. Short black hair with bangs.

Simple black dress cut high in front, low in back. She had on sunglasses and her voice, in English, was completely neutral. Then she sat down and slipped off the glasses and the accent. It was Katya Slobodkin.

She touched the hair. "You like it? Is wig."

"I like it. Are you following me?"

"Yes, but don't worry, I'm harmless."

I switched to Russian. "You come here often?"

"Why not? Speak English, OK."

"Why?"

"I don't want to be identified as Russian whore. Can I have Diet Coke, please?"

"Diet Coke?"

"I love Diet Coke. I am crazy for Diet Coke. I have friend, she says this is Jewish Champagne."

"You're Jewish also?"

"All Russians are Jewish also, don't you know, Artemy." She was tipsy. "I'm Katherine in here."

"Pretty name."

"Sorry?"

"Nothing."

"Would you like to dance?"

I shook my head. It scared me, being close to her. She was flirtatious and smart, vivid, funny and whole. Outside it was dark and cold, and Lily, beaten up and broken, lay in a hospital bed.

I said, "This is a coincidence. You and me, we just happen to be in the same dub at the same time?"

"No."

"No what?"

"Is not coincidence."

"Tolya fixed this?"

She shrugged. "What's difference, allow me one secret."

"Momo knows where you are?"

She said softly, speaking her mix of Russian and English, "Yes. He knows I am working. We don't discuss details. I think you're in trouble." She leaned her head back against her chair; I could feel her hair against my cheek.

"So you came to help me?"

"You think I can't help you? Your girlfriend, how she is?"

"She's conscious."

"Good."

"She doesn't know who the hell I am," I blurted out. "She doesn't know me."

"I've been thinking about this thing," Katya said. "I can take you to meet more whores, if you want. This is easy part," she said. "But this is not what you want."

"I don't want the whores. I want whoever beat up Lily."

She looked closely at my face. "Not someone who tries to hurt you in Pigalle?"

"How do you know?"

"I hear things."

"All I want is the guy who hurt Lily. That's all. That's all I want."

In her seductive way, she was pumping me; this was an interrogation, a test. Katya wanted something from me.

She said, "Many of pimps have signatures when they

168

punish girls. They think is cool, as you say. Sniper rifles. Car bombs. AKs. Knives. Hammer."

"Go on."

"There's all kinds, you know? I knew of Serb pimp who prefers Muslim girls because this gives him religious high, keeps war going. Add to thrill."

"Jesus Christ."

"Everything in name of Jesus Christ."

"It's like all the crap from the whole goddamn Soviet Empire is leaking into the rest of the world, like some kind of bloodletting."

"Bloodletting, I don't understand," Katya said and polished off her Diet Coke as soon as the waiter put it on the table. Around us was the buzz and chatter of people talking, laughing, drinking. The music played.

I explained and she said, "Yes. Bloodletting. Maybe take the infection eventually with it. Maybe not."

She stiffened suddenly. A quartet of ghouls in tuxedos had arrived. Katya said, "Dance with me. I don't want these creeps to see me. Dance with me, OK? I won't eat you."

The band had changed. A trio played slow music now, Gershwin, Porter. On the dance floor I could feel her tight against me, her face buried in my shoulder.

A few feet away, one of the thugs caught my eye. He was a short, squat man with sloping shoulders and thin blonde hair. He put his arms around a girl in a transparent chiffon dress cut to her naval. Absently, as if it were a little animal, he petted one of her breasts. He had on sunglasses; these guys always lived out the stereotypes.

My skin crawled. I had seen him before. It was the

creep who slapped me like I was a woman in the bar near the Place Clichy.

Suddenly, Katya saw his face. She pushed me off the dance floor towards a dark alcove at the back of the candlelit room and I was aware of her body. I tried not to think about it or who she was or why she was here with me.

Her voice was frightened. "Look at him."

"I'm looking."

"You know him?"

"No."

"You saw him, Artemy, you recognized him."

"OK. I saw him once somewhere. Who the fuck is he?"

"He is this guy they are calling Zhaba or Zhabo. Some corruption of word, but he is corruption of human being who likes hurting women. Who likes picking up desperate girls when they are crossing border."

"You've seen him before?"

"Yes." She pulled herself further into the corner; she made herself small.

I said, "What do they call him in English?"

"They call him Toad," she whispered in my ear. "This is man who has for signature to break girls' fingers. Rape. Kill."

"Lily?"

"Maybe."

"What's he doing here?"

She shivered. "I don't know." She felt me pull away. "Stay with me."

"You expected him? You came here because you knew he was coming?"

"No!" Her breathing was shallow with anxiety. "You think I want to be in the room with this thing?"

"Tell me how you know him."

In the alcove, using me as a shield, Katya leaned against the velvet-covered wall, her eyes always on Zhaba.

"You have some light?"

There was a plastic lighter in my pocket. I got it out, flicked it on. Katya put her right hand up close to my face. The fingers were crooked.

"God."

"I don't think God is interested."

"It was him?"

"Yes."

"Is that why Momo sent me to you?"

"Yes. But he says this is my decision to tell you or not."

"Where does Zhaba live?"

"He doesn't live. He moves around."

"You were surprised to see him here?"

"Yes."

"This isn't his normal turf?"

"No."

"Where's he from?"

"Hole in ground. Hole in hell."

We stood in the dark against the wall, watching the flickering scene, the couples, the low light, the music, the money.

I said, "This club, you come here, you've been here before?"

"Don't change the subject. Sure I been here before."

In my mind, Katya *was* the subject. She was a hooker in love with a cop; she recognized the man who probably attacked Lily.

I said, "The girls here go to bed with the customers?"

"Do you see beds?"

"What do you want, Ykaterina Vladimirovna?"

Her arms around me, Katya said into my ear, "Kill him for me. For Lily. Then is all over."

Over her shoulder, I looked at him. I thought of him working Lily over. I memorized the face as best I could. He stood in a tight group of men. Women in their gorgeous bright dresses circled behind them, watching, waiting. One woman put her arms around Zhaba from behind. Another offered the man beside him a drink. Mostly they stayed back, though, while the men did their business. It was like some tribal dance.

It would be easy. Katya could lure him into a car. I could find a dark empty place, under a bridge, in an alley. I could find a soft spot under his chin. Get a knife. Use the gun. I had the gun.

It would be finished. It would be over. I could do it. I could do it, and I imagined the squat body, saw it crumple, saw him die. Maybe I would take my time.

When I turned around, I saw Katya's beautiful, complicated face. Who the hell was she? What did she want? How did I know this Zhaba really was the thug who hurt Lily, and if I went for him, how would I get out of France and take Lily home and care for her?

I said, "Not here."

"Yes. Anywhere. Please." She whispered in my ear. She reminded me what he did to Lily.

172

I started to move out of the alcove.

The band was playing "Autumn in New York". Katya felt me pull away, but she held on to me. Then she let go and whispered again, in Russian this time, "Kill him."

14

"Where is he?" Katya was frantic.

Did he feel the danger? Did his cronies tighten the circle and move him out of the club?

He was gone. I'd hesitated. I'd lost him.

Did he see us? It didn't matter. I knew his face. I knew what he looked like. I threaded my way through the crowded club, tripping over one man who swore at me, bumping into couples on the dance floor. Without a coat, I ran into the street.

It was late. Cold. The guys at the door shook their heads. They didn't see anyone, they said, and I didn't know if they were lying. Maybe he paid them off and got in a waiting car.

I scoured the streets around the club until I was shaking from the cold, but he was gone.

"Katya, listen, I'll get him," I said when I got back inside the club. "I swear."

She saw I was cold. She put her arms around me and we moved back onto the dance floor. She held onto me so I would feel the heat from her; you had to be dead not to feel it.

Over her head, I saw Tolya, who had left the room earlier. Now he came in through the double doors at the far end of the room. The two women were with him. Other couples came and went the same way. A man in a fancy tux strolled through the door, one hand going instinctively to his fly.

Katya followed my glance. "You understand?"

"Yeah."

"You're American, so you disapprove?"

"I don't know. It looks like a bad movie. How do the girls feel about it?"

She smiled. "They feel this is for money. And make-believe."

"What?"

"You're looking for someone?"

"I thought he might come back."

"He won't come back." She put her head on my shoulder for an instant and said softly, "Anyone else?"

I thought about Levesque. "I'm not sure."

"There is no one else." She moved closer, reached up and kissed me. "Come with me."

"No. Thanks, but no thanks."

"It could be interesting."

She smelled wonderful. We were walking across the room and through the double doors. We were in the elevator. It had tufted-silk walls, little gold mirrors, a padded bench. We were alone in the confined space, and Katya was very good with her mouth. By the time we reached the third floor, I was panting.

★

The brocaded room had a big bed, candles, a TV, stacks of videos, a sound system, flowers, Champagne in a bucket. I tried to think about Lily. I fixed the Toad's face in my memory some more. I tried to make myself laugh at the whole set-up, but Katya laughed with me. I concentrated hard on the carpet, but she unzipped her dress, let it fall on the floor, stepped out of it. She was naked.

I fumbled in my pockets for cigarettes, then sat on the edge of the bed. "Don't."

"Why? It's for free."

"Just don't."

Maybe she was offering me a trade; as barter for killing Zhaba, was she willing to cheat on Momo? It wasn't why I stopped her, though. I stopped her because, for once in my miserable life, I was going to act like a grown-up, like a human being instead of like a dog in heat. Or a guy.

I've slept with a lot of women I shouldn't have slept with; I've followed my dick pretty much all my life. Lily was lying in some hospital now, raped, beat up, away from home, her fingers broken, not knowing who I was. I was here with Katya, this stunning naked woman who offered to service me in ways she was recounting now, breathing them in my ear, half English, half Russian, curled on the bed, laughing, letting her fingers run around my ears, neck, hands.

No one would know. Katya was a pro who did this for money, or barter. It was only business, as she promised me anything I wanted, here in this warm room

in the middle of the night. I had plenty of booze in me.
I wanted her a lot.

Don't do it, asshole, I said to myself.

She sat up. "Are you all right?"

"Why?"

"You don't want?"

"I do want, but I can't. Help me here."

"Of course."

"You show me this Zhaba, this toad, you point him
out, you ask me to kill him, then you bring me upstairs
to fuck me. You're Momo's girlfriend."

"That is different."

"Why?"

"It just is. You've never been to whores?"

"No."

She got up and, naked, went to the video and slipped
a tape in. "You like to watch something?" She had me
picked for a soft-porn guy. The picture was a blur of
romantic narrative and naked bodies.

I said, "Who goes to whores? Who are the men?"

"Everyone. Your friends. Men think we do things
wives don't do, girlfriends don't do."

"What do you do?"

She whispered in my ear for a while longer. She
smiled. "Guys need this. East. West. Some daddies, nice
guys, wife, two kids, they stop on way home. Nice guys
like you. People who got everything and want to buy
other thing. Exotic piece of ass." She grinned and turned
her own smooth, tight, lovely ass towards me.

"Why not? Some guys like sex, no relationships. Too
messy. Check it out. Buy it. Fuck it. Stock market up,

people rich, happy, spending, shopping. This is nice thing, like drug, you know?" She giggled and offered me her wonderful tits. "No one admits this, but is true. Tell me what you like."

"I don't have any money."

"I said I was not asking for your money."

"What? For what?"

"I told you."

"You want me to kill him?"

"Yes."

"So this is a trade arrangement."

"Something like that. US, Mexico, European Union, yes, is trade."

"Put your clothes on."

"No," she said and started unbuttoning my shirt.

An hour later, I put my clothes on. I said "Thank you" because I didn't know what to say.

"I thank you, Artemy," Katya said. "Was very nice."

"So who the hell owns this place?"

"Don't you know?"

"Not Zhaba?"

"You think I would be here if it was him, this piece of garbage from underneath earth?"

"Then who?"

"Guess."

"I can't."

"Try. One try." She was laughing.

"OK, Eric fucking Levesque."

"I don't know who is Levesque."

"I give up." I was impatient.

She laughed as if my not knowing was part of the game.

"But you know this, of course," she said. "The owner is your friend Anatoly Sverdloff. Bye bye, Artie."

I didn't go to my hotel. It was freezing out, but dry, and the moon was white and cold like a fluorescent bulb that lit up the empty streets. The hairs in my nose froze as I left the club, but I walked anyway, even when the wind blew, stinging my face like an infection. I needed the air. I felt lousy about what I did with Katya and the cold sobered me up fast.

If Tolya Sverdloff owned a club where Katya Slobodkin worked, who could I trust? Paris was an alien place where everyone I met was foreign, like me, where you slid on the surface, looking for a foothold. I could never get under the surface in this city that flirted with you, teased you, trashed your sanity with its beauty, then pulled its shutters down.

I kept walking. It was three in the morning by the time I crossed the river. A cloud skittered across the moon; it felt like snow again. I was losing Lily. The creep who attacked her had been in the club, and all Katya wanted from me was to kill for her.

On Boulevard Saint-Germaine there were still lights in a café; through its windows, I saw people talking, drinking, laughing, animated, distant as people on the moon.

All my life I wanted to come to Paris. People love Paris, I thought, walking faster. Musicians came and played great jazz here when they couldn't get work at home. People write songs about Paris, and novels, they love the buildings, the food, the style, the language, the way the city fits together. But it was too beautiful and too cold, and it had fucked me over and swallowed me up. A lone taxi passed and I flagged it down. It was very late when I got to Martha Burnham's. I leaned on the buzzer.

"What?" Through the crackle of the intercom, she sounded pissed off.

"I have to see you."

"Phone me."

"You don't answer your phone."

"It's the middle of the night."

I lied. "Lily asked me to come."

The door clicked open and I went in and took the elevator to the top floor.

Martha had a studio apartment with Indian bedspreads for curtains, a futon to sleep on and a set of wind-chimes in the window. It felt solitary and somehow lonely. There was a stick of incense in a jam jar.

Wearing a huge red-plaid flannel bathrobe, Martha bolted the door, gestured to an orange beanbag chair, then sat cross-legged on the futon.

"Listen, I'm sorry I woke you up."

"I figured you'd come. How's Lily?"

"What?"

"You were lying when you said Lily asked you to come." It wasn't a question.

"You never went to see her."

"I went."

"So you saw what they did to her."

180

She reached to the low driftwood table, picked up some paper and a plastic bag of grass and started rolling a joint anxiously.

"Yes."

"When?"

"What's the difference?"

"Help me here."

"You want to drink something?"

"Coffee would be good."

Still holding the rough joint she'd rolled, she lumbered to her feet and went around the counter into the open kitchen where she filled a saucepan with water.

"You never told me you put a security guy with Lily. He tried to keep me out."

"I said I tried to call you."

"You saw me through the window at McDonald's?"

"Yes. You took one look at me and beat it out of there. I don't get it, Martha. Why? We're on the same side."

"I was with a girl who was in trouble."

"Not good enough."

"I'm scared."

"What of?"

"Everything."

"I don't really believe that. You don't scare that easy. You want to tell me some other stuff about Lily's visit? I know there's things you didn't tell me."

"It was between her and me."

"Your secret."

"Fuck you."

She turned around, her back to the stove, elbows on the

counter between us. She fiddled with the leaves of a plant in a red and yellow pot, looked up at me and said, "This wasn't some girl thing, you know, we were working, we were trying to fix something. I'm still trying." The water boiled and Martha fixed up mugs of instant. "Milk?"

"Black."

She brought the mugs, put them on the table, sat down again, rolled a second joint and offered it to me. I shook my head. She lit her own.

Martha said, "Look, this stuff sucks. Girls get beaten up and killed and no one really gives a fuck so long as they don't do it in front of the Louvre."

"They care if it's an American."

"Up to a point."

"What point?"

"She didn't die. She'll go home. The cops will write it all down somewhere and file it and apologize to the embassy."

I hesitated. Martha was volatile and furious and she smoked the dope like it was going to save her life. If I told her about Zhaba, she might run off the rails.

"How come some thug who normally beats up hookers attacked Lily?"

"Maybe because she came to see me."

"How would they know?"

"Maybe they got it off a cell phone," she said. "I don't know how. Maybe I mentioned it to someone at the shelter, that I was seeing her, because I was so excited, and the word got around. Maybe I told a friend on the phone. I feel shitty about that. I feel maybe it was because of me."

"Or me. How come she really called you, after all those years?"

"I thought she missed me."

"Bullshit."

"I wanted to believe the bullshit."

The coffee tasted like old socks, but I drank some. Martha pushed herself off the floor and went to the window where she stood for a minute, looking out. She fiddled with the wind-chimes that hung from the ceiling over her stove, then said, "It's going to snow again."

Martha was ready to snap. I clutched the coffee mug and kept my mouth shut.

"She said she wanted to keep this whole business between us," Martha said. "She said she couldn't tell you. Specifically, she said so."

"She threw away anything that would connect her to it, right? Air tickets. Receipts. She cleaned her desk like she was hiding something."

"Yes."

"Why?"

"I need a drink." Martha went to the kitchen, pulled a small tray of gray ice cubes out, dumped them in a glass, poured some vodka on top, sat down for the third time.

"She said she made you give up being a cop because she was scared for you, and now she was sticking her own nose in bad stuff and you'd worry. You'd make her stop and she couldn't stop."

"You saw how Lily is. Whoever did this shit could be anywhere." I leaned close to Martha's face. "I'm running out of time here, and I need Lily to remember and she can't unless you fucking help me."

Martha squinted as she sucked up some ice. "I'm so thirsty."

"Help me." I was at the end of my rope. "You want them to do you next?" I grabbed her arm.

"You bastard." Martha twisted her arm out of my grasp, reached behind her and fumbled for a tape, then slid it into the video player. "Lily made me swear not to tell anyone."

"So what's the tape?"

"I swore."

"What's on the goddam tape?"

"Lily. She made me tape her. She sat there where you are and told me."

"Why?"

"In case someone killed her."

15

Lily's voice: "OK? OK, Marti?"

The picture settles. Lily's smiling at the camera. On the screen, wearing her gray pants suit, her aunt's silver pin in the lapel, the diamond earrings I gave her. Her hair is video orange, but it's long, same as it was when I left her at the train for Paris. She pushes it up off her neck, fixes it with a rubber band, says, "Hold the camera still, Marti, for Chrissake. Hold it on the back of a chair if you have to." She puts her hands up to her hair again.

Martha's voice: "You ready?"

"Let's go. Marti?"

"I'm with you, honey, I'm all set."

"I'm Lily Hanes and this is what happened to me in London on December twenty-ninth and thirtieth."

Martha's voice: "Do you want me to ask you questions?"

"Not unless you think I'm leaving something out."

"Got it."

"I'm recording this in Paris at Martha Burnham's apartment on the night of January second. I called

Martha from London and said I wanted to come and see her. I was going to Paris anyway the next day, with Artie, but I told him I was going a day early to see a friend." She hesitates, then seems to look out from the screen at me. "If you're watching this, Artie, if you are, I'm sorry I didn't tell you. I needed to do this."

I lit a cigarette and watched Lily.

"I had some bad times: that night in the pub, first of all, then on the wheel on New Year's Eve. Artie knew there was something wrong. It started the day we got to London. The twenty-seventh. I was in the apartment alone, wandering around. I was kind of restless. Artie went over to the Keyes office. I did some unpacking and then I saw this file with his stuff. It didn't have a name. I glanced through it. There were notes about a model agency in Paris, and I thought maybe it was a front for prostitutes, there have been a lot of cases I knew about, so I made a few phone calls." She grins. "OK, I made a ton of calls. I called everyone I know who works with prostitution, there are a lot of women's groups, journalists. Martha, of course. I couldn't help it. Maybe it was nothing and I was restless, or I'm paranoid, but I couldn't leave it alone, it was like a scab on your nose and you have to pick it."

"Who did you call?" Crouched on the floor, face almost against the screen, I was talking at Lily. Behind me I could feel Martha watching.

Lily goes on. "A friend at the *Guardian* was working on this stuff. She told me about a string of massage parlors, one especially where there was a lot of activity. So she gives me an address and I end up in north London somewhere, Walthamstow, some nondescript back street where a few dead trees straggle out of the pavement and women with white legs are pushing strollers. One of the strollers has a broken wheel and it tips over. The woman screams at her kid." Lily pauses. "Is this OK, Marti? I'm not going too fast?"

Lily, who used to work on TV, is fluent. She tells her story without missing the details, she knows how, she makes you see it. She re-starts her account.

"The place is named Sexy Riviera Tanning Salon. It has a frosted window, and inside there's a creep behind a table with some phones on it, and three girls in bikinis and fake tans, sitting on orange plastic chairs. Another guy is talking to the first one about a delivery. He's a squat man with thick white skin that reminds me of dough, coarse pastry dough, and he has blonde hair like a baby, very thin, that falls over his forehead. He has on sunglasses, and a gold cross around his neck, and when I come in, he says to the guy behind the table, 'Who the fuck is she?' He's talking something that isn't Russian but sounds like it."

I knew it was Zhaba in the massage parlor. He was on it even then. It began in London when he saw Lily.

Lily goes on. "I say to the first guy, 'I want to meet one of your girls.'

"'Fuck off,' he says.

"'I'll pay.'

"'How much?'

"'A hundred pounds for one girl for fifteen minutes.'

"It's so outrageous, he probably figures I'm into women or I'm pimping for some man or God knows

187

what, which is what I want him to think. I realize if the second guy's not Russian, maybe he's Serb. Maybe it's Serbo-Croat he's talking.

"I point at the girl closest to me, and she gets off the chair. I follow her through a door into a back room. She's a kid, really, her ribs are sticking out.

"'How old are you?' I ask.

"'Eighteen,' she says, but she's lying. She speaks a little English and we get by with that and some pantomime.

"I shove money in her hand.

"'How long have you been here?'

"'One year.'

"'Where are you from?'

"'Vienna.'

"'Originally.'

"She shakes her head; she doesn't want to say.

"'You work anywhere else?'

"'Sarajevo. Prague.'

"'Where did you learn English?'

"She's watching me like she's penned up, like she's caged. 'From other girls,' she says.

"'Only?'

"She nods. 'We don't go outside.'

"'Never?'

"She's terrified, looking at the door, at me. 'I don't want to talk. I need job. Five hundred girls every month are coming in England.'

"'From Vienna?'

"'Every place.'

"'Thanks,' I say.

"She whimpers, and makes a gesture towards the door with her head. 'Don't saying nothing.'"

Lily drinks some water, then goes on, "I give her more money, I give the resident pimp some money. The delivery guy watches me. He makes me nervous. But I've already made it rough on the girl so I get the hell out.

"I go home and check the Sexy Riviera Tanning chain with people who work on prostitution, who confirm they're moving girls into London, Paris also, all over Western Europe, from the East. The pimps move them in, then take away their passports if they have one. Most of the girls are illegals, so if they run away they have no place to go, they end up homeless or dead, or they're deported to the same ugly places they came from, and someone there kills them or puts them back on the job. This is what they call ethical foreign policy.

"Listen, I know everyone thinks I'm Mrs Trying-to-Save-the-World, but this is different, OK? I mean, I had started nosing around last fall when I was in Vienna, and it was like I'd crossed into some alternative world, some dark hole in the universe where women work the side of the road, if they're lucky, if they're not actual slaves, and men haggle over the price of a blow job. I could feel the shit up around my ankles. I'd been working on this for a while when I saw Artie's file."

Lily leans forward; she licks her lips as if her mouth is dry and says, "Can I have some more water, Marti, sweetie, please?"

She starts talking again. "I went to the massage parlor on December twenty-ninth, a few days after we got to

189

London. The next day is Saturday. I decide to get my hair done for New Year's, only Richard, where I've been going for years, is away, so I think I'll just go to one of those cheap places you can walk in off the street. There's one near Notting Hill Gate, so I go in and it's pandemonium. Women getting dolled up for New Year's, guys waiting for them, picking them up, kids yelling, the staff running around like crazy. The girl who's washing my hair does that thing they all do, asking stupid questions – been on holiday yet? – but I don't pay attention.

"So I'm sitting in the chair and the guy is about to dry my hair when someone says to him, 'Phone call for you,' and he says, 'I'll be right back,' and he disappears.

"After a while I begin to think, Jesus, he must be talking to Mars this is taking so long, but someone brings me a glass of Champagne, and I'm reading *Hello* magazine, and thinking: man, this is the life. I begin to doze. Then I feel it.

"Someone's behind me. I look in the mirror and it's not the guy who's doing my hair. It's the man I saw the day before at the massage parlor. The thug with the baby-blonde hair and doughy face. He just stands there looking at my reflection in the mirror. No one notices because the place is so busy. Then he puts his hands on my hair. He plays with my hair." Lily stops, visibly shaken.

"He puts his hands on my hair. I feel his fingers on my neck. It gives me the creeps worse than anything I ever had happen, these thin, oily fingers on my neck, only he doesn't do anything or say anything, he just plays with my hair. It takes maybe ten seconds, then he's gone. All I can feel afterwards for hours are those fingers on the back of my neck."

Lily puts her hand up to her forehead and wipes away the sweat.

"I don't tell anyone because it sounds insane, like I'm in a nightmare. Afterwards I go into a pub to meet Artie, I'm late. I don't tell him. I know he'll stop me. Later, I ask him about the case he's working for Keyes, he says someone forged a check on a dead guy's bank account. But that's after New Year's Eve. I see him again New Year's Eve, the creep who put his hands on my neck."

In spite of myself, I said to the screen, to Lily's image, "Where? Where did you see him again?"

She says, as if she's answering me, "I see him on the London Eye by the river." Lily pauses. "You can turn it off now, Marti," she adds, and the tape stops.

"They took it like a scalp."

Martha held the picture of Lily close to her face. The tape had ended, and she was crying.

"They hacked off her hair."

"How do you know?"

"You showed me the picture. She left here with long hair and a few hours later, just like you figured, someone chopped it off. Her hair. Like they did it with a knife."

"Where?"

Martha switched off the TV and pulled out the tape. I tried to take it out of her hand, but she shook her head and said, "It's mine."

I said, "Lily thought something would happen to her."

191

"Yes."

"Why didn't you tell me before?"

"Because I promised. She didn't want you to worry. She wanted it between us." Martha picked up the vodka bottle and poured some more into her glass.

"I wanted to solve this my way, I wanted to help her." She held out her hands, palms up. "I came up empty. I let her down."

"Did Lily mention any names? Did she know the name in the case I'm working?"

"No. She said you never told anyone the names or put them in the file until you finished."

"What about a thug named Zhaba? Serb, probably."

"I don't know. There's a ton of them out there. Who is he?"

"I think he's the guy who threatened Lily in London and beat her up here."

The dope, the vodka, Martha was spacy now, affectless. I had to keep the talk going. She was holding back. She knew something and she wasn't saying.

To give her some time, I changed the subject. "You ever hear of a guy named Eric Levesque?"

"Who?"

"Eric Levesque."

"Yeah, I knew him, so what?"

"You knew Levesque?"

"Sure. Why?"

"You talked about that with Lily?"

"It didn't come up. Why would it?"

"You didn't tell her?"

"I told you, why would I?" Martha fumbled with her

glass. "She asked me about the prostitutes, so I told her what I knew. She wanted to see where I work, I told her I'd show her. She never made it. Because of me." She looked up. "Or you. She got interested in your case and someone wanted to warn her off. It's your fault." She sucked an ice cube. "Is that brutal?"

"Pretty brutal. What's Levesque?"

"He's dead."

"What else?"

"He was an investment guy. He owned stuff."

"What stuff?"

"I don't know."

I got up. "You want me to take off?"

"He owned a model agency."

"You're telling me this didn't come up with Lily? Come on, lady. Your friend is dying."

"Am I speaking English? Christ, I told you. It didn't relate. Levesque's agency was a real one, not a front. Lily was only interested in the prostitutes, the whores, the bitches."

"So how come you knew Levesque?"

"One of the girls who worked there left his agency. She was doing crack, she went on the street and ended up at my shelter in real bad shape. It's a long time ago."

"You met him?"

"Yeah, he came to see me when he heard about her. He didn't live here. The business was an investment." She took another slug of vodka. Her tone changed. "Honey, it was really strange."

"Strange how?"

"I expected some real scum-bag, you know. And he

193

was very nice. He lived in California most of the year. He was this gallant guy who was horrified by what happened to his girl. He wrote me a huge check for the shelter more than once. The best guy I ever met, pretty much. We kept in touch. He came out at night to help when he was here. He spent all kinds of money getting the girls fixed up. He got them doctors. He even got one her papers."

"What did he look like?"

"Nice."

"How old?"

"Your age. Fortyish, or would be now."

"What happened to him?"

"He went down in some plane crash off the West Coast. Bodies were trapped in the fuselage, but he was there, he was on the passenger list." Her eyes filled up. "What's your interest?"

"The case I'm working involves Levesque." I added, "You were more than friends?"

She wiped the snot off her face and stopped crying. "We were only friends. He liked pretty women."

"You wanted more?"

"I only met him a few times. I don't have great luck with guys, honey." Martha smiled ruefully.

"You said you were married."

"Long time ago. A nice French boy I met in college. It was pretty romantic stuff in America. Then we got to France, turned out he wanted me to be a nice French wife, a *petite bourgeoise,* you understand what that is? The right number of courses for lunch and a yogurt after supper. I left New York and ended up in the suburbs of Rouen. You can imagine."

194

"You have a picture of Levesque?"

She pushed herself off the futon and found the big leather bag. From it, she pulled out the pack of photographs she'd produced at the restaurant. She took off the rubber band. She seemed obsessed with the pictures.

"It's not here," she said.

I kept my mouth shut. She was distracted. She searched her bag. She rummaged through her drawers. She was nuts for this guy and the picture was all she had.

"I can't find it," she said.

"He ever talk about his wife?" I was rummaging for information now.

"A little. Not really. They got married as kids. Then divorced."

"It wasn't Levesque running the whores?"

"He was an innocent. Like I said, he was about as good as there is. What's that?" She suddenly looked at the door.

"What's what?"

"Someone's outside," she said. "These doors are like paper. Someone's out there. Someone's been listening to everything we said."

I got up from the beanbag, switched off the lights, reached into my pocket for the gun, peered through the peephole in the door. "I don't see anyone."

"There's someone there."

I unlocked the door and opened it very slowly.

"There's no one," I said and shut the door.

"Maybe I'm paranoid. This thing with Lily." She picked up the photographs and put them back in her bag.

"I wish I could show you. Eric, I mean. Levesque. You'd see right away."

"See what?"

"The resemblance, honey."

"Resemblance to who?"

If getting Martha to talk meant playing these games, I'd sit here and play them all night, but time was running out, I could hear it drain away, hear the suck and gurgle.

"You want me to stick around tonight, Martha?"

She smiled. "Best offer I've had in years. I'll be fine, honey."

"You're sure?"

She hesitated. "I'll be OK. You want me to call you a cab?"

"I need air bad. I'll find one in the street. Anything else we should talk about?"

She looked at me. Extracted the snapshot of her and Lily.

"You take it. You should have it."

I put the picture in my pocket. I kissed her on the cheek, pulled on my jacket and said, "Tell me who Levesque resembled."

She opened the door. "Honey, he looked like you, and he was the nicest man I ever met. Artie?"

"What's that?"

"This piece of shit who hurt Lily?"

"Yeah?"

"I'm thinking the Iron Curtain, I'm thinking the middle of the middle of old Europe, you know?"

"Like where exactly?"

"My daddy was in the army, you know that, Artie? He was a colonel in the US Army." She saluted.

Martha was off her rocker now; she was rambling, imitating her father. "Anyone who messes with my country, he'd say, anyone who does that, I will mess right back with them. They call it a Cold War, kiddo, but it's hot, all right. He talked a real lot of crap. He was stationed in Berlin when I was a little girl. He used to show us the Berlin Wall. They call it the Iron Curtain, he'd say, it runs down through Germany, Czechoslovakia, Vienna, Slovenia, all the way down, and he'd tell us about the bad people who were called Communists."

"Go on."

"So the border now, you know, it's right where that fucking Iron Curtain used to run, right across Europe."

"I'm listening," I said.

"So you cross over, and you'll see them. The whores. Everywhere. Bars, hotels, along the side of the road. Try crossing over, OK? You got that?"

"Where? Where do I cross?"

"It's all I have. I swear to God. It's all she told me."

"Lily told you?"

"Yeah. She told me. So remember, Artie, it's a hot war, honey. Real hot."

197

16

It was almost dawn when I got to the rue de Rivoli. The
building where Lily was attacked was silent, the room
where the concierge lived still dark. I was so tired, I
stumbled out of the cab.

In my pocket were a couple of credit cards; I slipped
open the front door with one. It was dark in the hallway.
I moved carefully to the stairs, up the two flights to the
apartment where they found Lily. The cops were gone.
No one bothered me. From an apartment somewhere I
heard a puppy whine. Otherwise, it was very quiet.

The door opened easily. I closed it behind me.

I didn't know what I was looking for, but there had
to be something that told me why they beat her up here,
in this place. It was Tuesday morning. It was a week
since they'd hurt Lily. Raped her.

Say it, I said to myself. Raped her and hacked her hair
off.

I felt my way through the place in the dark, hands on
the walls, feeling the pebbly surface of the plaster. In the
living room, I could make out a stain on the floor where

they found her. The rug had been removed. Some forensic lab somewhere in Paris was laboring over it. Pointless stuff. Trying to match blood samples, but who to? Some Serb hood named Zhaba? The man on the wheel in London? The creep who fingered Lily's hair at the salon in London? I was pretty sure they were the same bastard. I crawled around the floor, desperate.

Lily comes to Paris because of me, first because of something she sees in the Levesque file, then because she feels threatened. She makes a date with her old friend Martha Burnham who works with battered prostitutes; a few hours later, she's beaten, raped, out cold in this apartment. Who called it in? I shivered. I was so strung out, I never asked. Was she really out? Was she conscious? Who made the call?

As my eyes adjusted to the dark, I could see the long narrow corridor that led from the living room. Off it was the kitchen with an old stove, rust-stained linoleum on the floor and cracked green paint on the walls. More doors. More rooms. I checked the doors. Two bedrooms. A bathroom. The floorboards creaked.

A shadow crawled over the wall as a car passed under the street light. I looked at my watch. Almost five.

God, I was tired. I slid down against the wall in the hallway for a minute. Adrenalin kept me barely awake. The boards creaking again, I scratched at the floor, looking for anything, a pin, a cigarette butt, a scrap of paper. On the cold floor, there was only more dust.

In one of the bedrooms, I reached under the metal frame of the bed, with its bare mattress folded over double. The room smelled musty, shut up, dead. My fingers touched something cold and metallic stuck between the floorboards. It came loose. Another car went by outside. Its headlights flashed into the room and I saw I was holding a coin. It was a Czech crown. Did Martha mention Czechoslovakia? Did Momo?

Martha Burnham was half cracked. This was only a coin. I ran my hand along the floor again, felt something, raised my hand close to my face so I could see what it was. On my hand were tiny cuttings of hair. Red hair. Lily's hair.

A light flashed from the living room. Someone was here. Someone had followed me to the apartment. I took the gun in one hand.

The concierge held open the door. It was the same sullen woman I'd met before, only now she was furious because I'd messed with her building when she was in charge. Behind her were Tolya Sverdloff and Momo Gourad.

I got up off the floor, the coin in my hand.

"How the hell did you find me?"

Gourad was pissed off. "How? Very difficult, you know." He tapped his head sarcastically. "I use my little gray cells, you know? I knew you'd come here. I knew you'd have to see for yourself that there is nothing to see."

"Who found her, Momo?"

"I did."

"Why didn't you tell me?"

"It's classified."

"Bullshit."

200

Momo said, "You're way off limits. The minute you come through the door, you fuck with the crime scene."

"No one else is fucking with it. No one else is doing anything, isn't that right, Momo?"

"Your satirism is not great."

"Sarcasm," I said.

"I put myself on a limb for you."

I turned to Tolya, whose tux was a mess, the jacket rumpled, wine stains on the shirt. "What are you doing here?"

"You disappear from the club without telling me, I go looking for you at that dump you're staying in, I run into Gourad who's also looking for you."

"Now you found me."

Gourad said, "I came to the hotel because my chief is asking about you. He doesn't like you running around Paris. He sent some idiot to talk to you the other night, you weren't there, he was sending a bigger idiot today. I was going to warn you to stay the fuck away from anything to do with this case for a few days."

"That's it?"

"It's fucking serious, Artie."

"You know and I know that Lily was beaten up here, she was raped here, they hacked off her hair here. Tell me something, Momo."

"What's that?"

"Who called you? How did you know Lily was hurt?"

He shifted his weight from one foot to the other.

"Tell me."

"The concierge heard something."

"What kind of thing?"

"Someone banging on the floor."

"Who was it?"

"It was Lily."

"She was conscious?"

"Yes."

"When you found her?"

"Semi-conscious. Yes. I'm sorry."

"You took pictures of her lying there." Numb, I rubbed my eyes. "And she was still conscious?"

The concierge stood by, mute. Tolya said to Gourad, "I'll take him back to my hotel."

"All right. But sit on him."

At Tolya's hotel I left him in the lobby and went to the bathroom. When I got back, Tolya, the black coat over his shoulders, was talking to someone. His back was to me; I couldn't see who he was talking to. Then he shifted to the left. It was Joe Fallon. Tolya was talking to Joe Fallon.

Joe looked up and put his hand out. "Hey, how are you, Art? I've been thinking about you. I was just going for breakfast. Couldn't sleep."

"You two know each other?" Tolya said.

Joe said. "We knew each other back when. We met up again recently. How's it going, Artie? How's Lily doing?"

"She's conscious."

"Good. Great. I'll be in the office all day. You have that number? Call me. Or we could have some lunch. Or I could call you."

I picked up a pen off the concierge's desk and wrote my number on the back of a hotel brochure.

"Fine." Joe shook my hand again, nodded at Tolya and went out of the door, looking for coffee.

Tolya said, "What the hell are you doing with Fallon?"

"He's a friend. You said you didn't know him."

"I didn't remember until I saw his face. I met him once at some party. In New York."

"So?"

"Fallon's from New York. He's in business. He moves around. I don't like him."

"Why not?"

Tolya said, "Let's get breakfast."

"I like him."

"OK, fine. Let's eat some breakfast."

"I don't want breakfast. What's wrong with Fallon?"

"I don't like his type." He was speaking Russian.

"What type?"

"Pretend Americans."

"So long, Tolya."

"Where the hell are you going?"

"I have a job to do."

"You're in trouble, man. You're in trouble with the company you work for, with Carol Browne, with the cops here, with yourself. Just stay cool. We'll work this together, we'll get Lily better, we'll take her home."

I always hate how I'm in hock to Tolya all the time. Now, I hated it worse because I knew where some of his money came from.

"You're just taking off? For where?"

"None of your business."

"What is my business?"

"Whores."

"Grow up. You're way over your head, you're running around like a crazy man. I know this thing with Lily makes you unhappy, but you're nowhere on this case."

"You're going to fix it, right? Like always?"

"You have to know, whatever you do, Lily will be safe. I'll be there. I have my guys on it, she'll have a nurse." He paused. "How come you're so pissed off at me, Artyom?" He looked tired. He was sober.

"I ask you if you know who runs hookers here, you tell me no, then it turns out you have a whorehouse like something from a bad Bond movie."

"It's not mine. I put some money in. It's an investment. They run it right. No one gets hurt. Everyone makes money, including the women. Especially the women. I fucking hate your fucking sanctimonious moralizing."

When Tolya gets angry, his huge body puffs up, his face gets purple.

"Listen, my cousin Svetlana loved you. This makes you family. But I don't have to put up with this shit. I'll take care of Lily because she's my friend, too, and I love her and I love Beth and I'm her godfather. But I'm fucking tired of your suspicions. You know who I am and what I do and you can come down off your high moral horse, man, and cut it out, and when you decide to dismount, then give me a call."

"Go to hell."

"Fuck you."

I walked to the door. Tolya brushed past me, and all

he said was, "If you want me, you know where to find me. I'll be with the whores," and set off down the street, his coat flapping in the wind.

"Lily?"

After I slept a few hours, the rest of Tuesday I sat with Lily in the hospital, watching her, waiting for Martha's call. She had promised to call. She promised. I had picked up some maps. I wasn't sure where I was going, but I had maps and they were on my lap while I sat with Lily. Outside the hospital window, snow fell in thick slanted curtains.

During the day, once in a while, I touched Lily's hair where it stuck out from the bandages. Sometimes I held her hand, or talked, and sometimes she talked back a little.

"Do you know who I am? Sweetheart?"

She didn't answer and I said, "Do you remember Martha?"

"I remember Martha," she whispered. "My friend."

"Yes."

"In love with me."

"Everyone's in love with you."

Lily smiled and closed her eyes.

Lariot, the doctor I'd met earlier that week, came by. He was wearing a joke tie, bright pink with cartoon doctors on it. He told me Lily was getting better. Physically, she was improving. He chose his words carefully, but he was frosty; he didn't like me. I followed him into the hallway.

I said, "If I have to go away for twenty-four hours, is it all right?"

He turned to go with the brisk gestures of a man consumed by busyness.

I grabbed his shoulder. "Tell me."

"Please let go of me."

"I'm sorry." I repeated myself. "If I go away for twenty-four hours, if I'm back by tomorrow night, is it OK?"

"Yes," he said. "She'll be all right."

Later, Momo dropped in to see Lily, shook my hand, left. The snow was still coming down, but I went into the courtyard for a smoke and stood under an overhang just outside Lily's room. I was standing, smoking, not talking, and watching the snow when I heard her scream.

In the doorway of her room, I slammed into Tolya. Lily was in bed, trying to sit up, a look of absolute terror on her face. I knelt next to her, put my arms around her as best I could, but she pushed me away. Tears streamed down her face.

Lariot hurried in. "What happened?"

"Lily?"

She closed her eyes.

I said, "Someone was here."

"That's impossible," Lariot said.

Tolya found his security guy who was in the toilet, fired him, called another one, and got an orderly who showed up ten minutes later with a cot. Tolya was already working the phone.

"What are you doing?" I said.

"I'm going to stay with her," Tolya said.

I didn't answer.

He said, "I don't know what the fuck happened or who was here, or if there was anyone, but I'm going to live here until she's ready to go home, and then I'll take her home. We'll take her home, Aryom, all right? You do what you have to get the creep. If you need to take a trip, go."

Tolya could always read me. I nodded. He pushed his hand in his pocket and brought out a wad of cash. I shook my head.

He said, "In case. In case. Take it."

I took the money. I kissed Lily's cheek and left, but I had smelled him. I knew Zhaba had been in Lily's room. I could smell him.

17

"You should go now," she said, opening the door. "You must get out of Paris right away."

The last few days, I'd visited Katya Slobodkin more than once. I'd stopped by on my way to and from the hospital. You could see the hospital from her apartment. I could talk to Katya; I could talk about what I'd seen and where I'd been and she believed me because she had been there.

Katya knew whatever Momo Gourad knew, maybe more. He wasn't telling me everything, but she told me because she thought I'd kill Zhaba for her. She wanted him dead. The way she saw it, Momo, who was official, couldn't do the killing, but I could. I was foreign, I wasn't a cop anymore, I had nothing permanent at stake in Europe; I could take Lily and go home.

She didn't mention the night at the club, just kissed me three times Russian style, pulled the belt of her pink bathrobe tight and poured me some of the tea she was drinking. Outside the windows, the snow was piled high and soft on her terrace.

She said, "I think you should go. I think you're asking too many questions. People are angry at you, Artemy."

I looked around and realized the door to the bedroom was shut. "I know that."

"Momo is asleep," she said. "He came here earlier from the hospital."

"I want to know how you're involved in all this."

"I told you. I know the creep. I want him to be dead."

"You asked me to kill a guy, Katya. I'm not some enforcer, I can't just knock off a guy."

"Because he hurt your Lily," she added. "And me, also."

"It doesn't work that way."

She smiled wryly. "You're such an American. Don't you believe me?"

"I don't always know."

"Because I'm Russian or because I'm a whore?"

"Stop it. You think I'm in trouble?"

"Yes."

"If I don't find him, he'll come for Lily again?"

"Like today at hospital."

"You heard?"

"Yes."

"And he'll come back?"

"Yes."

"Where am I going, Katya?"

Katya's robe fell open in front and she gathered it up and pulled the belt tight, then looked at me.

"You're blushing, Artemy," she said.

I shook my head.

She said, "You remember I said I would ask around about some girl I heard got beat up like Lily?"

"Yes."

"I heard about girls that work the border. Czech. German."

"I heard something like that, too," I said. "Where?"

She sipped her tea. Then, switching from English to Russian and back again, said, "I have heard there is shit-hole on Czech-German border. You cross at Raitzenhaim. On the Czech side, you look for signs to Teplice. This is European Highway 55."

"You've been there? You know this place?"

Katya withdrew; she didn't talk about herself much. "It doesn't matter how I know," she said. "You have what you need?"

I knew she meant a weapon and I nodded.

"How is Lily?"

"She's a little better."

"But she still doesn't know who you are."

"No."

The phone rang and Katya picked it up quickly. She listened, then hung up.

She put her hand on my arm then, and said, "Go, Artie. Please, get out of here now."

"Who was it?"

"Just please go."

"Who?"

"Momo's boss. He's looking for you."

"Why?"

She didn't answer.

"Tell me."

"Some people start to think maybe you are involved."

"That I hurt Lily? That's fucking insane."

She reached for her bag, a large yellow Hermès sack made of expensive reptiles, and pulled something out of it. "Here is something else."

"What is it?"

She spoke in Russian now, very softly. "It is a picture of Zhaba."

I held the picture up to the light.

"He changes his looks sometimes, sometimes a mustache, but you'll know him. You saw him at the club. You have picture now. You'll know from the smell, very sweet, very specific, and from tattoos on knuckles. You talked to your friend Anatoly Sverdloff?"

"What's there to talk about?"

"He's your friend, but you think he is some pimp," Katya said. "Look, the plane is faster, but it's snowing pretty bad, so the train to Dresden may be better, also no metal detectors."

"Thank you. Can I kiss you goodbye?"

"Sure. Yes." Katya wound her arms around my neck and kissed me on the cheek. "Be careful."

"Thanks."

I looked at the bedroom door and she said, "I'll tell Momo you were here."

"If you want."

"You don't trust Momo?"

"I trust him," I said. "I don't want to make trouble for him. He's still official. This is my business. You take care of Momo, OK. And Katya?"

"Yes?"

"How did you get the picture? Of Zhaba?"

She smiled slightly. "Why do you care? I give you this picture. It is enough."

"I want to know."

"I slept with someone."

From the street, after I left Katya's apartment, I tried Martha Burnham. There was no answer. At the hotel, I shoved some of Tolya's money across the desk and asked the manager to check the trains and planes. Berlin. Dresden. Prague. Anywhere I could make a connection.

The door opened and Momo appeared. He was out of breath.

"What's the matter?"

"I followed you from Katya's." His coat was heavy with snow. He took it off and shook it out.

"I have to go," I said.

"Where are you going?"

"The hospital."

"I'm all you've got, Artie, you know that? So don't come around Katya's because you want to look at her."

"You wanted me to meet Katya. I don't know what your game is."

"There's no game. I thought she could feel comfortable with you."

"Russian to Russian?"

"Yes. To talk. Who is Stuart Larkin?"

"What?"

"A bank in Puteaux put in a call. Some crazy American running around talking to Larkin, who worked for them."

"Worked?"

"He went on leave Friday night. The bank asked him to go. What is this?"

"Nothing, honestly, it's just a paper case. This case I've been working for Keyes, it's a security firm."

"I know what is Keyes. Come on."

"Where to?"

"I want to show you something."

I followed Momo out to his car.

"Get in."

"What?"

"Get the fuck in the car, Artie, and let's stop dancing around this. The bank wants to know where you are. I said I didn't see you since a while."

"Thank you." I got in the car and said, "Larkin sent me a copy of a video tape."

"What kind of tape?" He started the car.

"A surveillance tape, the bank one afternoon, something I've been working on. Nothing."

"What?"

"You mentioned a guy named Levesque."

"Go on." He pulled the car away from the curb.

I told him as much as I knew about Levesque, that he was dead, that someone forged his check, that I figured it was connected to the attack on Lily. I could see he thought I was making connections out of nothing. He was a good guy, this shambling intense cop who was in love with a Russian hooker, but he was a kid.

"How old are you, Momo?"

"What kind of shit is this?"

"How old?"

"Twenty-seven. You want also to know my sign?"

"You started early."

"I was a boy-genius. Forget it. I've been eight years on the job, including two in America. It's enough."

"OK."

"You're thinking of doing some traveling?"

"I don't know."

"I'm all that can cover our ass. Your embassy wants to know, the bank wants to know, my boss definitely wants to know everything there is to know about you."

"Your boss looks like a jerk."

"My boss is a jerk, but I can only keep him off you if you help me."

He pulled up at an anonymous gray building. I looked at my watch.

"What is it?"

"Come on."

Inside was a duty officer and a woman mopping the floor. I followed Momo down two flights of stairs to the basement.

It was a morgue. The girl was in a steel drawer he pulled out from the wall.

The first thing I saw was the hair. It was chopped with a knife, or a pair of shears, rough cut, jagged edges, pieces sticking up. The first time when I'd looked at her up on the waste-ground where she was murdered, maybe I didn't notice. After the video Burnham showed me of Lily, I could see the hair for what it was. Whoever attacked Lily had killed this girl. He took hair for a souvenir.

She was tiny and pale. Stored in the cold tray, waiting

for an autopsy, tagged and bagged, as they say, she barely looked fourteen; she could have been ten years old.

Looking down at her, we stood in the cold room. Momo was smoking to keep from weeping. He was a hard-ass cop, but he was a boy, he could still feel stuff. What scared me was I didn't feel anything at all, nothing. I was cold as ice.

The room was lined with steel trays; each tray had a number and a body. I looked at my watch.

"You're in a hurry?" He was angry. "You can't respect this girl for five minutes without thinking about your own misery?"

"What?"

Momo crossed himself.

"You're lucky, Momo, you know that?"

"Why's that?"

"You've got religion."

"Sure."

"And Monique and the kids, and the cheese soufflés. You've got Katya," I said. "I mean that nice, OK, about Katya."

He kept quiet.

"I'm sorry."

"It's OK. Are you carrying, Artie?"

I didn't answer.

"Tell me."

"I'm not doing anything that's going to put you in the shit. I swear to you."

I looked at the girl some more and all I saw was the hacked hair. Momo pulled back the covering and showed me where her joints had been smashed, all the hard surfaces, worse than Lily, knees, elbows, fingers, everywhere. With a hammer, someone smashed her up like she was constructed out of sticks and boards.

"Teeth, too," Momo said.

"What?"

"They smashed her teeth."

"Who was she?"

"Who knows? Some girl, a kid from nowhere, returning to nowhere, no story-line, no plot, no characters, just one like a million others."

"Someone will work this officially, give this a story?"

"For a while."

"Unofficial?"

He shivered. "Only me."

"You?"

"Yeah."

"Because it's a pattern?"

"Because of your Lily. Yes, now I have a pattern."

He closed the drawer and we started out of the cold room where everyone except us was dead.

"I'm getting a divorce," he said.

"For Katya?"

"Yes," Momo said. "You know I used to go a lot."

"Go where?"

"Hookers. Escort services. All the time. You're surprised?"

I was silent.

"A lot of cops, you know, relieve the tension. Other guys. Your typical guy who goes to hookers may be forty-five, athletic, good-looking, successful, married, kids, but he likes sex without involvement, and his wife would kill him if she knew. Kill him, maybe literally. You tip over into that world, you discover everyone's doing it, every second guy. There's a million women out there you can fuck, if you want."

It was what Katya told me.

We got outside, where Momo's car was parked. He opened the door, we got in.

"You're shocked, man, aren't you?" he said. "It's not your scene at all."

I stared at the floor. "Hey, it's a choice, like they say. Momo, listen, the next twenty-four hours, put someone with Lily. All the time, I mean. Can you do it?"

"Tell me where you're going."

"OK."

"Where?"

"You'll do it, for Lily?"

"Yes."

"I'm going near to a town name of Teplice. The German-Czech border."

He said, "I'm not going to stop you because you leveled with me, and because I work for a bunch of losers. Be in touch. Keep me up with where you are. Otherwise, it's my ass."

"I'll be back tomorrow night latest. You have my cell phone. I'll call. I have to go."

"I know guys everywhere."

"Can you buy me some hours, Momo? Tonight, maybe? Can you keep your boss off my back until the morning? I can get a plane."

"Then get out of your hotel now. Don't check out.

Just take what you need. I'll drop you at the airport, you can spend the night in a hotel there."

From the car, on the way to the hotel, I tried Martha Burnham again, but her machine answered and her cell phone was switched off.

Momo took me back to my hotel. There was a substitute guy on the desk who didn't pay any attention to me, and I went up, stuffed a few things in my bag, put the gun in a drawer. In spite of Katya's advice, I was planning to fly; the metal detectors would screw me up if I took a weapon.

I strolled back out the front door. I knew I had to go east fast. I believed Katya when she told me about the border. This was where Zhaba worked; this was the hole in the ground where I would find him. I had to go before it was too late, for me, for Lily.

Momo drove me to an airport hotel where I got a room and slept. I got up early. I had one more thing to do before I left Paris.

18

"I'm in Paris, Mom, Paris." I yelled in Russian into the phone as if the yelling would make her understand. "Paris."

I heard the call bounce off the satellite, relayed from Paris to Haifa. The phone was OK. It wasn't the phone. It wasn't the phone in Paris or Israel or the satellite that wasn't working right, the silence wasn't technical. It was my mother. She couldn't understand me.

She doesn't ever know me when I call now, doesn't know my voice. She entered a world of her own making years ago, after my father died, after he was blown up by a bomb in Israel where we went to live when we left Moscow. In the good days when he was still in the KGB – he said they were good days – he was a tall, handsome man. Afterwards, after they had to leave because my mother was a noisy dissident Jew, they went to Israel and he got smaller. His only pleasure was hanging out with the generals who sometimes consulted him on intelligence.

My mother survived the bomb. She hated Israel and she wasn't interested in America. All she ever wanted was Europe; Paris was her obsession.

My mother had dreamed about Paris all the time. She had a collection of tattered paperbacks about the city. Sometimes she cooked us French recipes she found in magazines she paid a fortune for in some back-alley shop on the Arbat. She had a large map, too, and most nights she spread it on the kitchen table after supper and worked on her itinerary for the trips she never took.

Now she was in a place where I couldn't reach her and never would. I couldn't reach Lily, but Lily was different. Lily was coming back. I had to believe it.

I sat on the edge of the bed in the airport hotel, holding the phone, wanting so bad for my mother to know I made it to Paris where she wanted to go all her life.

I kept on talking. "I'm in Paris. I've seen the Place de la Concorde. I've seen the Eiffel Tower. The Left Bank. The Louvre. The Impressionists, you know Mom?"

I was lying now. I hadn't seen the things she cared about, the great pictures, the theater, the opera, the Luxembourg Gardens, the famous sewers, the bookshops on the Left Bank, the jazz clubs. She had constructed her Paris out of the pieces of novels and ancient travel guides and the battered map.

I wanted her to know. I wanted her to remember and I said, "The Seine. And Notre Dame. It's so beautiful. It's as beautiful as you thought, Mom."

The line went quiet. Someone took the phone away from her, but I kept talking for a while. I couldn't remember the last time I cried. Maybe when Svetlana got blown up in Moscow. Maybe then. I put the receiver carefully back on the hotel phone.

PART TWO

19

For me it was only Lily, but for Momo Gourad it was war. This business with the women, it was his war and I could hear it in his voice the next morning when he called to tell me Martha Burnham was found dead at her shelter.

"This morning," Momo said. "The caretaker found her."

I was on my way to the airport when he called. She had been dead for eight, maybe ten hours, sprawled on the floor in her down vest, hat, skirt, sweater, her bag next to her, the contents dumped on the floor. Shot, Momo said. I had seen her very early Tuesday morning, three, four in the morning. That night they hunted her down at her shelter.

"What about her hair?" I yelled into the phone, but Momo said her hair wasn't touched. They were taking prints and blood to get the DNA, see if it matched what they found with Lily, with the girl behind the billboard. I knew it would match. So did he.

"Momo?"

"What's that?"

"I'll keep you in touch."

"Good."

"No, I mean it, I'll call you. Whatever I get, I'll give it to you."

"Thank you."

"Is Katya OK?"

"Yes."

"Is she part of it?"

But all he said was, "I'll give her your regards."

By the time I got to the terminal that morning, half the flights were late or scratched. There was a blizzard coming in across northern France; freezing weather and floods in Germany over the weekend had turned the country into a skating rink. Air-traffic controllers in Amsterdam were on go-slow.

At seven in the morning, the airport was already jammed with people, yelling, arguing, whining. It was Wednesday. Europe was open for business, but nothing moved, including my flight to Dresden. Katya said take the train, but the plane would be faster. I could be back with Lily that night or the next morning.

At the Hertz counter fifty people were screaming for rentals, even though the highways were jammed with protesting French truckers. A man in the Hertz line told me that the eighteen-wheelers were walled in by the weather. He was a Brit with a bald head and a briefcase and those expensive shoes you get made to measure. He was talking into a phone and when he snapped it shut, he said to me, "I'm getting the train. Would you like a lift? I have a car. I kept a taxi waiting just in case."

★

The Gare de l'Est was bleak and cold. A wild-eyed kid tried to carry my bag for tips. I yanked it away, gave him some change, waited restlessly in line and got a ticket to Dresden. The train left at 8.20.

The station was packed with people trapped by the storm. They put on extra trains. When I finally climbed on, it had old-fashioned compartments, the kind I hadn't seen since we left Moscow, my mother, her Agatha Christie in her hand, my father staring out of the window, tears on his face.

There was a window seat in smoking. I climbed over five German soldiers so young they had blonde fuzz on their faces. Going home, one said in English.

The train was jammed. Heaving my bag onto the shelf over my seat, I sat down and rubbed mist from the window.

Suddenly I saw a man on the platform who looked like Joe Fallon. His back was to me, he had a heavy suitcase in one hand and a black leather backpack. I couldn't see his face, but it looked like Joe. I stumbled over the Germans, who were too polite to complain. I scrambled to the door where people were piling in luggage and yelling at each other.

"Joe?" I leaned out. "Joe?"

But Joe was sucked up by the chaotic crowds and I never made out if it was him or my imagination. Then the train pushed out of the station.

The snow came down against the window in big, relentless flakes. It was six and a half hours to Frankfurt, where I would change trains. I called Lily a couple of times and got the nurse. On and off, I tried to read a copy of *The Quiet American* I'd found with Lily's stuff. I used Zhaba's picture as a bookmark; the face was imprinted on my brain, the thick white skin, pale eyes, thin blonde hair, high forehead. The train was hot. I started to sweat.

My German soldiers snored and I stood in the corridor for a while, leaning against the window, holding my book, watching Europe out the window – France, the border, Germany, Saarbrucken, Kaiserslautern. I could have moved nuclear samples or humped cash, guns, drugs, women. I could have brought a ton of Semtex on board. The global economy. Only the weather could shut it down.

All around me, businessmen yakked into their cell phones and tapped on their computers, then gave up when the phones went dead. The signals were lousy; millions of people trying to get through tied up the networks if they were working at all.

The further we went, the more I felt like a tourist trapped somewhere on the wrong side of the border. But the immigration guy barely glanced at my passport. He didn't know I was on my way east looking to kill a man.

In Frankfurt I changed trains, grabbed a sandwich, stood up in the bar-car to eat it and watched the landscape. Weimar, Leipzig. I finished the sandwich and drank a warm beer, watching the scenery get flatter as we rumbled into the borderlands where the Iron Curtain once ran twelve hundred miles.

Alongside the tracks were parts of broken trains; I could see the rust through the snow. All that remained of the railway sheds were piles of shattered brick. Smoke stacks spewed filth, streams were so polluted you could see the thick green algae through the ice. I called the hospital, where a night nurse told me Lily was asleep and Tolya was in her room. I got through to my machine in New York to check for messages like I do every day, but all I heard was the voice of a cop I used to know asking me to his stag night at El Teddy's, four hang-ups, and Joe Fallon in Paris, unable to reach me anyplace else, wanting to take me to dinner if I was still in town. More hang-ups. Then Momo Gourad. Where are you? Call me.

For another half hour I tried calling. I left him more messages. He was my only life-line.

In spite of the weather, the train was on time. We hit Dresden at 7.47 and I got a cab to the airport car rental. I thought about the fire bombing in Dresden, about the way people got their feet stuck in hot tar and were burned alive. They couldn't move their feet, so they stood there and burned to death. All I really knew was what I read in Kurt Vonnegut, though. For me, in a way, it was only fiction, more or less.

At Hertz, I signed for the car I'd reserved. Then I slid Zhaba's picture across the counter. The agent looked down. Politely, because all Germans seemed polite, he shook his head. Never saw this one, he said. You are police? I said no and asked for directions. He tugged his earring and spread out a map.

The roads out of town were empty. The snow and ice had scared off the tourists and most of the commuters; people stayed home in bed or hunkered down in airports.

I used some of the cash Tolya gave me for the rented Mercedes, which held the road in spite of the weather. I drove slowly in the dark, skidding a couple of times. I was heading south for the border, where Katya figured Zhaba worked.

At the gas station where I stopped for a drink, at a roadside café where I got a sandwich, I showed the picture. I made noise. I complained. People would remember me. Someone would talk. I wanted him coming after me. I wanted him out in the open. I wanted it over.

I ran into a Dutch film crew and a famous French actor at the café; they were making a low-budget feature about Albanian refugees. The old Iron Curtain road had become fashionable and the Balkans were Europe's Vietnam all over again.

It was flat borderland here, and I drove, trying to stay awake, fiddling with the radio, listening to news in foreign languages.

No oceans, no mountains, just flat, bleak countryside, easy pickings for the hoards that had run over it, up to the Baltic, down towards the Adriatic. Turks and Swedes, Mongols and Prussians. Most of all, Russians.

Except for the weather that slowed me down, it wasn't far. I saw the signs for the border, and at Raitzenhaim I crossed into the Czech Republic, where I pulled off the road. There was a gas station, a bar and a supermarket where all you could buy were big pieces of Czech cheese, garden gnomes and women.

20

"Mister."

A voice called from the side of the road, and through the murky night I could make out women, some standing, others leaning against buildings. It was snowing. Hard to make out their faces. I was out of cigarettes and I needed one really bad.

It snowed on the garden furniture that seemed to be the staple of this gloomy duty-free pit-stop; the dwarfish figures with Santa caps stood near the plastic window boxes along the side of the road. There was soaking wet astro-turf rolled up into three-foot wheels. Some of the hookers leaned against the stuff.

A car in front of me pulled up sharp so I almost rammed it, then parked on the shoulder. A woman in a clear plastic raincoat darted out, inspected the gnomes, picked up a three-foot statuette and struggled with it until a man came out of the shed. They bickered for a while. Then she paid and dragged her prize triumphantly into her car.

A week ago I was in London feeling happy, now I was

trapped behind a woman buying a gnome. I parked and went inside to get cigarettes.

A few yards further along, the supermarket was run by a Vietnamese couple. North Vietnamese? South? Who can tell the difference these days? Nobody lives where they come from anymore; nobody lives anyplace. They were residents of the Czech Republic now, and they sold cheap make-up, canned fish, chopsticks, plastic toys, stuff only people in the East would have wanted, maybe still did.

This was where the Iron Curtain once ran, three rows of barbed wire, the land between the wire mined, the fence electrified, guards with dogs. All gone now, and there was only the duty-free and the snow.

The big cars swished past: Mercedes, BMWs, snappy Golfs, the stylish Audis, SUVs. People stopped for drinks or gas, then took off again, going somewhere, moving on, heading for home. Inside, a few tourists, stranded by the weather, fingered the lousy goods. Three Czech hoods hung around the duty-free liquor. An American in a pink ski jacket grabbed some Juicy Fruit and a few cans of Coke, looked at the hoods and beat it back to his rental car.

I wanted to get back to the road where the women were, but the creeps, two short, one tall, were watching me. They were big-shouldered men in their twenties, stubble on their faces, gold chains looped around their necks. They looked stupid and pissed-off. Maybe they were friends with Zhaba.

I roamed the aisles, fumbled with cartons of Marlboros. I bought some, then showed the Vietnamese woman the picture; she shook her head. No, she said. Don't know.

A display of beach towels that featured Siegfried and Roy and Michael Jackson, dripped on a line outside. Banks of dirty snow, a foot high, had frozen over into hedges alongside the road.

I got in my car and called Paris. I left the window open a few inches so I could breathe.

"How is she?" I yelled into the cell phone, trying to hear Tolya's voice. "How's Lily?"

"Sort of –"

"Sort of what?"

"Where are you, man?"

The signal broke up. I shouted. "Tell me you're with her."

"I'm with her."

"In her room? Swear on your kids."

"I can't hear you."

"Hey, Mister." The voice came from the side of the road and I squinted into the snow.

"Mister! Over here!"

The phone went dead.

"Mister."

I punched a button and the window rolled down further; a stinging wind blew snow into the car.

"Mister. Over here. Cheap."

The girl who lurched to the side of the car was wearing thigh-high white plastic boots with stiletto heels, fishnet stockings with a hole in them, hot pants and a fake zebra jacket. She held a red umbrella over her head.

This was where the hookers worked. Katya said so. Zhaba worked here, she'd said. He was here. Somewhere behind the screen of snow-laden trees there were houses, or hotels, where they took the customers.

The girl signaled me to drive forward a few feet and pull off onto the shoulder, then she leaned through the window.

"Cheap stuff," she said again in English.

"How much?" I stuck my head out into the snow.

"Hundred dollars," she said.

"That's not cheap."

"How much?"

"That depends."

Two other women materialized as soon as I climbed out of the car and I showed them Zhaba's picture. "I want him."

"For money?"

"Yes."

She looked at the picture, but one of the others shook her head as if in warning and said, "We don't know him."

I looked at the girl in the white plastic boots. "What about you?"

She hesitated. "No."

"Ask around." I gave her a twenty.

"Maybe."

I pointed back to the shop where I bought the cigarettes. There was a bar next door. "I'll wait."

She held her hand out again. I gave her another twenty, made sure all the women saw me do it, looked at my watch. It was eleven. I pointed at the dial, said I'd wait until midnight. The word would get around some rich American asshole was spending money. I didn't expect the girls to give Zhaba up, but someone would know him if he was here, if he had been here. I could wait. I headed for the bar.

21

SEXDOLLS.COM was his website, though he said he had a second one called "happypoking". The guy in the bar told me his on-line business was determining the "fuckability' of girls at various bars, hotels and rest stops along Europe's highways, especially here, European Highway 55. Name's Finn, he added, with a matter-of-fact smile, How do you do? He was the kind of guy who made quotation marks in the air with his fingers when he said "fuckability".

I'd parked the car and gone into the bar to wait for the girl in white leather boots and get out of the cold. It was a cavernous shed with a bar, tables and chairs, a jukebox, some slot machines and a couple of Jean Claude Van Damme posters on the wall. But it was warm. From the jukebox Tina Turner belted out a song I didn't know.

Behind the bar, a guy was wiping down the surface with a stringy cloth. In the back of the room was a second door with a beaded curtain. Every time someone opened the front door, the curtain shivered in the blast of cold air, the colored beads clinking.

There were a couple of girls at a table. They looked

about fifteen. They wore miniskirts, tight spandex tops – one silver, the other gold – and spike heels. Chatting to each other, they eyed the door and looked unhappy. Business was bad, but it was late Wednesday night in the middle of winter.

I bought a beer, which was when Finn motioned me to his table. He looked like a regular who knew his way around. He was wearing a red sweatshirt with his logo on it: SEXDOLLS.COM and a picture of nesting Russian dolls, except instead of the usual babushkas, the dolls were whores.

"Some weather," I said.

He got up and put his hand out. "Terrible. How do you do?"

"Yeah, how you doing?" I made myself eager, gregarious, a guy looking for action. I gave him one of those sincere two-hand shakes you see guys do.

"Great."

"Good."

"Please sit down." He had an accent I couldn't make out. On the table was a lap-top that he had connected to his cell phone.

"Thanks." I sat down. He sat down. I said, "Where you from?"

He said, "I am from Finland. Near Helsinki. You are American?"

"American, yeah."

"Ah. Good." He grinned.

He was a big guy in his early thirties, well built, prematurely gray; the eyes were small and bright, dark buttons in the pale northern face.

235

I said, to make conversation, "Where you headed?"

"Nowhere. I come here special. I get a train. The train doesn't return tonight because of this storm."

"You come here a lot?"

"Whenever I can." He sighed. "It is wonderful this part of Europe, very small, very easy to travel, you know? The Czech Republic, Austria, Serbia, Bosnia, Slovenia." He sighed again. "It is so lovely, Lubljana in Slovenia, so untouched, you know, wonderful resorts by the lakes. So many places for visiting, and having fun." He sipped his beer very slowly, as if he were costing out every sip.

"Let me buy you another." I went and got a couple of more bottles of beer.

When I got back to the table, Finn turned his lap-top computer in my direction, plugged it into his cell phone, punched a few buttons, the thing lit up and he was on line.

He said, "Please take a look and enjoy while I'm going to the toilet."

Drinking beer, I looked at his website. It was a guide to a dozen European countries, the hookers available, the kinds of services, where to find them, the "fuck-ability" of the girls. I remembered what Lily said on the tape Martha Burnham showed me: "It was like I'd crossed into some alternative world, this dark hole in the universe where women worked the side of the road, if they were lucky, if they weren't actual slaves, and men haggled over the price of a blow job."

Lily had been here, or she had known about it. Now it was me tipped into this bleak world and I knew there

236

was worse down the road. I clicked through some of Finn's pages. Was this what men were like? Was I one of them? A wave of nausea rippled through me. I reached for my cigarettes to try to get rid of the smell.

On the screen, I read the breezy words. All places "dissected" by fuckability. The word appeared over and over and made me numb. All clubs and girls rated for convenience (7-10 at Bar Nina outside Teplice, for instance). Or another entry: "Little for the genuine fucker at this club." There were escort services, street girls, clubs that featured boys, girls, he/shes, kids. Everything for the fucker on the move, it said.

There are things I feel pretty bad about. I've slept around more than was a good idea, even after I met Lily, and I felt lousy when I thought about it. Katya, for one. And Tolya's investment in the club in Paris made me furious. But this tidal wave of sex for sale was something else; I felt I was drowning in shit.

Finn returned to the table. "Nice graphics, yes?" He sat down, eyed the beer, said, "Thanks."

"Groovy," I said, "How did you think of the name for your website?"

He smiled, pleased as punch. "You know these little wooden dollies they have in Russia, these matrioshka, you know, and now sometimes guys are calling the whores by this nice old-fashioned name 'dolls'. You don't think this is sexy idea, girls nesting inside each other, always one more, always one fresh one?" He turned off his computer, the cell phone signal had cut out.

"You come here for business?" I gestured at his computer. "Or the girls?"

"Same thing. You bet. You? First time?"

I nodded.

He smiled at me, glad to help a fellow traveler, give him the lay of the land. For a while he gave me a rap on sex and how much healthier it was, this straightforward attitude to "fucking" as he put it. No pretense. Somehow, guys who use hookers always feed you this kind of garbage.

He was a regular here and in all the border towns. Other places up and down the line, he said. Plenty of good fresh girls here, he added, especially since the Balkan wars. Lot of girls needed the money. I put my picture of Zhaba on the table.

He glanced at it. "I never saw this man. Who is he?"

I shrugged.

"A gangster?"

"Maybe."

"They have gangs here who are running these borders, every territory, different gang. Not such nice guys, maybe, but keeping places safe, girls very clean, you know?"

I held up my glass. "One more for the road?"

"Very nice."

We clinked bottles and he chugged his beer now he knew there was plenty more where it came from and for free.

The bartender turned off the jukebox and switched on a TV over the bar. I looked up. CNN was reporting the worst storms in Europe in twenty-five years. The bartender switched to a Czech sports show.

Desperate for news from Momo, I tried Paris. The

signal on my cell phone was gone. I went to the pay-phone on the wall. It was broken.

It was after midnight. The girl in white boots didn't show up. I figured I'd give her another half hour because where the hell was I going? Back to Dresden? To Prague to try and get a plane? I was stranded and, without a line to Momo, I was as cut off as if there was still a barbed-wire fence.

Finn said, "So, really is first time for you?"

"First time."

"Maybe we get some bargains because of weather." He gestured to the girls at the table in the back of the room.

They walked slowly towards us. One girl hovered near Finn. The younger girl leaned over me so I could check out her cleavage. She had small hard tits. She tried kissing me, then went for my zipper; between my legs, I felt her hands working.

I said, "No thanks, OK?" but Finn knew the ropes.

He pulled her away from me by her hand, then grabbed her breasts and felt her up, moving his hand slowly over her left breast, cupping it, pinching the nipple. He put his hand inside her sweater, and said to me, laughing, "Competition is very hot here, you see, these girls, you can just be grabbing their asses, and check out quite thoroughly." He pinched her again and said, "Very nice. How much?"

The girl answered in German. He pinched her ass again and glanced at her friend. "For both?"

She shook her head.

He said, "Too much."

The girls left the bar. Finn shrugged.

"Anyway, I already had that one before," he said. "She doesn't do blow job well and requires a condom for the blow job, like 98 per cent of the time they all do. Not like Vienna where you can get anything. Or Sarajevo where there is thousands of whores, so much loveliness, many clubs. Maybe two hundred, three hundred, very tight control by gangs who come after wars," he said. "But Vienna may be best, meaning girls are very nice with you. If filled with plenty booze you could fall in love in Vienna, as I did." The smile was sheepish.

"Vienna two weeks ago I am on business, insane fees, but nice room in pretty house, and you can being sure of a wonderful fuck that is worth this amount. Her name is Maria, nice lean body, long black hair, kissing, sucking, fucking without a condom with this gorgeous girl who is doing everything to give me feelings she is madly in love with me and enjoying every poke and second." He leaned toward me. "I am filled with so much drinks I could start to get caught in this romance." He chuckled.

"Yeah?"

"Am I repeating? I am sorry." Finn gulped his beer greedily. "I may give some advice?"

I looked around. "Sure."

"Prices usually in German marks, OK? Good sex here for about equivalent forty US. Girls are grateful for tips because she is often seeing little or nothing of your payment after the bar and her pimp take their share."

"Who are the girls?"

He misunderstood me. "These girls are from flabby

and ugly to fresh and young, also once in a while the beauty, Miss-Universe types. You are always finding something for your taste because there are so many. In this bar, generally I would say looks are 6-8, attitude maybe is a 5. Ask for one who is very young, so you will not get some disgusting old bitch."

"You're very scientific. How young?"

"Fifteen is OK. Age of consent fifteen in Czech Republic, so fourteen, even thirteen can be nice, fresh." He grinned. "But here you need to be on guard constantly, make sure you repeat two times at least aloud what is on the table for you and everyone should see exactly which hour your time period starts. Wrong addition is yielding too high a bill."

"What's the big deal if you pay an extra five bucks?"

He looked surprised. "You are ruining this system. Spoiling girls."

"So you come often?"

"Every month," he said. "Twice. Sometimes I go other places, but this is excellent. Girls constantly begging me for drinks, so I will keep coming back." The bright button eyes were greedy. "You know, in this bar once, two girls are kissing me all over, for over fifteen minutes, right here, and one is grabbing me in my pants. A third would have joined in," he added, "but she is not my type. I give this bar good fuckability rating. There is nicer bars around here, better drinks, but for the fucker there is nothing to buy."

"I got it."

He finished his beer. "Very nice to be talking with you." He got up.

241

"You're going?"

He said, "I have business, then I look for bargains."

"What kind of business?"

He grinned. "Cementing international relations." He turned serious now. "Last time I am here I was cheated by this girl. Bitch," he said, his tone changing. "I paid, she did not deliver. I want a refund."

"How much?"

"Seventy-five German marks."

I grabbed his sleeve and shoved Zhaba's picture in his face. "If you see this guy, tell him I'm looking for him."

"OK, sure. So check out my website."

"I'll be sure to check it out."

"Thank you." He stood up and held out his hand, and I shook it. He pulled on his thick green parka, zipped it, packed up his computer, and, with a wave, turned to go, then said, "As we are saying, happy poking."

22

The girl in the white leather boots showed up half an hour later. She brought a friend who wore fake leather jeans and a pink fur jacket. "What's your name?" I said.

The girl in the pink fur said, "Chanelle."

"Does she know him?" I asked the first girl.

"Show her."

I showed Chanelle the picture of Zhaba, but she hesitated. She had a small, flattened face; the features looked as if they had been smashed out of putty.

"Give her some money," the first one said.

The two tens I gave Chanelle she split with the other girl, who stuffed the bill in her jacket pocket and left, her white boots tapping across the floor until she disappeared through the door and into the night. Chanelle, as she called herself, stayed by my table. I showed her the picture again.

"Maybe I saw him sometime," she said. "I don't know."

"You know someone who knows him?"

"Maybe."

"You want a drink?"

"OK."

"How much do you charge?"

"What for?"

"What could I get?"

"Anything."

"Without a condom?"

"Sure. For money," she said and I felt shitty for asking. She looked about fifteen.

"How old are you?"

"Eighteen." She turned to leave. I tossed some money on the bar and followed her.

Outside was another woman; she was about forty, this one, with big blonde hair, stone-washed jeans, gold chains around her neck. She had some sparkle, though, as if she'd had another life once upon a time. The younger girl had eyes as impenetrable and dead as fish.

"My friend," Chanelle said, shaking from the cold. "Show her picture if you want."

The friend shook my hand. "I am Amber."

"It's your real name?"

She laughed. "What's the difference?"

"You speak English?" I said.

"Yes." she said. "Something."

"Russian?"

The two of them looked disgusted. Russians were bad news even now, but Amber smelled a sale. "Also little," she said.

"Don't worry. I'm not Russian."

"American?"

"Yes."

"Lucky you."

I opened my wallet and said, "A hundred?"

"Dollars?" Amber asked me.

"Sure."

"Fine," she said. "Yes. Where is your car?"

The three of us got in the Mercedes, the two women in back, and they directed me up a muddy track off the side of the road. The car slid for a few feet on the ice, then came to a stop.

"You can park there." She gestured to a short stretch of road near some bushes.

"Where'd you learn the English?"

"In school," she said.

Up a sloping path, about a hundred yards away, was a building. It was a Soviet-style apartment house, three stories, holes in some of the windows, rough boards nailed over them. The ground was frozen and there were dirty crusts of snow. Garbage cans overflowed and there were slabs of wood and concrete blocks in a random heap; it looked like a war zone.

She called herself Amber, she said, because most of the girls took "professional' names. She came from a provincial town in Bosnia, had spent some time in Vienna where she worked as a nurse's aid; the Austrians despised the Balkan refugees and let them know it. Jobs were hard to get, she added as we went into the building.

She led me down a long corridor smeared with graffiti. Half the light bulbs were burned out. From outside you could hear the wind scream.

Chanelle, the younger girl, followed us down the hall, but when Amber opened a door she continued walking. I figured she had a room of her own.

Two straight chairs, a table, a small window draped with some faded fabric, a couch covered with a dirty spread, a single bed. Amber's room also contained a dripping sink. Above it was a bottle of purple schnapps. Amber found two glasses, then poured the stuff in them and offered me one. I gulped it down. It was thick, sweet, strong.

Amber, who talked a mix of bad English and bad Russian to me, finished her drink, tossed off her thick jacket and made to take off the crocheted black sweater she wore underneath it. I shook my head and sat on the chair and asked her to sit down.

She said, "You look healthy. You have money. You don't like me? You want someone else? Younger? Different color?"

"I'm healthy," I said. "But I didn't come for that." I put Zhaba's picture on the table. I put the police picture of Lily next to it. "This is what I came for."

Amber, who told me she had a couple kids of her own in Bosnia with her mother, poured herself another glass full of the thick purple liqueur; she held it up to the light, made a face, knocked it back, then peered at the photograph. "Someone you know?"

"Yes. A friend."

"I would like to help."

"Why's that?"

"I'm garbage, but I'm my own garbage most of the time. The pimps don't bother with me so much now." She added, "I'm too old and too cheap."

She thought Lily was one of them, but I let it go.

"What do they bother with?"

I needed her to trust me. If she knew Zhaba, she wouldn't talk unless there was something in it for her, unless she trusted me. Maybe not even then.

Amber gestured at her sweater again. "You paid. You're welcome. They don't usually look so nice, so polite, these guys, as you." She looked around. "We could go into Teplice. Nice hotel." It was a diversion. The picture of Zhaba scared her.

"It's OK. Who do they bother with, the pimps?"

She wandered around the room now, moving heavily, tugging at her sweater, then sitting down on the bed.

Softly, I said again, "Who do they bother with?"

"Young. They like fresh girls, young, that wants to get out of shitty life, Albanian, Bosnia, Ukraine, doesn't matter, so they promise them jobs in West, take passports, move girls to Paris, London, Middle East. This is big traffic," she said. "Once, it makes me very angry. Now I think, what can I do? Vienna is big town for trade of whores." She spat when she said it.

"Is that where the pimps work out of?"

"They move around."

"Russians?"

"Russians at top. Also Albanian gangs. Serbs, especially." She winced. "Especially if they can find Bosnian girls. They continue the war only now they got girls instead of guns."

It was what Katya had told me.

"You?"

She nodded. "The little one you met also is from Bosnia. You want to talk? You have more lovely dollars?"

"Sure."

247

"She could use help." Amber went to the door. "She has baby. She takes care of her kid, not like whores who abandon children. In Czechia near German border are child-homes full of kids left by whores."

Amber left me alone in the dismal room. There was an electric heater and I switched it on, but the bars that turned red were cold. From the road I heard traffic heading south to Prague, then Vienna.

The door opened. Amber came back with Chanelle. She pulled her sweater tight around her little body and looked at me warily. Amber spoke to her. I offered Chanelle a cigarette and cash. She took both, then sat on the bed, legs crossed. Her legs, in her tight jeans, were thin as sticks.

"What do you want?" she said in English.

I pointed at the pictures of Lily and Zhaba. "I'm looking for a man who beats up women like this. He beats them, he breaks their fingers, and sometimes he rapes them, and cuts their hair off for a trophy. Do you understand?"

She nodded.

"Is this him? Your friend said you knew."

Slowly, Chanelle rolled up the sleeves of her pink sweater and showed me the bruises on her elbows. One of them had been badly set and the bone stuck out at an awkward angle. She said softly, "I know who does this beating."

"Who? Is it him, this Zhaba?"

"If I tell you, they'll come again and break my head this time."

"I'll find a way to protect you." I lied to her because of Lily.

The girl helped herself to the purple liqueur. She lifted the bottle to her lips and sucked some out. It left a smear on her lips. She wiped her mouth with the back of her hand, then lit the cigarette and glanced out of the window into the night. She patted the bed beside her. I went and sat next to her. I could smell her. She had on plenty of perfume but she was just a kid. I wondered what she thought about, how she was inside. If she had any insides left.

"There are ways to protect you," I said again. "I could help you."

"I will take more cash instead," she said. "Also I want to eat."

There was a greasy plastic menu and I ordered the two most expensive bottles of wine on the list and steak for all of us, though Chanelle wanted fish. There wasn't any fish, except the herring that passed for an appetizer. It came out of a jar.

The restaurant was up a back road from the building where the women lived. The village consisted of a couple of farm houses, a derelict gas station, a shuttered shop and, in a low, stained stucco building, the restaurant. Lights were in the windows, there was a Pils sign on the door, and Streisand was singing "Send in the Clowns".

Another day had gone by and I still had no hard information about Zhaba. It made me impatient and crazy, but I knew I had to take it easy now or Chanelle would back off. She wore a white knitted cap with a yellow pom pom.

The half-dozen tables in the restaurant were all occupied by men. There was a stuffed fish on the wall. The bartender, a man with a pencil mustache and not much hair, worked frantically serving up the booze, and there was, from a kitchen somewhere, the heavy smell of meat frying. It was night in the middle of Europe in a village whose name I didn't know, and I was eating herring with a couple of hookers called Amber and Chanelle. I scanned the men in the room. Zhaba wasn't there.

Amber drank a couple of glasses of red wine. Chanelle drank steadily but left her food untouched. The older woman reached over and stabbed Chanelle's herring up with her fork and ate it. A tall man I recognized from the Vietnamese supermarket glanced at me and Amber saw me stare back.

"Leave it," she said. "He's nothing." She went back to her food, but added, "Like he thinks he is in movie."

"So what's your movie?"

"*Terminator*." She paused for effect and flexed her arms, though there wasn't much muscle. "Some day, I say to myself, I'm going to get money and come back and . . ." She looked around at the creeps hunkered down in the dim room, the smoke rising, Streisand singing, the stink of fried food. Amber chortled and dragged my cigarettes across the table.

I looked at Chanelle. "You want to talk here?"

Her voice was low. "Here is OK. Nobody speaks English, also there is noise. No one thinks you are talking except for sex." She put my hand on her thigh. "Fake it like this is business, OK?"

Her flesh was warm through the jeans. It was hot in the restaurant. She pushed her plate aside, leaned her arms on the table, leaned her chin on them. In one hand she clutched the glass of vodka she was drinking now. I leaned forward.

"This woman you show us who gets hurt, she's also whore?"

She meant Lily. I said, "No."

"So why?"

"She tried to help girls who got hurt."

Chanelle snorted. "She's crazy. What's to help?"

I kept quiet.

Amber leaned over and put her arm around the girl. "If she's not whore, somebody big is very angry, because is not normal to mess around other women."

"Who?"

"I don't know."

"What about him?" I held up the picture. "This one they call Zhaba."

They looked at each other. Chanelle shook her head. "We don't know."

"You said you knew. You showed me your arm."

"I don't know." She turned petulant.

"Is he a boss? He collects the dolls?"

"I said I don't know."

"What do you want?"

"I told you. Give us money."

"Then tell me where to find him. Tell me where he works. Is he here?" I looked around. "Is he?"

"Wait," she said, and I knew now it was bullshit. She didn't know. Neither of them knew.

251

"I can't wait."

By two in the morning, loud bad Czech rock on the stereo, everyone in the restaurant was stupid drunk. The tables were crammed with empties, beer, vodka, schnapps. The owner took away the piles of dishes. A couple more girls wandered in. You could feel fights brewing up, the men laughing too loud, yelling, joking. One of them looked at the women with me and called out something dirty; the other men laughed harder.

I threw some money on the table, we got up, Amber and Chanelle took my arms.

"Pretend we are threesome," the older woman said and called out to the men about her good fortune finding this handsome American at the border. I could make out just enough Czech to get the drift. Something in the pit of my stomach lurched.

We went out into the frigid night where the snow was still coming down, piling up, the road frozen solid. Chanelle, in her high-heeled boots, stumbled. In the apartment they offered me more liqueurs, but all I wanted was to know where he was.

I said, "I have to go."

Amber said, "You want this guy?"

"I want Zhaba, yes." I leaned forward.

Amber put her mouth against my ear. "Maybe we heard about him. He moves around very fast. We hear the rumors. He has whole set of tools he can use. Hammer. Knives. Serb guy, OK? Probably Serb." She nodded at Chanelle. "Give her one hundred more dollars."

I looked in my wallet. "I have mostly French money."

Amber looked at the girl, who nodded, and the older woman said to me, "OK, give her equal amount."

"What else?"

"Nothing here."

"Listen, just tell me the fucking truth. You can keep the money."

Amber said, "OK, so we don't know this bastard."

I was angry. I was exhausted. I wanted to sleep and I didn't know if she was lying or not. Chanelle's eyes were shut.

Amber put her hand on my arm. "OK, so go to Vienna. Look in Black and Blue Club, OK? I give you this for free."

"He's there?"

"Maybe."

"Thank you."

"You're welcome."

"Where are you from?"

"Small town in Bosnia."

"What's it called?"

"Visno."

I gestured at the sleeping girl. "Her town, too?"

"Yes."

"You have family there?"

"There is no one there."

23

The car lights were on.

"Momo?" I was talking into the phone, walking down the sloping road, away from the women. Through the dense snow and fog, I could see the lights. Did I leave my car lights on?

I began to run. The signal on the phone was lousy.

"Momo? Where was she from, the little girl behind the billboard in Paris, what was her town?" I was shouting into the phone, but before I finished, the signal went dead.

My feet tried for traction on the icy surface; my whole body was stiff from the effort, from trying not to fall on my ass, trying to stay awake, feeling someone on my back. I knew the car battery was dead. My shoulders clenched up, my gut churned. I got to the car. I climbed in. I turned the key. Nothing.

Someone had jimmied the door, been in the car, turned on the lights. I could smell him. I climbed out again and opened the hood. The snow was falling faster than I could brush it away.

There was a screen of thick bushes between me and the main road and I could hear the traffic pass. No one could see me. My socks were wet, and I thought how much I hated wet socks. Idiotic, but the fatigue made me concentrate on the socks. I was distracted. Then he was there. I could smell him. I smelled the sweet aftershave. Suddenly I knew what the smell was: it was the stink of over-ripe apples, like the disinfectant they used to clean up after the drunks in Moscow buildings in the old days.

He was behind me.

He yanked my arms back behind me so hard my knees buckled. The ice-cold blade of a knife was against the back of my neck.

Knives scare me. Knives are slow and cold. The creeps who use them enjoy it, they like cutting you, the feel of the flesh and bone, the blood, they like doing it slow; all this was running on a loop in my head, even while I felt the cold knife on my neck, my wet socks, the warm trickle of my own blood mixing with the snow.

Was it him or was it only one of the hoods in the restaurant who had seen me with the women? Did they know him?

He shoved me onto the ground. I tried to say the name, but he kicked me and mumbled – Czech, Serbo-Croat, I couldn't figure it out. I was dizzy. He ran the blade along my neck, not cutting deep, just playing games. No pain, only the terror and stink of the guy pulling my arms back hard enough to break them. He was going to snap my arms like toothpicks.

In Russian, I swore at him and, from behind, I felt his muscled body tense up with rage. Through the bushes, I could see the headlights. Cars passed. A few yards away, there were cars. Lights.

Without any warning, still holding my arms, he shoved me onto the ground, face in a drift of fresh snow. He pulled me up, shoved me back on the ground again. I could feel the big squat body, the force like an ox, a bull. It was what he had done to Lily. She would have smelled him before he raped her. She was conscious. Conscious enough to bang on the floor of the apartment near the rue de Rivoli.

He jerked me up a third time. In the snow in the muffled light from a passing car, I saw his knife. From the road came the sound of voices, someone arguing; a hooker and a potential client were drunk. There was snow in my eyes. I thought about Lily. I was frantic. I grabbed for the knife.

I got it. I got the knife. I stabbed at his leg. Then I cut him hard. Deep. I could feel bone. He whimpered. He moved away. I lunged at him again. He ran and I followed him, sliding on black ice under the new snow, crashing through bushes, following the noise, his stink. I ran towards the village where the restaurant was, but he vanished between the buildings. Maybe he went for cover in one of the houses. Maybe in the restaurant with the men. He was one of them.

The muscles in my shoulder had been ripped, my face was burning, my feet were numb. I got back to the car, felt in my pocket for the cell phone; it was gone. On my hands and knees, I scrabbled in the snow and dirt; the phone wasn't there. I trudged up to the supermarket where a young guy was reading a Vietnamese martial arts comic book. He took some cash off me and went out with cables to jump start the car while I tried Momo from the pay-phone.

At his station house the line crackled with static. I finally got him on his cell phone. I was panting, out of breath, terrified.

"Artie? You hear me? The phones are fucked all over France. You there?"

"I'm here."

"You anywhere near Vienna?"

"Near enough. Why?"

"Someone saw him check into a hotel in Vienna."

"Who?"

"What?"

"Who checked in?"

"I can't hear you?"

"It wasn't fucking Zhaba who checked in, Momo. He was here. What hotel?"

"Not Zhaba," he said.

"What?"

"It was Levesque. The guy who checked in. He registered as Eric Levesque. He had the passport," Momo said, then the line went dead.

I went to Vienna because of Momo. There was no point hanging around after I cut Zhaba. Almost from the beginning I'd set myself up as a decoy. Now I figured he'd follow me to Vienna the way he'd followed me so far. I was a threat now. Amber had told me he worked out of the Black and Blue in Vienna. Or maybe she was lying. But I went because there was no place else to go. I moved forward because I couldn't go back.

The airports in Germany were still closed, according to the radio. Prague, too. My phone was gone. Some blind momentum pushed me down the empty road.

On the road, I followed the tracks a snowplow left. I tried not to drive off the road. My shoulder was killing me, but I followed the plow, driving snowblind, trying to make out the news on the radio, in Czech or German, not understanding. There was nothing outside except the endless flat road and the snow.

My eyes closed. I jerked myself awake over and over and when I saw a turn-off, I managed to drive down it. There was a road-side café with a crummy hotel. I banged on the door until a woman in a hairnet let me in. In the room where I dragged my suitcase, I fell onto the bed in my clothes and slept. The nightmares lasted until I woke up in a room that was too hot. The radiator belched; grit mixed with snow on the window sill.

In the morning, in the dull half light, I swung my legs over the edge of the bed, felt a sharp pain in my shoulder when I sat up, looked at my watch, saw it was Thursday. Wednesday morning I was in Paris, then last night the border. It was Thursday. I felt like a tourist on a bad trip; it was as if some travel agent on acid had booked all the wrong places, but I had paid and there was no way out.

Keep moving, I thought. Hurry. I hobbled into the bathroom with its cracked tiles and stood under the thin trickle of warm water. I saw my right shoulder was swollen and I poked around for broken bones. It was so tender I yelled out loud. Then I remembered my phone was gone, lost in the snow, stolen off me by the thug with the knife.

In the café, the woman in the hairnet was making coffee. She offered me some stale cake – no deliveries had come through for two days, she said. An old TV stood on the bar. I switched it to CNN while I drank the coffee and ate a Danish.

Three fishermen in Russia had fallen through the ice the night before. In Holland, people went to work on skates; there were icicles a foot long as far south as Budapest; the only European airport east of Paris that was open was Zurich.

The pay-phone was broken too, but the woman let me use her phone. While I watched the TV, I called the hospital over and over; I couldn't get through. I swallowed the last piece of sticky Danish and paid; I was using Tolya's cash up fast.

Then I was back on the road and there were signs for Prague now. Prague. The fabulous little city like a Disney construct that I only knew from the movies, movies about Mozart, movies about tanks rolling down the beautiful streets in 1968. The Czechs really took it up the ass from the system that destroyed them. Long time ago.

That morning, the snowplows were still on the roads. I kept driving. There was no place to go now except Vienna.

24

In Vienna, the hotel manager, obviously glad for a customer, sidled out of his office. He smiled with his long teeth showing, led me into the bar off the lobby and offered me coffee and a slice of *sacher torte,* a flat black chocolate cake with jam inside so sweet it would rot those teeth. When I thanked him, he said, "We Austrians live to serve."

It's about two hundred miles past Prague to Vienna, and I'd stopped at every gas station to call Lily. Once, I got through to her; she whispered into the phone. She didn't say my name, but it was her voice. As soon as I got Zhaba, I'd go back to Paris and take Lily home. Home. It was like a mantra now. I got to Vienna, I checked into a modern hotel near the center of town. Later I dumped the car at Hertz.

The snow had stopped, but the temperature was down; everything had turned to ice. The garbage workers in Vienna were on strike and black plastic bags poked up through the frozen snowdrifts like weird sculptures.

The hotel manager sat opposite me, still smiling. I pushed some of Tolya's money discreetly into his hand and got him to reserve a seat for me on the first flight to Paris the next morning if there was anything going, or a train if there wasn't. He helped me cancel my cell phone, then called a friend of a friend who sold phones. For cash, inside an hour, I had a new cell.

I went upstairs, unpacked my bag and left the hospital my new number. I left it for Momo, along with the name of the hotel. God knew if he was getting the messages. All I got were answering machines or over-worked cops at his station house or lines that filled up with static. I didn't know if he was getting the messages. I didn't know if he was even alive from one day to the next.

Sitting on the velvet bedspread that was the color of puke, I worked the phone, running down local hotels, looking for Eric Levesque because Momo said he was here. I went through the motions. I didn't have much luck, but Levesque was a side-show now; I was in Vienna for Zhaba.

Zhaba had been chasing me down the road, playing cat and mouse; I wanted him out of his hole, but I was running out of Tolya's cash, so I made a stink about my room which the manager agreed to change, then I persuaded him to cash a check for me. I wasn't sure if I had anything in my account, but I didn't care. I'd get it back to him later. Some other time. I asked him where the main police station was. He gave me directions.

Outside, there was the clang of shovels on cement as

261

workers tried to chip away ice. Women in dark-green loden coats and high-heeled fur-lined ankle boots minced carefully along the icy streets. The men wore the same green coats, with brushes in their small-brimmed hats. Through the window of an old coffee house – the window filled with cakes and marzipan – I watched a couple meet. Both of them wore the green coats. The man removed his hat, she took off her glove and held out her hand and he kissed it.

Vienna was built to show off an empire: the buildings were big, grandiose and dark, all Baroque curlicues and grime under the frozen snow. The boulevards were big, too, like Paris, but with more bombast.

It weighed you down, Vienna; it was probably full of Nazis. You couldn't tell them from the rest of the people in the street unless you figured every guy with a brush in his hat for one of them.

What did I know about Austria? Vienna? *The Sound of Music!* Freud? Mozart? Cake? It was a border town, everything about it was Western except that it was stuck in the East, further east than Prague even. For a while, after the war, they split it like an orange into four segments. Now it was a neutral nowhere with a lot of UN money. "We live to serve."

Posters on the walls advertised politicians and opera. I was hungry. Mostly, the restaurants were empty; the tourists were gone, and every tourist restaurant I passed claimed the biggest schnitzel in town at bargain prices. Vienna obviously took its clichés pretty seriously. Maybe it had to. What did it have except tourism, and there weren't any tourists except me as I strolled along, whistling "My Favorite Things". The words went around in my head all day ("snowflakes that fall on my nose and eyelashes"), but I switched the lyrics off and listened, in my head, to John Coltrane's miraculous version.

After I got lost walking in circles and wandered away from the Ring Road, I found myself staring at a huge statue of some guy on a horse. Some emperor carved in stone, covered in snow. I looked at the street sign: Josefplatz. I found a taxi.

The driver, an Israeli who talked too much, claimed he was an expert on crime in Vienna so I passed over my picture of Zhaba. He shrugged. I sat back, lit a cigarette and tried my phone.

"Lily? Are you there?"

At the police station, I showed the cop on duty my passport and told him in a loud voice that I was an American businessman. I owned a travel agency.

He barely spoke English. Four sodden Austrians, huddled in heavy coats, waited patiently on a bench to the right, eyeing me while I talked at the cop. New York, I said.

Oh ja, he said. I love New York.

He was a big guy with a sad stupid face, but I didn't care. I bullied him some more. I wanted someone in charge, I said. I had received a threatening phone call at my hotel and I was worried. I was American and I wanted a senior officer to pay attention or I'd call the embassy.

A door on my left opened and an officer in uniform

came out, gave a crisp little bow, shook my hand, welcomed me to Vienna. How could he help? Please come into my office. Please sit down. I told him about the threatening calls. More than one? he asked. At least three, I said. Maybe four. As soon as I'd checked in that morning. The hotel was hopeless. They moved my room. Very short beds, I said. Not really adequate, and the frightening phone calls! I took out the picture of Zhaba and handed it to him. His expression never changed.

This man, I said. I had noticed him in the lobby.

You took his picture? the cop asked. Yes. I had my Polaroid camera, I said. I was photographing the lobby because it was my hobby to take pictures of hotel lobbies. He was watching me, I said, and I was worried, so I took his picture. Smart, huh?

The officer summoned a secretary in a tight turquoise sweater and bright pink lipstick who wrote down my name, my address, my cell phone. I gave them all the information, said how much I admired Vienna, how pleasant the people were, how lovely the women, the pastry. How I planned to send my many clients from my travel agency on vacation to Austria. Then we all shook hands, the officer, the secretary, the cop, me. I fawned, mentioned my aversion to all politics that interfered with international accord and tourism. We wished each other well. He said he'd be in touch. Don't worry, he said, and I thanked him and smiled a businessman's smug smile and he responded with a good cop smile. Vienna seemed like a good place for make-believe. I strolled out of the station and down the stairs to the street.

By the time I got back to the hotel, I figured that half of Vienna would know I was there. It was freezing. I went into a store and bought a blue fleece shirt and a hat, complained about the foreign sizing, then stopped at the Café Mozart because it was packed with tourists. There were models of cakes made out of plastic in the window.

Inside, a small group of Japanese tourists looked pissed off at the weather. I ordered cake with whipped cream and complained about the service. The waiter wasn't interested. I used my new cell phone to check out some more hotels; I was looking for Eric Levesque, but there was no Levesque. No one by that name, not in the last few weeks, no, sorry. Very sorry. I was jittery. Couldn't sit still. Had to move on.

Maybe Momo got it wrong.

I walked some more. I found the American Bar, a tiny box that was all mahogany and mirrors, like the inside of a humidor. There were green leather seats and Tony Bennett and Bill Evans on the sound system. The bartender, an American kid who talked jazz non-stop, made good martinis. I saved the toothpicks from the olives in the martinis. Said I collected them. Who could forget an asshole who collects olive picks?

Where was Zhaba?

Later, at the hotel, I went upstairs, switched on the TV. While I changed my shirt, I watched Austrian kids whack each other around; half were anti-government, half pro. Jorge Haider appeared on the screen. He was a good-looking man and I knew what Lily would say: political beefcake, she'd say, and oozing charm. This was a country that was a sucker for charm. God, I missed her. I missed her in bed, I missed her brains, her nutty political views, her curiosity. Lily is interested in the world and it makes everything, even the most mundane, alluring. She gives it all a buzz. Like Martha Burnham said, she turns your head. She had turned mine. Poor Martha.

Around nine, I went to the lobby and talked on the phone to my machine in New York. I talked loud. I talked about the locals. Then I cracked jokes about Nazis and Freud with the bartender who didn't understand any of it, or maybe he was pretending.

Where the fuck was Zhaba? A four-year-old could have found me. The guy at the hotel never heard of the Black and Blue Club, or he wasn't saying; neither had the kid at the American Bar.

It was bitter cold in the street. Outside the opera house, big white lights lit up the night like day. A group of men and women in eighteenth-century costumes strolled by, everyone in wigs, the men in knee-pants and stockings. One was smoking. Another skirted some cables. The movie crew in heavy jackets messed with tracks and lights on the icy street.

There was a bar nearby and I went inside. Two actresses, their huge blue silk skirts hitched up over their knees, sat at the far end of the bar eating sandwiches and drinking beer. It was warm inside and I climbed on a bar stool.

On the bar was a copy of *Hustler*. There were also copies of some local rag in English. The pleasures of Vienna. I got a beer, took out a pack of cigarettes and

266

glanced up at the TV over the bar where CNN played. The bartender watched me drink. He was young, handsome and bald; when I took out a smoke, he held out his lighter.

I said, "You're from Vienna?"

"I'm from Vienna. You're American?"

I nodded.

It was still early. The bar wasn't crowded, he was in a talkative mood and I wanted his confidence, so I asked for another beer, told him my name, held out my hand.

"I am Walter," he said.

I glanced at the copy of *Hustler*. He saw me do it and snorted. "For customers," he said.

"But not for you."

"No."

"How come?"

He smiled. Behind the bar he had a catalogue from a New York gallery propped up.

I said, "You're an artist."

He looked happy. "You are perceptive," he said.

"Thanks. You weren't always a bartender?"

"Very good."

"For an American, you mean." I kept the tone light.

"I am an artist, but no one comes to Vienna for this, only for the past. For the nostalgia. Or for sex." He looked up. "So, you too?" Walter added, practically crackling with irony when he said it.

CNN droned on. The screen was filled with images of people stranded by snow. "Bad weather." Walter smiled as if it somehow pleased him. "Nothing moves. Not even the garbage."

Walter had his own conversational agenda. I said, "What kind of art?"

"Art that no one buys. The rich want old stuff, even gangsters want ancestral portraits." He lit up and sucked in the smoke. "I'm sorry. This is stupid talk. What can I do for you?"

I went carefully. "Maybe some nightclubs?"

He fumbled behind the bar and took out a newspaper. It was eight sheets of listings.

"It's English," he said. "Excuse me one minute." He tossed me the paper and went to the end of the bar where the two women in big skirts were gesturing at him.

While he was gone, I glanced at the paper. There was plenty here ('This guide shall help you to find your preferred girls without making bad experiences'). There were sections for "Street Prostitution", "Call Girls", "Escort Services", "Bars", "Peep Shows". There were price codes: "Oral sex in the car", "Oral sex and intercourse in the hotel".

Walter returned and tossed a couple more papers at me, a Vienna newspaper named *Kurier* where he marked the section labeled "Hostessen", and a magazine, *S.O.Z*, advertising prostitutes in Vienna, complete with phone numbers, pictures and the services on offer. Most of the girls were in the Gurtel district.

I went back to the English paper, which included "a small dictionary with sexual terms". I drank my beer and got up to speed with terms such as *Algierfranzosich*, "the girl licks your ass-hole"; *bis zur Vollendung/mitSchlucken*,

268

"the girl will give you a blow job until you cum(!) into her mouth and swallow your sperm".

Walter glanced at me. "Something is funny?"

"Nothing," I said and looked out of the window; there wasn't much traffic, but cabs passed from time to time.

Walter spread out the papers on the bar and picked up a felt-tip pen.

"You're looking for something special? Girls? Boys? Good club for boys is name Vienna Boys' Choir." He chuckled.

"Sure," I said. "Girls. Good-looking. Expensive. From Bosnia, maybe."

I pushed the magazine across the bar. Walter flipped the pages, marked a few entries, gave it back to me. "The girls are OK here," he said. "Clean, but expensive. They charge double for the Champagne."

I said "Thanks", put some money on the bar and added, "You ever hear of a place named the Black and Blue Club?"

He shrugged. "Not so much for tourists like you."

"Who for?"

He looked at my clothes. "For big money."

"I'm not that kind of tourist."

"Everyone is this kind of tourist. All forms of human exchange are corrupt: sex, money, death, irony. This is my belief." Walter laughed. "Too much irony, bad for the soul. You are going to Black and Blue?"

"Maybe."

"To other clubs?"

"Sure."

269

"You should be careful."

"Why's that?"

He glanced at the door where an old man entered, his arm around a young boy. "In Vienna, everyone is whores," Walter said.

25

The Bee Gees singing "Staying Alive' blasted my eardrums when the doorman pulled open the heavy padded door of the Black and Blue Club. On my way here I'd seen plenty of women, even in the cold, working the streets. Once you started looking, you saw them. Girls, too. Little girls, twelve, thirteen, some pretty. They were everywhere.

Maurice Gibb always sounds like someone just stepped on his balls. The doorman who doubled as a bouncer took the money I gave him and I was ushered in out of the ghostly street where the snow was ankle deep.

The club was a black lacquer box with mirrored walls. On the long black bar and little tables were lamps with blue glass shades. Women sat with men at the tables drinking Austrian champagne. At a corner banquette were men who took their style cues from *The Sopranos;* there were plenty of leather jackets, big rings, silk suits, loud shirts.

The smoke was thick. We were underground and the

signal on my cell phone was dead. I found a phone and tried Momo's station house, got through and was instantly cut off. I checked my messages. Nothing from Momo. At the bar I got a drink and looked around. Zhaba wasn't there. Not yet.

Disco music thumped relentlessly. On a crowded dance floor, topless girls danced with customers to the Bee Gees and Donna Summer. It was Seventies Night at the Black and Blue. I scanned the place for Zhaba, and while I was watching, I saw Walter arrive.

The bartender I'd met earlier was wearing tight black jeans, black tee shirt, a pin-striped double-breasted jacket. He saw me. "Any luck?" he said.

I bought Walter a vodka and tonic, then another.

He said, "You're looking for someone?"

I picked up my beer. "Maybe."

Where was he? Where was the blonde hair, the sloping shoulders, the smell of rotten-apple aftershave?

In the gloom, my eyes darted all over the place. Once I thought I saw him, but it was someone else. And everywhere there were girls. Hookers. Dancing. Drinking.

I thought about Finn again, the guy on the border. Sexdolls.com. Happy Poking. "You can haggle. You must say two times out loud how long is your time period." He went to the border once a month, sometimes more, and there were a million Finns. Tens of millions. The women only lasted a few years. There was plenty of turnover and I began to see the edges of the industry and how many women it consumed, how lucrative, how big it was.

You'd have to turn the girls over constantly if you wanted them fresh, like Finn wanted them, if you wanted them like the girls on the dance floor in the Black and Blue. It was bigger than drugs.

"You come to this kind of place a lot."

Walter snorted. "When I'm invited." He added, "For the art, of course. This is special art form."

"Tell me you're here accidentally tonight."

"No."

"What?"

"Let's sit."

"I'm happy like this."

We leaned against the bar. Again, once or twice, I thought I saw Zhaba, but it was always someone else, some other guy with sloping shoulders and fine blonde hair. Walter turned his back to the room, leaned on the bar and said, "Why is it you wanted girls from Bosnia?"

"I have strange tastes."

"I can go away if you want."

"I'm sorry." I signaled for more drinks.

"I know some refugees. From the war."

"What kind?"

"Women. Friends."

"Here?"

"Here, there."

"OK." I slipped the picture of Zhaba out of my pocket and showed it to Walter.

In the dim light, he squinted at me. "What are you?"

"A tourist. What about you?"

"I told you, I'm an artist, and I think you're a cop."

"So I'm a cop. What about this guy."

Walter peered harder. "Sure, he's a pimp. I've seen him lots of places."

"Here?"

"Here," he said. "Yes."

"What other places?"

"You should ask him," Walter said.

"How can I find him?"

Walter shrugged.

"You want money?"

"I don't mind money."

I gave him some of what I had left from Tolya's cash. He put it in his pocket and said, "Wait here."

I waited. I watched the men and women. My shoulder hurt, I worried about Lily. In the distance, halfway across the floor, I watched Walter talk to some women, head down, laughing with them.

He came back over. "OK," he said, "I can tell you something."

"What?"

"Let's have another drink."

"No. First tell me." I didn't know what his game was. "You want more money?"

"No."

"Why not?"

"I prefer you get this bastard."

"So where the fuck is he?"

Walter said, "I don't know, but I know his town."

"What town?"

"In Bosnia."

"What's it called?"

"He comes from the town named Visno."

26

"She was from Bosnia," Momo said as soon as he saw me in the coffee shop.

"How the hell did you get here?"

"The girl behind the billboard, the one you figured for Albanian?"

"Yes?"

"She wasn't Albanian. The town is called Visno."

"Like I thought."

"Yes."

"Him, too. Zhaba."

"How do you know?"

I thought about Walter. "I met someone. I'm fucking glad to see you."

It was the next day. I'd spent all day running down false leads in Vienna, looking for Zhaba, coming up empty. I went back to the bar to look for Walter, but it was his day off. The Black and Blue Club was shut until late. The weather was still lousy and I couldn't get a plane.

Around five I went into the hotel coffee shop and

ordered a ham sandwich. On the counter was a bowl of Mozart candies for sale, chocolate balls with marzipan in the middle, wrapped in gold foil, with a picture of the man himself in a wig. On the wall was a bad mural that I guessed was *The Merry Widow*. Otherwise, it was all brass and glass, shiny green plants and waitresses in dirndls and blouses with puffy sleeves. And then Momo, right there, in the coffee shop.

It was after six when Momo Gourad slipped into the seat opposite me, picked up the menu and ordered a schnitzel with a fried egg and anchovies on it, boiled potatoes, rye bread and hot chocolate with whipped cream. "Some fucking trip," he said.

"You got my message."

"You think I'm an idiot? You practically broadcast it by satellite that you were here. I've been on four trains today."

"He's here."

"Who?"

"Zhaba."

"Where?"

"I don't know, but he's been following me from the German border. He was there. Now he's here, I think. I can't find him. How the hell did you get here?"

"I had help. There's nothing else moving except a few trains on this miserable continent."

"So what are you, Momo? You're connected. You're not exactly my idea of a bumbling Paris street cop with a taste for American movies." I played with my cigarettes. "Are you?"

The waitress brought his veal. He picked up two slabs

of rye bread, made a sandwich and then chomped on it for a minute. He sat back and sipped his hot chocolate.

"I was really hungry," he said. He took off his good tweed jacket and folded it carefully, put it beside him and fooled with his shirt collar.

I said, "Talk to me."

"Just let me go to the toilet. I'm going to burst."

Momo ambled away. I reached into his jacket pocket and helped myself to a couple of his business cards. Maybe I could pose as a French cop if I needed ID; I had nothing else.

Sighing, Momo returned and ordered apple strudel.

"So," I said.

"I love the movies, honestly, I love them. Westerns. Cop movies. All my life." He smiled. "I hate Jerry Lewis, in case you're worried."

"I didn't ask about your taste in movies. We've done that. I get it. You love American movies."

"You think this is a cliché? French guy who loves American movies?"

"So it's not a cliché. It's yours and yours alone. You're unique."

"Thank you."

"Stop stonewalling."

"What's this stonewalling?"

I kept my mouth shut.

Momo said finally, "The girl behind the billboard came from a town called Visno. There've been other killings, other women, same town. We think whoever killed the little girl beat up Lily. There were some similar marks."

"DNA confirms, you have that?"

"Yes."

"The kid was raped?"

"Yes."

"Martha Burnham?"

"Yes."

"The semen matches, the DNA?"

"Yes."

I said, carefully, "What about Katya Slobodkin?"

He looked at the table. "None of your fucking business."

"Where the fuck is Visno?"

"It's up on the Bosnia-Serbia border. There was a lot of fighting around there. Gangs ran it. This turd Zhaba comes from Visno, he grew up there, he pimps for women he knew in the town. Them, other women who come from the East, Ukraine, Russia. He runs them into Western Europe."

"He's a pimp."

"Yeah. And an enforcer. You can get anything in Bosnia. Drugs. Weapons. Women. The only successful multi-ethnic business is crime."

"I figured for sure we were looking at Russians in the beginning," I said.

"You thought. I didn't think. Maybe you always think about Russians. In Paris it used to be North Africans. Then they started coming in from the East, like I said. Russian, Ukraine, Belorus, Rumania. Some of them eleven, twelve years old. We couldn't stop it. After the Balkan shit it got worse because the gangs were vicious, there were no cops, nothing to get in their way.

Fucking UN couldn't do a thing. NGOs either. Pricks like Zhaba are just the muscle, but they don't care who they murder – girls they deliver, cops, it doesn't matter. They get on a truck or a plane or in a car and hightail it back to whatever the fuck hole they come from. These are countries who do not care to help us extradite. We can't touch them."

"I'm listening."

"We couldn't even get close there were so many of them. Then we started seeing signatures in certain assaults, especially if the girls escaped from particular clubs or out of the territory of the guys who controlled them. In this case, it was a hammer. Someone broke the girls' fingers." He paused. "And the hair."

"Like Lily."

"Yes. I mean there are a hundred towns, dozens of gangs, in some places like Kosovo there are foreign troops but no local cops at all. All we've done is turn these places into free-fire zones for the criminals. The gangs are the new government. With a specific place like Visno, we can start focusing on one gang, one creep. It was the kind of detail that could give us access. It's like a can opener. You can get a little leverage, put a name and a face on it."

"Like Zhaba."

"That's how we identified him. We started tracing the girls who came from Visno. You helped a lot."

"He's a Serb?"

Momo said, "He's part Serb, part Croat, even had a Muslim grandfather. Which makes it worse, you know? A guy who pimps for women from his own town. That's how it works; they work on women they know or know

279

about, and bring them in, move them around. Like produce to market. This is corporate Europe, Artie, the free market. The Russians, who are at the top of the tree, already got web sites to market girls. The best women, they move them on to America, service the guys who make the big bucks. We're talking billions."

"Why don't you pick him up?"

"He's not easy. Zhaba moves fast. I'm waiting."

"Waiting for fucking what?"

"Until he does something that leads me to his boss."

"I'm going to Visno," I said suddenly.

"There's no one there."

"You've been?"

"This gets out and my kids don't eat, OK?"

"OK."

"I've been there."

"You didn't find him."

"No."

"He has a base there?"

"Maybe. I don't know."

The waitress brought the strudel and put it down. She had a powdery face and dark circles under her eyes; her thick brown hair was done up in braids.

Momo ate a piece of the strudel, put his fork down, muttered "Stale", then said out of the blue, "I worked on prostitution in Paris, I took some leave to look at international stuff. The boss said I had to quit, the economics were wrong. Trade relations were more important and a lot of countries were angry because we were interfering over this business of prostitution. I didn't agree."

"You stayed on your regular job as far as the brass knew because it gave you access? You pretended you were a good boy?"

"More or less."

"But you went freelance."

"Yes. I had a friend. He worked for the War Crimes Tribunal in the Hague. He was a homicide cop from Lyons, and volunteered to take me through some of the shit that went down during the Bosnian War. There were bad people on both sides, but these Serbs, they were monsters. I met some of the women. People were investigating this stuff one case at a time, one murder at a time, it was taking years."

"What happened to your pal?"

Momo picked up his hot chocolate. "Someone executed him. He made too many enemies. He was at the site of a mass grave doing the forensics, and someone came up behind him and strangled him and pushed him into that hole in the ground with the corpses."

I listened.

"You know what got me started in the beginning though, Artie? I wonder if they have any chocolate cake." He looked for the waitress.

"What?"

"I was undercover once in some horrible place near the Bois de Vincennes that was a front. It was full of sad little girls, all under-age, boys too, you could get a little boy there, and there's a customer, a middle-aged jerk with a Pierre Cardin tie on. He says, 'The place to go if you want a really good time is Kiev. There's everything under the sun you could want." Sex tourism, it's his

281

thing. He says this. He doesn't care they're moving these women around like cattle. He doesn't give a shit. He wants a good time. You go on vacation, you deserve sun and sex. I got so pissed off I volunteered for the international job."

"Which is how you met your friend that died."

"Yeah."

"Why didn't you tell me all this before?"

Momo didn't answer.

"You didn't trust me?"

"I didn't tell you because when I saw you with Lily I didn't think you could necessarily take it."

"You thought I was cracking up. I want to go."

"Visno's a shit-hole."

"I don't care."

"It isn't easy."

I leaned over the table. "I need to see." I slid the picture of Zhaba across the table.

Momo said, "How did you get this picture?"

"A friend gave it to me." I looked at the picture. I had to be sure. "This is definitely him?"

"Yes."

"You're sure?"

"Sure I'm sure. We both know it's him. You want me to tell you his brand of condoms? I'm sure."

"What's his real name?"

"He has several names."

"Tell me one."

"Boris Zhabovich is the one I hear most. Sometimes Ratko. Sometimes Zultan. Sometimes Bob."

"Bob?"

282

"Bob, Pierre, Franco, Werner, all names, any names, every country. Europe is one big happy family."

"What about his last name?"

"Whatever he needs. Russian. Serb. Croat. Bosnian. Austrian. He doesn't give a fuck what you call him. But I need him out there, Artie. Eventually he's going to do something stupid again, and big, and I'll be there, waiting for him, and the rest of them."

"You want him for bait."

"Yes."

"You don't give a shit about him."

"Sure I do. But there's bigger."

We were going in circles. "Who?"

"I don't fucking know."

I yelled at the waitress. "Hey, Miss, gimme another one of those nice beers, OK?" I was talking loud. People in the coffee shop looked offended, which was the point.

Momo smiled. "Artie?"

"Yeah?"

"You really think if you make a lot of noise, you'll flush him out?"

"I don't know."

He wiped his mouth on a paper napkin, unfolded his jacket carefully and put it on. "You want to take a walk?"

I told the waitress to forget the beer and put some money on the table. "Where are you staying?" I asked Momo.

"I have a cousin who runs a hotel on the edge of town. It's a dump, but it's free. They make a living. They claim Stalin spent the night. The Pensione Schonbrunn makes this big deal that Stalin slept there, but my cousin claims the old bastard stayed at his place too."

"You mean tourists go because they think Stalin slept in the bed?"

"Why not? Stalin was a celebrity."

"Shit, it's cold," Momo said when we were outside. I didn't answer.

"I don't know this guy Tolya Sverdloff, Artie, but he's a good friend for you. He's been with Lily every minute, you know." We started walking in the frozen night. "He sleeps in her room."

We walked fast because it was cold; we walked away from the center of Vienna, beyond the center and the Ring Road, beyond the neon, past a white building with a gilded Art Deco dome. After that, we threaded our way through a market, the stalls shuttered up tight, and eventually came to a subway station. A couple of benches stood outside. We sat down. I was so cold my eyebrows froze, but I owed Momo Gourad and I didn't ask any questions. He had been watching my back. He'd kept his boss off me. He did what he could for Lily.

"You can get more sympathy for a bunch of veal calves being shipped out of England than for women," he said, looking around.

There was no one on the street.

"You meeting someone?"

"Yes."

A harsh wind blew, and I looked at Momo. "It's him, isn't it?"

"I made a connection with a cop here I used to know. I'm not sure. We put out a line. We promised him he'd be meeting a guy with big money. It was worth a try. Christ, it's freezing." He blew on his hands and pulled down the ear-flaps on his Russian-style hat. Then he took out a pack of cigarettes and bent double to light one. "You think we're a little old to be squatting here in the dark, Art? You think Clint ever does this shit?"

"Clint Eastwood is an actor, man."

"You know what I mean."

"No, I do not think Dirty Harry ever gets his pants wet sitting on outdoor furniture by a subway station in Vienna."

"I'm glad you made Zhaba bleed up on the German border," he said. "I was really pleased when I heard. I have no moral confusion about this at all."

The wind whined. I looked at Momo. "You knew?"

He hesitated. "You hear things." He looked at his watch again.

I said, to cheer him up, "Gene Hackman in *French Connection,* he stood around in the shitty weather a lot."

We sat on the bench, talking about movies and smoking Momo's French cigarettes that made me cough.

"So, Momo, you met Katya how? On the job?"

He grinned. "Yes. Before she left Russia, she was a doctor who did forensic work, but it paid her shit and she wanted out. I met her once, but I told you, didn't I? She got screwed up in some deal trying to get herself out, and there was some bad stuff when they stole her passport. She won't talk about it, but she had a rough time. Then she called me. I remembered her and I said I'd help. She came to Paris. You like her?"

"I like her," I said.

"She thought she was safe in Paris, but they came after her."

"When?"

"A year ago."

"They hurt her because of you, your work?"

"Yes."

I thought about me and Lily. "I'm sorry."

"I love her." Like a kid, he blurted it out.

"I figured."

"You think I'm nuts, falling in love with a Russian hooker, don't you?"

It was important to him, so I said, "No."

"You like her?"

"I like her a lot." I felt guilty as hell about Katya. I wanted to tell him, wanted him to absolve me; I'd done enough damage. I bit my tongue.

We waited. I knew Zhaba wasn't coming.

"Let's get the hell out of here," Momo said finally. "We'll start again in the morning."

There were no cabs. I didn't want to get in an empty subway train and neither did Momo. In a train, you were trapped. We'd started to walk when we heard a car behind us. We ran like crazy, turning a corner where we banged into a Pizza Hut. I could smell the sauce. I could see the lights inside.

Exhausted, I shoved through the door, looked behind me and saw Momo dragging himself up the street. In the restaurant, four teenagers were drinking coffee, the remains of a pizza on their table. They looked up, then went back to the coffee.

"Momo?" I turned around.

He was gone. I ran outside. I could see him in the distance, sprinting towards me. He had seen someone and disappeared down a side street, now he was back, running in my direction. I yelled out "Momo", but the words were sucked away by the wind, and a few seconds later I heard the shot.

27

"What happened?"

Momo shook his head. "I was running, and someone took a fucking pot-shot at me. I couldn't see."

"You think it was him?"

"I don't know. There's a taxi."

We took the cab back to the center of town. As we passed a big hotel Momo said, "Let's stop here. I want a decent drink."

We climbed out. A row of foreign flags above the entrance whipped in the wind. Momo was shivering.

I looked at my watch. Hurry, I thought, hurry. I was already making a plan which didn't include Momo, who only wanted Zhaba for bait.

The lobby was all brocade and gilt and crystal chandeliers. Five men were checking in. Squadrons of porters surrounded them, piling fancy luggage on carts. I counted three Vuittons, an Hermès, a Gucci and a complete set of Halliburtons. Momo followed my gaze.

"Fuck a duck," he said, applying the language skills he acquired on the job in America.

"What?"

"Let's sit over there so we can watch. Come on."

We went into the bar and sat at a table with a view of the lobby. Momo ordered Cognac, selected a few almonds from the dish of nuts and munched them. He stared at the men in the lobby. The hotel people danced attendance. The piles of luggage disappeared into elevators. One by one, carrying expensive overcoats, the men filtered quietly into the bar and gathered at a large table in the back against the brocade wall. Momo was pop-eyed.

"What?"

He whispered, "Jesus fucking Christ."

"What?"

"What do you see?"

"I see some businessmen, a Chinese, a Jap, maybe; the one with the black mink is probably Russian. A couple of Euro guys. So what?"

Momo finished off his drink and ordered another. He was still whispering.

"They can't hear us," I said.

"You never know."

A pair of waiters brought the men trays of drinks and snacks. I was impatient. "What?"

Momo pulled his chair closer to mine and leaned over.

"Every year," he said, working on his drink, "every year the big European crime bosses meet somewhere – them, their friends from Asia. It was Beaune in France one year. Don't laugh. I swear to God, it's true. One year on the beach outside Malmo. They go to some nice hotel and they divide things up. The Russians, Japs, Italians. The French. They discuss problems. Like the G8."

"You're fucking kidding me."

"I'm not kidding you. They hold focus groups. They discuss what people are paying for whores, or drugs. Fix prices. Split up territories. Talk about what kinds of new stuff you can sell. Which new designer drugs are coming onto the market. Illegal workers. Body parts. Nukes. They have fucking seminars, Art. They discuss product branding. I'm surprised they're in Vienna; usually they go for some kind of resort. I heard they were going to Capri this year, or Scotland. They don't advertise exactly. The fact they're meeting in Austria means there's bigger money here than I figured. A lot bigger. It's an honor to host the meeting."

"And no one does anything?"

"What can you do? They look like businessmen. They act like businessmen. They behave very nice."

"You think our guy is tied in?"

"Yeah, now I'm sure he's tied in, but Zhaba's not in their league. He's low-level, some kind of asshole enforcer, pimp, muscle. Like we said, like we knew. These guys are the money." He finished his drink and got up.

On the way out of the hotel, Momo stopped one of the assistant managers in the lobby and slipped him some cash. "Your guests, just checking in, they're staying the weekend?"

The young guy shrugged and said, "No, only two nights. Tomorrow for the opera and the Egon Schieles."

"How did they get here with the weather?"

"I don't know. Private planes, perhaps. Private trains. After Vienna they go to Salzburg."

"How come?"

"Maybe they like Mozart."

Momo pulled me out of the hotel.

I said, "How do they decide who gets the best room?"

"I'd fucking hate to be the travel agent," Momo replied as we walked to my hotel. We stood in the doorway waiting for a cab to take Momo back to his cousin's place.

"Give me a match, Momo, OK?"

He reached into his pocket, dug out a pack of matches, lit my cigarette and his own, then passed the matches to me. I put them in my pocket. Momo said, "Listen, Artie, about Visno."

"What?"

"You guessed right. Zhaba does have a base there."

"I want to go."

"I understand. Give me another day in Vienna and we'll go. I'll take you. Just sit on it until I set it up there with some people. It's a rough place."

"Tell me again when you left Paris?"

Momo looked away. "This morning."

"Tell me how you knew I made him bleed up on the border. You said you were glad I cut him."

He blew out some smoke and looked to see if his cab had arrived. "I told you. I hear things."

"You sure?"

"I'm sure." His cab arrived. He opened the door. "See you tomorrow," he said.

I went to bed and tried to sleep, but I kept thinking about Lily. I put on the light and got out a cigarette. I found the matches Momo had given me. On the cover was the logo of the Black and Blue Club.

28

The Strauss waltz played through the airplane's loudspeaker. Outside a squadron of snowplows came towards us in formation, seeming to move to the music, lights blinking through the fog that had draped itself over the airport like a soft, sodden blanket. We sat on the runway and waited.

It was the next morning. While Momo was still asleep at his cousin's, I was already at the airport. They boarded us, then we sat waiting for the fog to lift. For two hours we sat. Then the seat-belt lights went on, and we taxied down the runway. I thought I heard ice cracking under the wheels.

It was the only flight that made it out that morning before the snow started again. After we left, they shut the airport.

Even after take-off, the Strauss waltzes played incessantly, one after the other, the Skaters' Waltz, the Blue Danube, other tunes I couldn't name.

Momo wanted Zhaba, too. He had been at the Black and Blue Club, like me. But he would do it legit. I couldn't wait.

There was a map spread over my lap. Vienna, Serbia, Bosnia. It was so close; I could have driven to Visno in less than a day. It was a cramped, crowded, vicious part of the world.

"A Waltz in the Sky" was the airline's motto and they played Strauss waltzes the whole trip. As the plane shuddered into the black clouds, a thunderstorm came up. I clutched my plastic cup of orange juice, trying not to watch the liquid slosh side to side, the motion making me want to puke. Thunder crashed somewhere close by, a flash of lightning split the low clouds. The flight attendants, petrified, sat down, hanging on to the edge of their seats.

The flight was only an hour. I tried reading. Next to me was a Canadian guy from the UN who was completely calm. He was small and compact, short gray hair, yellow turtle-neck, jeans, polished loafers. He ignored the weather and worked steadily on some document on his tray table, looking up to smile reassuringly a few times. He ate a sandwich he made from cheese and bread he carried in a cool-pack.

"Name's Albert Lucas," he said. "You can call me Al," he added with a chuckle, then picked up his sandwich. "Don't worry, it's often bad on this run. I've seen much worse. Nothing to worry about. Have a sandwich. This cheese is terrific. A very nice Reblochon. Try some. You'll feel better. Cornichons? Chocolate? *Linzertorte?*"

The stink of ripe cheese made my stomach lurch and the Strauss waltzes played, but I was glad for Al's company. There was more Midwest than Canadian in his accent; he'd been to college in Buffalo and lived in Chicago. We chatted the rest of the way. I told him I was a travel agent looking to do business in this part of the world, let him know I could be interested in some contact with the locals, even some kind of R&R. You never knew who had the information you wanted, and something Al said made me figure him for a guy who liked women. He was full of information. He knew his way around Bosnia where he was based, part of SFOR. "The Stability Forces," he grinned.

A lovely country, Bosnia, he said mournfully, but broken. Broken countryside. Busted economy. Did I need a lift someplace? He was headed up north towards Tuzla. I told him as it happened I wanted a good look up there – the mountains, the old vineyards. Told him I knew someone back home from a place named Visno.

He made a face. "Nothing in Visno," he said. But he'd give me a lift anyplace. Sure, he said. I can give you a lift wherever you want.

For the rest of the trip, I talked to Al. The waltzes played until the plane bounced onto the tarmac in Sarajevo. Al put on his orange sheepskin coat, bundled up his papers and his lap-top, put the remains of his lunch in the cooler. I followed him off the plane. His loafers had pennies in them.

In the terminal, I checked my pockets. All I had with me was my passport, the maps, a return ticket to Vienna, the last of Tolya's cash and Momo's business cards that I'd swiped. Figuring I'd be back that night, I hadn't checked out of the hotel in Vienna. I wore the blue fleece shirt and my heavy jacket. I had some gloves.

Americans don't need a visa for Bosnia. We're the good guys, more or less. The other thing I didn't have was a weapon. I could have picked one up in Vienna, but I couldn't risk it at the airport.

At Sarajevo Airport, Al went through the diplomatic line, I waited with the Bosnians and the tourists. On the other side, plywood was stuck up everywhere, half the lights were out, there were workmen drinking coffee and smoking and passengers yelling because the flights were all delayed. Most of the passengers were UN or military; they were bigger and better dressed than the locals, and they strode through the terminal like an occupying army.

Al Lucas hurried outside where sleet was falling on long lines of gleaming white vehicles. I followed. This army used big SUVs; the Nissans, Mercedes, Toyotas cruised in and out of the terminal, picking up, depositing people, all of them gabbing in Dutch, French, English, German, all busy trying to patch up the world. TV crews scrambled into vans, lugging silver metal boxes that gleamed with importance. On the other side of the road was a makeshift taxi-stand. Local drivers leaned against their cars, smoking and reading newspapers. The economy was bust here; everyone drove a cab.

"You coming?" It was Al.

A white Nissan, big as a tank, was parked in a temporary lot a few yards from the front of the terminal and Al got the keys out of his pocket.

I don't know what made me hesitate, but I looked around. Was it Zhaba I felt? Was he close by? Was he on my tail? Bundled in his orange sheepskin jacket, Al was waiting.

296

"Coming?"

"Sure," I said. "Sure."

Pulling away from the airport, Al snapped open a box of CDs and stuck one in the player. It was a great sound system, a Bose, and, Santana playing, we pulled onto the highway. Al didn't talk much on the way; he listened to the music; he ate from a jumbo-size bag of peanut M&Ms. He didn't seem interested in my going to Visno; he accepted my story.

Visno is up on the border between Bosnia and Serbia. A few years ago, it was all the same country. Then Yugoslavia was broken up like a bad jigsaw puzzle with the picture missing. More criminal fallout. The waves of crime that began when the Soviet Union broke up seemed to drench Europe. I thought of old war maps where the unstoppable enemy was always represented by a spreading red stain. It was about fifty miles to Visno. There was slush on the road and the big tires made a noise in it like someone sucking up the bottom of a drink through a straw.

Through the window, the broken suburbs sped by. This was my last stop. All I could do was hunt Zhaba one last time; on his own turf, he might feel safe coming out in the open. I didn't show Al his picture. I figured it wasn't exactly UN territory.

One more time. Last time, I promised myself, wiping sweat off my forehead, rolling down the window an inch, lighting a cigarette, accepting some of Al's M&Ms because he wanted me to, the nuts sticking in my teeth as we climbed into the hills. There was snow on the fields.

After a while Al said, "Hungry?" and I shook my head, so he kept driving. He put on the *Buena Vista Social Club*. The warm, lilting music reminded me of New Year's Eve. Outside, it was bleak. A light sleet fell and melting ice dripped off the bare trees.

The signal on my phone came and went as we climbed further toward Visno. Halfway, we got stuck behind a US Army convoy doing twenty-five miles an hour. One of the GIs looked out of the back of the truck, waved, gave us a V-sign; he was a nice-looking kid with headphones on. I waved back. Al was bitching now.

"Goddamn convoys," he said. "I spend my whole damn time stuck behind the military. You want to stop for something? Take a leak? Get a drink?"

His phone beeped and he answered it. He didn't say much, just listened and grunted some. Then he glanced at me.

"I need to make a stop anyhow, OK, Artie? You don't mind? It would take an hour or so and we could go on after. Or if I have to stay longer, I could fix you up with a taxi, take you to do your thing, bring you back. I mean I'll see you get back to Sarajevo, OK?" He added, "And I could show you something I bet you don't see at home."

I nodded. I felt disengaged, detached, removed from myself, the scene around me, the place I was going. At the next exit, Al pulled off the road. There was a brand-new gas station where he filled up, then he drove another mile. Overhead was a ramshackle sign that read only market. The letters of the first word, made out of crudely painted wood, had fallen off.

"Where are we?"

Al pulled his vehicle up, parked, and turned off the ignition. "We helped set up these markets so there was a safe place where the Serbs and the Bosnians could trade. Arizona Market, Virginia Market, this place. They'd rather kill each other, but we don't let them, so meanwhile they do business. We figure if we can get them to be interested in money, they might stop fighting. There's a café; we could get lunch."

The market was about two blocks by five. There were makeshift stalls selling clothes, parity hose, sneakers, shoes, crackers, plastic bottles of Coke, cosmetics, towels. Other stalls were laden with sides of beef and buckets of produce – potatoes, carrots, turnips, apples. The lanes between the stalls were ankle-deep in mud and slush; kids ran around everywhere. Somewhere, from a boombox, loud music played.

"We call it Balkan rock," Al said.

I followed him to a café. Outside were white plastic chairs. Inside, a hunk of meat turned on a spit. Three toothless old men sat around a table drinking coffee. Al ordered sandwiches and beer.

"So what's your business here?"

"We patrol the markets, make sure no one gets a knife in the back."

"It's that bad?"

"Sometimes."

"So they're not just selling lipstick and vegetables here."

"Very perceptive, Artie. You can get pretty much anything here."

I lowered my voice. "Drugs?"

"Sure. You want something?"

"No thanks. What else?"

"Knives, brass knuckles."

"Guns?"

"Anything."

"Women, too?"

He perked up. "I knew you were interested. I had a sense of that."

"How's that?"

"Stuff you were mentioning on the plane, you had a look." He tossed some money on the table. "German marks," he said. "It's all they want, but not for long. They'll have to make do with fucking Euros."

In the muddy market I followed him for a hundred yards, then again as he turned and made his way to a shack with a porch and some more white plastic chairs. Outside were a couple of guys in leather coats. One of them let me see the pistol he had in his belt. It was obvious they knew Al; they stood aside and let us through. A kind of dull dread was what I felt. I hesitated, then followed him in.

There was only one room, homemade curtains on the windows, a rug on the floor, a man in a suit in an armchair, an old woman making coffee. There was a woman in her twenties on a kitchen chair. She had crinkly hair dyed gold and a scared, sullen expression. Her eyes darted around as if she wanted to escape. She wore hot pants, an angora sweater and thigh-high, high-heeled boots. She was pretty except her skin was raw as if she'd been left out in the bad weather too long. The man in the chair barked something at her and she got up and paraded slowly around the little room. Her sweater was baby blue and it sparkled.

Al whispered, "You like this one?"

I could feel rage take over. "How do you mean?"

"You can touch her if you want. You can look at her teeth if you want even. She has great legs. Look at those legs, man." His tone was confidential. "She was supposed to be for me, but, listen, if you want her, she's yours, man. Honest. There's plenty more."

I looked at Al, a small, neat Canadian with an open face and a Chicago accent. I said, "How much?"

Al leaned down and talked to the man in the suit. He said to me, "Three thousand German marks."

"For how long?"

"Whatever you want." He sighed. "Of course, there's one price for locals, a different price for foreigners, but that's what makes the market. Foreigners make the market. So it's expensive, but you get the best goods. For three thousand you can have her for your property for six months."

"Where's she from?"

"Ukraine, I think." He looked up at the girl. "Where are you from, hon?"

She didn't answer and the old man slapped her lightly on the ass. She mumbled, "Kiev."

Al said to me, "You like her? You want her?"

I wanted to kill him, but all I said was, "Listen, I'll think about it, OK? I'm going for a little walk, get a drink, you know?" I faked the excuse as best I could.

When I left, Al was still talking to the man in the

chair. The woman glanced at me helplessly, but there wasn't much I could do.

On my way out of the market, I passed a stall selling hardware. I picked up a tire iron and a crummy hunting knife. There were a couple more white vehicles parked at the entrance, but I wanted a local. I wanted a local who knew about the women. I asked three or four drivers; no one wanted to go to Visno.

"I can take you." A thick-set woman eating a sandwich, she overheard me. "You need taxi?"

I nodded.

"For Visno?"

"First Visno. After, I'm not sure." I told her I'd pay her double for the whole day.

"What are you?"

"Reporter," I said this time. I didn't think she'd buy the travel-agent bit.

"OK. Other reporters been there. Good story, right?" She finished her sandwich, held open the passenger door of the old Skoda for me, and got into the driver's seat. We set off.

Her name was Eva. She had a placid smile but angry eyes, and she spoke good English. She was a dentist.

Eva never asked me what I was doing. I didn't show her Zhaba's picture. I didn't want to scare her off. Finally I said, "Do you live around here?"

"Yes."

"You know the market?"

She nodded.

"You know about the women?"

She turned and looked at me. "Yes."

"Tell me."

"They are selling women," she said.

"How does it work?"

"I hear stories," she said. "I hear they take women from Ukraine, Russia, other places, they take them to Belgrade, then across the border to this market you saw. They take their passports. They sell the women. They sell them again. The women can never buy their way out. Like slavery."

"Christ!"

"Yes."

"And there are foreigners involved?"

"Sure, one price for Bosnians," she said, "one price for foreigners."

It was what Al had said. I was betting Zhaba was involved.

"Are you cold?" Eva asked. "Heater stinks in this car."

As we climbed higher, the sleet stopped. It turned colder, but the sky was blue and the bare landscape was beautiful where the land had been terraced and there were remnants of vineyards.

Eva turned off the highway onto a back road, the blacktop cracked up from ice and snow, then, a few miles further, swerved onto a dirt track through a forest. She turned off the radio.

There was no one around. No sound. Just the rattle of the old car, a light wind, a few icicles that popped off the trees onto the roof and broken tree limbs that snapped as we drove over them.

"What do you know about Visno?" I said to Eva and my words, breaking the quiet, seemed crude and noisy.

"It was a spa town once. Twenty thousand people, more in summertime, right on the border. The border was in the middle of the town, one side Serb, one side Bosnian. It was famous for this. Also famous for the most beautiful women in Yugoslavia." She looked nervous. "Do you want me to drive you into the town center when we get there?"

"No." I was looking for trouble, but I wanted Eva safe. Also, she was my only means of transportation out of this silent place. "You can wait on the outskirts, if you want."

"I was in Visno for holidays once," she said suddenly. "Very pretty. It's a dead town now. After Serbs besieged this place and the Bosnian gangs killed some of them for revenge, Serbs slaughtered all men and boys. Some women walked away, some not. Some women are put in the rape camps."

"Rape camps?"

"Where Serbs put women after they kill the men. I meet a little girl one time, they make her have sex with her own father, they make her watch while they slit her brother's throat. Worse stuff. Stuff I don't repeat or think about. There was no work, no men, nothing. The place dies."

It was completely silent that winter afternoon, brilliant sunshine, no sounds. Eva drove along the dirt track for another mile until she reached a clearing, pulled up, kept the engine running. Broken chunks of whitewashed masonry littered the ground. Something

304

was written on one large stone that stuck up out of the still snowy earth.

"What's it say?"

Eva peered out of the window. "It says 'Welcome to Visno'."

29

The town had been picked clean. Like a pile of chicken bones tossed on a platter. The walls left standing, the skins of buildings without roofs, were pocked with bullet holes. Burned-out skeletons of cars littered the streets, the street lamps were twisted metal. This was a dead place.

It was cold and silent. The only sound was my own footsteps as I turned into what had been the main street. There were fragments of hotels, vacation houses, cafés. Over a doorway with no door was a sign for Dr Pepper.

In my right hand I had the plastic bag with the knife and tire iron. I wouldn't kill him if I found him. There was nothing in killing him, I suddenly knew. I would take him back to face the women; they could parade him in front of his victims, including Katya, especially Katya. Or Lily if she was OK for it. In my fantasy, he'd sit in the courts for years, then in prison, prosecuted and tried and locked up until he was old, until he was dead. I wasn't scared, just numb and very calm.

Somewhere from up in the mountain I thought I

heard the rumble of a convoy. If someone saw me, I had no excuse. I had no business here.

At the end of the street was what had been the spa. A few mock-Roman pillars still stood and there were some crumbling marble steps. I was climbing over a pile of broken sinks, trying to get a better look at the town, when I heard a car.

There was the purr of an engine. Crouched behind half a brick wall now, I saw the black Landcruiser traveling ten miles an hour. The car window was open. He leaned back in the driver's seat, puffing on a cigarette, and the bright afternoon sunshine lit him up. Lit up the baby-blonde hair. The doughy skin. Reflected off the sunglasses. He drove slowly as if he were surveying the real estate. The street sloped up slightly and I could follow his car from where I hid. At the top of the hill, he turned left and disappeared. I started to run.

It was a dirt road hidden by the trees. In the snow still on the ground, his tire marks made tracks and I followed them, running hard, branches scratching my face, lungs burning. I followed him through the patch of forest.

A mile further there was a clearing with a large wooden building. Bright-blue paint still showed on its façade and there were ramshackle cottages near by. Down a little hill was a pond with a pile of rowboats stacked alongside it, a wooden dock, the remains of a tennis court. It had been some kind of holiday camp once; there were rolls of barbed wire now in the yard where the Landcruiser was parked next to a rusty pick-up truck.

There was a light on in the main building. I scuttled into the parking lot and hid behind the truck. Then the door to the building opened and he came out onto the stoop, smoking.

It was him. It was Zhaba. The man I'd seen in the Paris club. The man in the photograph. A man who resembled Putin, the Russian president, on steroids; bland, pale, sloping shoulders, he wore stiff black jeans, loafers, a leather jacket; it was him. The thin hair blew in the sharp wind, and he wore sunglasses. I couldn't see the eyes.

He smoked. I waited. Did he know I was coming? Was he waiting for me? A phone rang, and he tossed his cigarette into the yard, turned and went back inside. I could hear his voice.

The sun was going down now, the sky streaked with color, and I crept around to the side of the building where I grabbed onto the window ledge and pulled myself up so I could see inside.

His back was to me. He was talking on the phone in an office that had an old oak desk, some rickety shelves with a few books, a cross on the wall and storage cartons on the floor. He finished the conversation. I dropped back down on the ground and waited. I thought I could hear my own watch ticking or maybe it was my heart.

It could have been five minutes or fifteen when he walked outside again. I managed to get around the side of the building and I could see him now in the front yard as he loaded some lumber into the pick-up truck. He got in, turned the key, drove towards the pond. After a few minutes, the sound of a hammer rang out.

So long as I could hear the hammer down by the dock, I knew he was busy. I was safe. I ducked into the building. The boards creaked under my feet. The light outside was almost gone. The dim room made me squint.

I looked at the oak desk. There was an ashtray stuffed with butts, a Sony shortwave radio, and a stack of paper. On the top was a smudged photocopy of a newspaper, and I realized I was looking at my own picture. It was a copy of an old picture from the *Daily News*, the year I solved a big case in Brooklyn. He knew my face. He had been watching me. He had my picture. Then I saw the box.

The storage boxes were piled on the floor. I pulled the lids off three of them, but there were only folders, books, rolls of string, envelopes, junk. The box on the bottom of the pile was made of clear plastic. Inside it was the hair.

There were skeins of blonde hair, hanks of dark hair, short gray curls, all of it tangled up together. I pulled off the lid of the box; I could see the textures now, silky, coarse, curly. Some of the hair was red. There was a tangle of red hair. The color of Lily's hair.

It was dark, but a light he'd rigged at the pond lit up the dock where he was working. Crouched on his haunches, a hammer in one hand, he was intent on his work, a cigarette hanging out of his mouth. The truck radio spewed news. From behind the truck where I waited, I could see the semiautomatic on the ground next to him.

As if he'd heard something, suddenly he picked up the gun. He couldn't see me but he was coming in my direction. The tire iron was in my hand and I tossed it at the pond where it clanged across the ice and skittered to the other side. It startled him. He turned and looked at the ice, then raised the gun and shot at random, at the pond, in my direction, turning in circles, looking for whoever threw a tire iron onto the pond, looking for me. This was what I wanted. Come on, I thought. Come and get me.

For an instant, I was paralysed, lost in this surreal place, up a mountain in Bosnia, and there was a disconnect between my brain and my body. Then I focused on him, what he'd done, and I moved.

I was fast. Everything that happened in the last couple weeks welled up in me and I was on him with the knife. It caught him on the cheek; I pulled the blade down over his fleshy face to his neck until I heard the skin rip. Blood poured out. There was blood on my jacket, my shoes, my hands. He stumbled and I grabbed the gun. Then he scuttled away from me on his hands and knees until he got to the pond. He tried to skirt it but he tumbled on it and he was heavy. The ice cracked.

"He got off easy." Eva spit it out.

She had followed me. She was waiting outside the main building. I went in and got the plastic box with the hair and without a word she opened the trunk of the Skoda, put it in and pulled out a bundle of clothing, then handed it to me. She gave me a bottle of water and a towel and I washed the blood off my shoes and hands as best I could.

The heavy army sweater and corduroy pants had belonged to her father. I peeled off my own stuff, pants, the leather jacket, the fleece shirt I bought in Vienna. Eva stuffed them in a dark-blue plastic shopping bag then gave it to me. She was silent all the way back to Sarajevo in the dark.

It was late, I'd missed all the flights out and the first plane to Vienna was at seven the next morning. Eva took me into town. The city felt convalescent, buildings still pocked with bullet holes stood next to the Gap and Armani. People strolled home from the movies or restaurants. A group of foreigners spilled out of a white UN vehicle, men and women, tall, well fed, handsome. They started up the street towards a club where a neon sign flashed. On the pavement, a pair of old men leaned on each other and laughed and laughed.

Eva dropped me at a cheap hotel that looked like an alpine chalet; she said it belonged to friends, I'd be OK there. She would pick me up in the morning.

The ceiling of my room sloped and I had to crouch to get to the bed. The wooden walls and ceiling were painted green. The owner fixed me a meat sandwich that I ate but didn't taste. The adrenalin wore off and I realized how crazy I'd been, chasing Zhaba into his own country, driven by fury. It would be a while before anyone found Zhaba's body in the pond, and I'd tossed the knife after him. His people wouldn't come for the cops on this side of the border.

Most of the night, I sat up. Outside, on the street opposite the hotel, was a club and all night I heard the foreign voices as men went in and came out. I heard women laughing. There was music.

I had never killed with a knife. For a minute, by the

pond, I felt triumphant, now there was no pleasure, no victory; it was thin stuff. After I cut him, when he was helpless, I let him sink into the pond. Let him drown. I watched him sink under the ice.

Could I have dragged him out? Sitting on the bed under the ceiling the color of grass, I didn't know.

"He got off easy," Eva had said. She was right.

It was over. I was done.

At five the next morning, like she promised, Eva picked me up in the Skoda. I left the plastic carton of hair with her to give to some international court, some UN committee, someone who dealt with justice. I had the shopping bag she gave me and I told her I'd send her father's clothes back. She said, "Keep them." Then I went into the airport and looked in my pocket for change to buy a cup of coffee.

The change was gone. My passport, my ticket, the francs and dollars were in my pants pocket, but the loose change I'd had in my jacket was gone.

The flight was a couple of hours late and I was in the air, the "Blue Danube" playing, the flight attendants in their little suits fussing over some businessmen, when I remembered. We were nearly in Vienna and I remembered that when I was running on the road to Zhaba's camp, loose change had fallen out of my jacket pocket; so had Momo's business card. I looked everywhere, I went through all my pockets, I couldn't find them. They were somewhere on the mountain.

30

Momo yawned and looked at his watch. It was eight in the morning, Sunday, and still dark, but he couldn't sleep. He splashed some cold water on his face, yanked on his jeans and a thick sweater and left his cousin's hotel where Stalin once slept. The cousin was there; he told me later.

"Mo?"

"Shh, I'm just going out for coffee."

"I'll make the coffee. It's Sunday. It's freezing," his cousin said, but Momo just smiled. He needed the air. He wanted to talk to Katya and the signal on his phone was lousy indoors. His cousin watched him go. He stood in the door and watched.

The cold air blasted him as soon as he opened the door. It was snowing again. He pulled his wool scarf tight around his neck and over his mouth, then dialed Katya's number. Except for an elderly couple on their way to early mass, the street was deserted.

Momo held the phone to his ear and walked down the front steps of the house to the sidewalk and then towards the street, which is when he probably saw them. He was preoccupied with the phone.

"Katya? Are you there? Darling?"

There wasn't time to run or duck back into the house, he barely realized what was happening, and he was still talking into the phone with Katya when he fell onto a bed of fresh fallen snow.

Momo's cousin was weeping when I called from the airport in Vienna. His face was still wet when I got to his hotel and he told me how it all happened, how a man got out of a car at the curb, pulled out a gun, shot Momo. It all happened as if in slow motion, Momo's cousin said. He tried to run out to stop them. He saw the blood on the snow.

"I told Momo I'd make the coffee," his cousin said over and over. "He wanted some air."

In front of the hotel were three police cars. A group of cops was examining the place where Momo had fallen but the body had been removed by the time I got there. His body left a heavy imprint in the snow that was stained red.

It happened around the time I was leaving Sarajevo. Someone was waiting for him. Someone who picked up his business cards in Visno, maybe, or discovered Zhaba's body. Or maybe they wanted Momo Gourad all along.

There was nothing I could do. I went back to my own hotel and called Katya Slobodkin. She knew. She knew when Momo called her that morning and he suddenly stopped talking.

She knew when she heard my voice.

She said, "He's dead, isn't he?"

I was finished here. There was a flight to Paris that evening. If it didn't go, I'd drive or get a train or a bus. If Dr Alpert in Paris was right about confronting Lily with what happened, I knew enough: I knew it was Zhaba who threatened her in London, who attacked her in France. I knew about Martha Burnham. The only thing I didn't know was who Lily met at the Ritz that night she was attacked, but I didn't need it. Zhaba was dead and there was a story I could tell Lily.

Packing up to leave Vienna, adrenalin gone, shuffling around the hotel room, I felt old and scared. I didn't know if the thugs who got Momo would come for me. I stood in the shower, let it run hot, couldn't tell if it was the water or tears on my face, but I had frightened myself with my rage in Paris and the Bosnian market, and with chilly determination in Visno. I couldn't shake it, the way it felt when the knife connected with Zhaba's face.

Wrapped in a towel, a cigarette in my hand, I watched the weather on CNN and listened to the garbage trucks outside. The garbage strike was over in Vienna. I stuffed the shirt I'd worn in Visno into the bottom of my bag, put on a clean one with jeans and Eva's father's sweater.

For days I'd been skidding across Europe, jittery, in a hurry, like a nervous skater, hunting down Zhaba, intent on my own desperate needs. Bring Lily the story. Hurry hurry.

But what if Alpert was wrong? What if, like people said, he was just an old crackpot looking to make good on his theories? What if all I ever wanted was revenge? If I told Lily what happened to her, she would have to

315

live with those images the rest of her life: Zhaba, the meaty white face coming at her; his clammy feel; the stink.

What if I told her and she couldn't shake the memory ever, couldn't wake up from the nightmare? As long as she got better, it would be OK. Even if she didn't know who I was, I'd live with it. I'd be with her.

Some of the phone lines were still down in France, but finally I got through to the hospital. It was Tolya on the other end.

"How is she?" I asked. "Tell me!"

He said she was getting stronger, she was amazing physically, everyone said.

"I'll hold the phone for her so you can talk," he said. "Lily? Are you there?"

There was time to kill until my flight out of Vienna. In a café I sat in the window, drank coffee and thought about Momo Gourad, who was crazy about the movies and Katya Slobodkin and who popped up his plaid umbrella when it rained in Paris. They killed him because he was an obsessive. He tried to make things better. He wanted to stop the trade where women were moved like cattle or slaves, but it was a tidal wave and it caught him.

I sat, killing time.

"I've been looking all over for you, man." Joe Fallon walked into the café, pumped my hand eagerly and added, "You said Vienna, right?" Fallon shed his overcoat, brushed snow off it, then hung it on a peg on the wall.

I was startled. "What are you doing here? When did you get in?"

"I just got in." He straightened his suit jacket. "Boy, could I use some coffee." He signaled the waitress and ordered in German.

"How did you get here?" I didn't know what to make of it, Joe showing up. It felt weird, but he was a guy who traveled and I was not sorry to see him.

"I got the first flight."

"The airport's open?"

"Thank God. It's been a nightmare. The whole continent is gridlock. My kid was due to meet me here, he never made it out of London. As soon as I got here I checked around the hotels looking for you, I couldn't get you on your cell phone, the signals are mostly fucked." He looked at some apple cake I had ordered. "Any good? I must have called sixteen different hotels looking for you. I gave up, then I was passing this place and I saw you." He stared at me. "Are you OK?"

"Yeah." I felt wary.

"Tell me how Lily is, Art? I wanted to visit but Sverdloff stood there like a guard dog in the doorway, wouldn't let anyone in, so I sent flowers. Yellow roses. That OK?"

"Fine."

"You want to talk?"

In Paris I had only told him Lily was sick. Now I told him the details, unsure why even as I talked.

"Who would do something like that? It's so horrible. You said you were working some kind of case for Keyes, you think it was related?"

"I don't know."

"Lily's still in Paris?"

I was wiped out. Joe was a nice guy. I knew he cared, but I didn't want to talk about it anymore and I felt uncomfortable about Zhaba. I said, "You have business in Vienna?"

"One of my companies does some work with the websites for the tourist industry here. Fun, right? Mostly I keep out. But I was in Paris, and someone had to tell them we didn't want their business anymore, and everyone has some bloody flu or other, including my kid, Billy, who's supposed to handle all the new media, and said he'd come, but got held up in London. So I thought, OK, I'll do this and then I'm out of here. God I hate this place. I always hear the bloody Nazis marching in, you know, the populace welcoming them." He drank some water. "I'm really doing it for Dede," he said.

"She told me she was going to divorce me if I worked with these bastards," Joe added. "She was kidding, but she couldn't stand it. She said it made her blood run cold, being in Austria, more than any other place. She hated that I even had a company who worked for them. I said, listen, it's only some tourist stuff, no big deal, and she said, yeah, well, where do you draw the line? She was sexy and gorgeous, but Dede was a straight arrow and I cleaned up my act for her, you know? After this I'm going home."

The waitress brought his coffee along with a slab of cake. He swallowed his coffee in one gulp. "I needed that." He ate a piece of the cake, then put some money on the table and looked at his watch. "I've got a couple of hours before my meeting, Art. You want to get some exercise or something? I could use a walk, I'm stiff as a board from the traveling. You have time? You feel like it?"

"Sure."

"There's a park."

For twenty minutes we walked; Fallon kept the pace brisk. We walked for a long time without talking and Fallon was good at it, being there, waiting for the conversation to start up, feeling how you were feeling. He had become a friend.

In the park, we started to jog, trotting past rides called "The Spaceshot" and "The Space Shuttle", past restaurants and bars, and the ferris wheel. We jogged into an avenue bordered by bare trees. The path had been salted. Fallon was faster. He slowed down to keep pace with me.

I said, "You know Vienna pretty well."

"I know it." He sounded bitter.

"How come?"

"I spent some time here. I never told anyone but Dede, I don't know why, but I felt humiliated by what happened. When I first left Moscow, I came here. They sent me here. They put me in a camp for refugees. Traiskirchen. About half an hour from Vienna. They put everyone there, everyone who ever left some shit-hole – Hungarians in '56, Czechs in '72, Ugandan Asians, Cambodians, Vietnamese, Kurds, the whole damn bunch. I hated it. I thought I was too good for it. I was white. I was Russian. You can imagine what an asshole I was."

319

"I know how you felt," I said.

"I know you do."

"We left Moscow for Rome on a train, second class. No one came to the station. Everyone was scared to come," I said.

Joe nodded. "I used to pick a few pockets in the camp, get enough money and I'd come into Vienna for the night." He smiled. "Long time ago."

We slowed to a walk. I looked at my watch.

Joe said, "You have an appointment?"

"I have a plane."

"You want to get back to Lily, I know that."

"Yes."

"Take her home, Artie. She belongs at home. If there's anything you need, you know . . ."

"Thanks."

After about a mile, Joe turned and we started back.

"Did you ever come across a guy named Levesque, Joe?" I asked, not wanting to talk about Lily.

"I don't think so. Who was he?"

"A case I was working. He's dead."

"Tell me some more. Maybe I can help." He laughed. "Mr Joe Fixit."

"He was killed in a plane crash."

"You making any progress?"

"Someone tried to forge a check on his account."

"What sorry son-of-a-bitch would forge a dead man's check?"

"It's weird because I couldn't get much on him except a woman in Paris he knew."

"Who's that?"

"A woman named Martha Burnham."

"What else?"

"I don't know. Keyes dumped me."

"And this Burnham?"

I said, "She thought Levesque was next door to God."

He grunted. "Different strokes, man. I am sorry about the case, but there's other firms than Keyes you could work for. Better."

"Gourad's dead."

"Who?"

"The French cop on Lily's case."

"You think all this shit's related, your case, Lily's?"

I got a cigarette out of my pocket. "He was executed. Gourad."

"Where?"

"Here."

"What else?"

"I don't know any more," I said.

We were back at the amusement park. In the snow, a tourist stood snapping pictures of the big wheel. Two hookers looked up hopefully. Joe Fallon didn't notice them.

"It's none of my business," he said, "but I know you're hurting bad and I understand. Lily's in trouble. I've been there. I was in that place when Dede was dying. I went nuts, all I did was bawl, I wanted to sue everyone or kill them. It will get better."

"Thanks."

"I know good people. If you want."

"I hear you."

He loosened his scarf and said, "The only thing that

makes me feel better is if I keep moving. Something wrong with my knees. I had the surgery, but it's shitty. If I don't keep moving, I feel like it's going to stiffen up for good. You want to do another loop with me? Another couple miles?"

"I'll grab a taxi."

Joe put out his hand and we shook, then he gave me a bear hug.

"You OK for dough? I didn't want to ask, and you can tell me to go fuck myself if that's inappropriate. Oh shit, I'm making a mess of this."

"No. I'm OK. Thanks. Really."

"I'll be in touch," he said. "We'll catch up in New York."

"Sure."

"So long, Artie."

I had half an hour left so I went to the wheel and paid for a ride. The place was almost empty. The guy who sold the tickets offered me the deluxe cabin, same price. I climbed in.

It had mahogany paneling, a table in the middle and lace curtains. I stood by the window. The cabin rose slowly. I thought about New Year's Eve and the wheel over London. I had tried to distract Lily by talking about *The Third Man,* her favorite movie. Nothing helped. Now I tried to remember the scene in the wheel here, but I couldn't call up the dialogue.

Down below I could see the frozen ground, the tourist taking pictures, the hookers. Vienna was spread out around me. Light snow was falling. Zhaba was dead.

I was going home. In the distance, I thought I saw Joe Fallon jog away into the park with the bare trees. He grew smaller and smaller and then he disappeared.

31

The church in Paris was full for Momo's funeral. It was two days after I got back from Vienna. I saw Monique, the wife who made the cheese soufflés, and the kids, and after a while it got to me. I went outside and tried to breathe the icy air.

Katya Slobodkin, in her fur coat and hiking boots, the blue cap on, came up beside me and put her hand through my arm, then slipped an envelope into my pocket and kissed my cheek. I asked if she wanted to go into the church with me, but she shook her head and walked slowly away.

Inside the envelope was one of Martha Burnham's crumpled snapshots, her name on the back. Seeing the picture, I knew it was Martha who had forged Eric Levesque's check, Martha who wanted to stir things up over Levesque because she found out about the prostitutes or she was bitter because he didn't love her or both. Probably both. But she couldn't give me the picture. I think she had planned to give it to me the night I went to her apartment, but she couldn't betray him that way.

In the cold Paris morning, I looked at the picture and everything seemed clear. It was Levesque Lily had gone to meet at the Ritz the night she was attacked. Levesque who set her up and sent her to the apartment where Zhaba was waiting. Everything was completely clear. I played back the last two weeks: the London Eye on New Year's Eve; Paris; the borders; Vienna.

Zhaba was the enforcer, a thug who did the dirty work. The ugly little Balkan wars were good for guys like Zhaba. It gave them some kind of purpose and freed up their gangs to score. But he was just a pimp. Levesque owned him. I shivered from the cold and also because, the picture in my hand, I knew who Eric Levesque was.

New York
January 21

32

As soon as I called him on the day Momo was killed in Vienna, Tolya got Lily out of Paris and took her home. "Too many dead people," he said into the phone. "Let me take her home now." I let him. I wanted to go with them, but he said it was safer if I came separately. And for Beth. In case anything happened, she'd have one of us. I also wanted to be at Momo's funeral, so I waited. Tolya got Lily on a private plane, took a nurse and doctor and went with them.

After I got back to New York from Paris I sat with her most of the day and slept in her room at night. From her hospital room I could see the East River, the buildings, the city. New York. We were home.

"Are you Artie?" Lily looked up at me and tried smiling.

My heart lurched. "Yes, it's me."

Sometimes she sank into a deep, soft fog, sometimes she lay in bed and looked up at the television suspended over the bed. She watched *Who Wants to be a Millionaire?* and one night, when a contestant won the million, she got all the answers right. She lit up. It made her feel smart again. "I won a million bucks," she said. "I won a million."

Other times, she was enraged because she forgot where she was. The rage swelled up in her, she was bloated with it. She remembered, then she stopped remembering.

"Not too much talk today," the doctor said, coming into the room.

I looked down at her still-bruised face and held out a bunch of purple anemones, which she loves. I leaned over her and said, "Do you remember anything about Paris?"

"Paris?"

"You went to the Ritz for a drink after you met Martha Burnham. Do you remember?"

"I think so."

"Who did you meet at the Ritz?"

She closed her eyes and Tolya put his hand on my arm. "Stop it now."

"Was it a man, Lily? Was it?"

"I think so." She opened her eyes briefly and said, "Who are you?"

I met Lily's doctor outside her room. White coat, Birkenstocks, sympathetic face, tired eyes, he listened while I pinned him to the wall. I was desperate. I told him about the old French doctor, Bernard Alpert, and his theories of confrontation. He listened carefully and I was surprised when he said, "I've seen this work." He hesitated. "Are you ready to tell her what happened? You're completely sure?"

"Isn't it too late? Alpert said a week."

"That's a little extreme, it's why people think he's cracked. I mean, why a week? Why not two, or three? If you want to do this thing, we'll try. Make sure you have it right, though, OK?"

"Give me another day."

Emerging from Lily's room, Tolya leaned against the wall and took out his cigarettes, glancing up and down the corridor. On the wall was a no-smoking sign. He lit up a cigarette.

"You're not mad at me anymore?" Tolya's face was stiff with fatigue.

"You were there for Lily. Thank you."

"Go home, get some rest, stay quiet for a few days."

"I'll stay here."

"No."

"What? Why?"

"In case they know you're back in New York."

"Who?"

"Whoever hurt Lily and killed the others, they know where you've been and what you've been doing over there in Bosnia. I heard something this morning, maybe something, maybe nothing."

"He's dead."

"Not him. The people he worked for."

"How do you know?"

"Come on, Artyom. You want me to spell out how I get information? We'll just start yelling at each other again. We both know everything starts and ends in New York, this is where they pull the strings, where the power is, the money. Trust me this time."

"I trust you."

"Then stay away from Lily."

"How long?"

"For a couple of days," Tolya said. "Until I'm sure they're not coming here looking for you. Or her."

"Will you stay with her tonight?"

"As long as you need me." He kissed me Russian style, three times.

I said, "Thanks. Thank you."

From the cab going home, I called Sonny Lippert and I was glad to hear the son-of-a-bitch on the other end. It was a cold, hard, bright day. Along the river, everything looked clean, the buildings in relief against a frozen sky.

The cabbie, whose name on the grubby license in the plastic partition read "Sunil", said, "You look like happy man," and I said, "Yeah. Happy to be home."

Home.

I'd only been by my place to dump my stuff and pick up clean clothes after I came home; the rest of the time I stayed with Lily. There was a stack of bills on the desk, striped tulips in a jar, a note from Lois and Louise, my neighbors: Welcome Home. I glanced at the mail, the bills, the invites to parties that were long over. I put one invitation next to my keys on the kitchen counter. I'd noticed it when I first got home.

In spite of the cold, I shoved the window open, stuck my head out and saw Mike Rizzi inside his coffee shop across the street, shutting up for the day. Mike leaned over the counter, wiping it down with a cloth. On the street people scurried to the subway. Opposite my window, in the sweatshop, the Chinese girls sewed wedding veils like they always do. The dog upstairs whined. The kids from next door had the bass up on some rap shit. I love the way my building has its own soundtrack.

I put Ella Fitzgerald on loud so I could hear it in the bathroom. Up to my neck in hot water, I let the heat soak into my bones. My shoulder was still hurting.

From Paris, before Momo's funeral, I had filed a report with Keyes. I told them it was Martha Burnham who forged Levesque's check. Unrequited love, I said, and left it at that. No one asked who had checked into the Vienna hotel under the name Levesque after Burnham was already dead. No one asked because no one even knew except Momo and me and maybe Martha Burnham.

It was a simple case of bad love, Keyes agreed; their client was satisfied, so was the bank. Stuart Larkin, I heard, went back to work.

If the customer was happy, everyone was happy. Eventually, in a couple of years, if no one claimed the Levesque money, no relative, no heir, the bank would turn the whole thing over to the government.

Lying in the bathtub, listening to the sounds in the building and the music, I waited for Sonny to call me with the information. Central Europe seemed far away, a dark, borderless place.

I dried off, climbed into jeans and an old sweatshirt, found a stale pack of smokes in the desk drawer. Sonny knew the guys in DC with the access, he'd get me what I needed. Where was he? I listened for the phone.

On my desk I laid out the pictures: Lily, Zhaba, Levesque. It startled me when a little tower of snow toppled onto my fire escape outside the window, but it was only one of the kids upstairs playing.

The answering machine cranked out the messages: the dentist about a check-up; Visa about late payments; Johnny Farone who is married to my cousin Genia in Brighton Beach to say they were expecting a kid, Happy New Year, come and see us. There was an old message from a real-estate agent asking if my loft was available for sale. Another from a woman I know who writes crime novels and who, if I wasn't already attached, I could be interested in. Sometimes I meet her over at Jerry's for martinis and fried calamari and talk to her about cop stuff. I went away, I came back, there were messages. I'd been in a different universe, but here life kept running on normal.

In the fridge I found a beer and waited, restless now, for Sonny's call. He called at nine.

"It's Lippert, man. I'm coming up on the last shuttle out of DC. I'm at the airport. I got what you wanted. You'll need back-up, so I'll meet you, OK Art? I'll be there. Sit tight. I'll have the information you need. You know what they say, man: Don't leave home without me."

We fell out plenty, me and Sonny, and there are times I don't trust his ambition, which is rapacious, but I know who he is. He would be there.

Someone was buzzing downstairs and I picked up the intercom. "What?"

"Artie? It's me, Mike."

"Hey, Mike. Come on up."

"For a second, OK? I got something for you."

I buzzed him in and shut off the answering machine. A few minutes later Mike appeared in my door holding a pie plate covered with a yellow checkered dishcloth. He came in, put it on the kitchen counter, shook my hand, hugged me. "Hey, how's Lily? How is she?"

"You heard?"

"I heard. Jesus, Artie. I heard."

"She's going to make it."

"Thank Christ. I even went to church, I lit candles, the girls, too. I brought pie for her, key lime, I made it fresh today."

"Thanks, Mike. How's everyone?"

"Everyone's real good. City's nervous. The market's on a roller-coaster. There are more poor bastards sleeping on the streets and the girls turning tricks, they get younger and younger. I worry about mine. You want me to sit with you a while?"

"Go home. I'm going to sleep a few hours," I lied. "Then I got stuff to do."

"You need help?"

"I'll let you know."

He said, "Let me know, OK?"

As soon as Mike left, I picked up the invitation I'd put in the kitchen, stuck a pistol and ammunition in my pocket and another gun in my waistband, went out and got a cab because my car was in the shop. I didn't wait for Sonny. I left him a message. I told him to meet me.

The guy behind the wheel was half asleep, the city

335

was dead; slush spewed out from the wheels as we turned up Greenwich Avenue.

The address was Little West 12th Street, not far from the river. I paid off the cab and looked for the entrance to the club.

33

The blast of heat, light and music sucked me in out of the freezing black and white night. It was like being enveloped in a comforting blaze, yellow, noisy, hot. And there was the music. Someone playing "You're Blasé", a tune only Stan Getz plays as far as I know, playing it like an amateur would play Stan's version. It was my favorite tune. It was as if someone was expecting me.

At the bottom of the rickety stairs, I gave a skinny kid with a ponytail the invitation and ten bucks, and went into the small, crowded club. There were benches along the walls and a few tables, and every seat was taken. Kids in jeans, mostly, and a few older fans were all intent on the trio on the bandstand, all tapping their feet, nodding their heads. In a shiny satin baseball jacket with jazz embroidered on the back, one guy hunched his shoulders, closed his eyes in some kind of ecstasy, then hissed, "Smoking!"

There was a small bar where you could get beer, wine, apple juice, but no one cared about the booze. It was Sunday night, when anyone could sit in. These were the kind of maniacs who went out to play in any weather.

A club without hookers looked good to me. No hookers, no strippers, no guys with thick necks or sex tourists like Finn. Just the music.

On the walls were famous jazz pictures: Dexter Gordon with the smoke from his cigarette swirling up; Miles Davis backstage at Carnegie Hall; Dizzy, cheeks blown out, playing his bent horn; Percy Heath and Horace Silver studying sheet music; Satchmo in Egypt by the Pyramids.

The trio on the stage, piano, bass, sax, wasn't bad. They finished and everyone pounded the tables, stamped their feet, clapped; the man with the sax put it gently on a chair, strolled through the crowd and held out his hand to me.

Joe Fallon was wearing a red polo shirt with long sleeves, the collar up, jeans, a black fleece vest. His face pink from playing, he took off his glasses, rubbed his eyes and said, "I'm pretty terrible. I took lessons for years and years, and I know a dentist who still plays a lot better than me. You like my little club?"

"Your club?"

"My kid, Billy's, really. I gave him and some friends the money to set it up and run it. I'm just the angel. A backer. Where else can I play?"

A guitarist came on, but he lost his way on the tune and the crowd booed him. He got it back together long enough to finish; clutching his guitar, skin sweating, he rushed out of the club.

I said, "Let's go get some coffee. I want to talk."

"Come in the back."

There was a kid thought he was Erroll Garner who started playing the piano, a tune named "Red Top". I followed Joe through the bar, down a hallway and into a back room that doubled as an office.

He put his arm around my shoulders. "It's so good to see you. How's Lily? You brought her home?"

"Yes."

"Good. That's good. If I can help . . . You hungry, Art? Billy's bringing some food over from Pastis, because I'm starving. He always brings extra in case some musician stops by. Anyway, I want for Billy to meet you. He's a good kid."

From the club, through the paper-thin wall, the music rolled in to Joe's room. The shelves were jammed with jazz books, original Blue Notes albums, postcards. A table held another stack of records, a couple of phones, piles of paper. There was an old leather sofa, a couple of armchairs. From a fridge, Fallon took a bottle of wine and held it up.

"White OK?"

"Sure."

"You got my invitation?" Fallon sat in a chair, leaned over and took off his loafers. No socks. "My feet are killing me."

"Yeah. They were killing you in Paris."

Joe smiled. "Feet. Knees. I'm a mess, Artie. I'm a fallible guy here, but then what do you expect when you turn forty, right, man? You've been home long?"

"Not long."

"Look, I know a great doctor at Sinai for Lily. He's a

neurological guy, the best, the Pope of neuros. And if your insurance won't cover, you know, hey."

"You left Vienna after me?"

"Next morning. Straight to London, got the first flight home. I should have called, but Billy needed me. Kids."

"No other stops?" I unzipped my jacket.

Joe glanced at me. "What are you talking about?"

"Making conversation." I took off my jacket so he could see the weapon.

"You've got a gun with you?"

"Old habit. I was a cop."

"You're not going to kill me, are you Artie?" He laughed. "My playing's not that terrible." He paused. "What the fuck am I talking about?" He poured the wine into a couple of glasses, then looked up as his son came through the door.

A carbon copy of Joe without the glasses, Billy struggled with a tray, set it down on the desk.

"Hey, Dad."

Fallon introduced us. The son was in his early twenties. He shook my hand, then set out the food, the steak and fries, the bread and salad.

"You eating with us, Billy?"

"I already ate. Have fun," he said and went into the club to catch the rest of the act.

Joe Fallon fell on the food. "I'm sorry," he laughed. "I was so fucking hungry."

I wasn't hungry. I watched him eat. He tossed me a pack of cigarettes. Out of the blue, he said, "Wasn't your dad KGB, Art?"

"What's that have to do with anything?"

"I was just remembering. He was a real guy's guy, wasn't he? He did the business. He had a real job, he went out in the morning and came home at night, and in between he stood up for the Party, the country, all that."

Joe couldn't shake his past, or mine. I kept on smoking and finished the wine.

He said, "Isn't that right?"

"Sure, I guess."

"Then they dumped him, I remember. My parents talked about it. It was a famous thing in our school. People whispered. It must have been tough on you."

I waited.

"Your mother gave the game away. She was always talking about politics. I never heard anyone else talk like that. Very seductive. She was really good looking, wasn't she? All us boys were crazy about her."

"Go to hell."

"Sorry. Christ, I didn't mean anything. It was a compliment. I loved your mom." Fallon leaned over the table, and put his hand on my arm. "I just had a really great idea."

I waited.

"Come and work with me, Artie. What do you need this security business shit for? We could have fun and you'd make some money, I was thinking of opening more clubs, uptown, in Europe maybe, put jazz back on the map, get the word out. Maybe set up a small record label, I've been wanting that. You could use the money, I know that. You don't want to be in hock to Tolya Sverdloff all your life."

"I'll make you a deal."

"Anything," he said.

"You tell me some stuff I want to know and I'll come and work for you if you want, OK? You have any socks?"

"What?"

"I need some air. It's cold. You'll need your socks."

He laughed. "I hate socks. I'll get some off Billy. He'll be here all night long. I'll get my kid's socks if you want me to put on socks so bad." He humored me; he thought I was nuts because of Lily.

When I looked at Fallon, I could barely remember little Joey Fialkov, the kid who fixed everything. He remembered me; he had the details of my whole life on file in his head.

I kept the tone light. "You still want to be in my gang?"

"What?"

"You wanted to be in my gang when we were kids."

"Sure," Fallon said. "Or you could be in mine. So what do you want to talk about?"

Joe Fallon put on the socks, then his shoes, the black sheepskin jacket, and what looked like Dizzy Gillespie's beret. He followed me out of the club.

We walked to the end of the street where the bike path follows the river. It was deserted. I had no real plan, but the underground club made me feel trapped, no windows, my back to the wall. It was Fallon's club, him and the kid who was a dead-ringer for him. On the river, thick white mist was settling on the water and you couldn't see the other side; Jersey was lost to view.

342

"These fucking socks are too damn big, they're all scrunched up. Jesus, Artie, let's go the fuck back inside. Or come to my house, or something, this is nuts."

Fallon played the part so well I started to doubt myself. Maybe I was wrong. Maybe it was only Zhaba who beat up Lily and killed the others. Maybe Fallon was only a good-natured businessman, rich, easy going, who loved Stan Getz, and I resented him for liking my music as if he'd stolen it from me. He dug in his pocket for gloves, then found a pack of smokes and offered me one. He lit one for himself.

I said, "I asked you in Vienna if you knew Levesque and you said 'Who *was* he?' not 'Who is he?', as if you knew he was dead."

"What? I don't know, maybe I thought he was dead. I meet a ton of people all the time."

"Did you think it?"

"Maybe I did. So what? Maybe I remembered after, I would have told you if I thought it was such a big deal. I probably did some business with him way back when."

"When was that?"

"Christ, who the hell can remember?"

"Give it a try, Joe."

"Do we have to do this out here?"

"I need the exercise."

"I honest to God don't remember, so give me a clue."

"He ran a model agency."

Fallon looked out at the river, one hand in his pocket. "I'm thinking."

"Good."

"I seem to remember something back when the

343

Soviet Union was opening up, you know, and I went back. People suddenly realized the women were gorgeous — what we always knew, right, but everyone else thought they were just fat old babushkas. Levesque, if he was the guy, he had this idea about importing them. One thing maybe led to the other, maybe he was on the make. Is that right?"

"You tell me."

"He had some kind of model agency or marriage bureau, something like that."

"Go on."

"A few of the girls got their name in the *New York Magazine*. 'Super Natashas', they called them. He made some dough."

"What else?"

"I think I heard something about him going down in a plane crash, though. I'm going to freeze my balls off out here."

We walked some more. By the time we were at Canal Street, a car rolled slowly by, blue and red lights flashing. A young cop on the job leaned out of the window, checking the path for drunks before they froze to death and the police got another bad rap.

The car stopped, the uniform leaned out again. "Everything OK?"

Fallon made a move towards the cop as if to tell him I had a gun, but I got in front of him and said, very pally, cop to cop, "Hey, how's things over at the First?" and mentioned a guy I knew who used to work there. We exchanged greetings, then they rolled up the window, pulled slowly away. Fallon was alone with me.

Fallon said, "Listen, Art, I'll tell you anything you want, but can we go inside? My place, if you want, it's a couple blocks."

"I had a real hard time getting stuff on Levesque, no pictures, no real files, no nothing."

"There were lots of guys like that cashing in on the Russian thing, so what?"

"There's something else."

"Can we please, please, go indoors. Listen, you know what, I'm going." He started to jog. "You can come or not, or fucking shoot me." He smiled. "But I'm not going to freeze to fucking death out here. You can get hypothermia like this, or frostbite, I was reading this book about Everest and how fast you can get it. I'm not doing business without my toes."

I grabbed his arm hard. "Not yet." I was buying time, hoping Sonny Lippert got my message and knew where to meet me.

"There was a woman."

Fallon smiled. "Ain't it the truth?"

"Martha Burnham."

He turned towards me, said, "What the fuck's a Martha Burnham?" His eyes flickered, the lids coming down double-time behind the glasses. He was nervous.

He said, "You know, I really hated you, Artie. It's amazing how the past can keep a grip on you, you can't even imagine how much I hated my life when we were kids."

"You wanted mine so you hated me?"

"Loved. Hated. Both."

"But you were the kid who could fix anything."

345

"Sure. It got me friends. My parents were nothing. My sister was training up as a Party hack."

"She was a scary girl," I said.

He was trapped in a past where he remembered every detail so clearly he could pick them up and examine them when he needed to; it was his way of laying blame for his childhood. Joey was the good-looking member of the family; the sister was a girl who let you feel her up, then reported you. I could still see her, her blouse pulled tight across her breasts, the young Pioneer scarf tied too tight around her floury white neck.

Joey's sister, with her ardent face, the pale, serious little Communist with the studious pallor, the blonde braids wound around her head, could sniff out dissent in the school hallway. When she sang Party songs, her eyes shone with religious fervor.

My parents used to laugh about the Fialkovs, but we loved Joey. Joey always knew there was something better out there and he made us all love him for seeing it.

"This is ancient history, Joe, it's bullshit, no one cares, not me, not anyone. If it's eating you up, go see a fucking shrink."

"You didn't know my life," he said.

"Lucky me."

"Then I met you in Paris and you were just another miserable fucker like the rest of us with a plateful of trouble, and I could help you."

"Like you always did."

"Something like that."

He was scanning the West Side Highway for a cab,

346

but none passed. I grabbed Joe Fallon's arm and kept hold of him.

He jerked out of my grasp. "Listen, I'm going. Come or don't come." Fallon started across the West Side Highway against the light. "If you shoot me it won't help Lily, though, will it?"

There was no sign of Sonny Lippert when we got to Staple Street. It was a narrow alley and Fallon stopped in front of a squat nineteenth-century house. He turned the key in the lock. "Come on in."

A light came on inside Fallon's front door.

I said, "Who's in there?"

"It's on a timer."

"After you."

"I'm glad you came, Artie," he said, and I followed him.

The living room had white walls, a high ceiling, pale floors with silky kilims on them, high windows, sky-lights. A Steinway piano stood in one corner. There was a pair of pale-green silk sofas, a red leather Barcelona chair, a low glass coffee table.

Fallon shucked his jacket onto a chair, went to a table in the corner, got a bottle of a single malt I never heard of, and poured the whiskey into two heavy glasses. He perched on the arm of the sofa.

"So what's this about, Artie? I mean what the fuck are you carrying on like Dirty Harry or something? What's on your mind?"

On the wall were a Diebenkorn, a Hockney drawing, a couple of Cartier Bresson photographs. Fallon saw me

347

look at them, smiled, kicked off his shoes. He pulled off the socks that were too big for him.

I said, "You ever have any dealings with Yugoslavia?"

"What?"

"You heard me. You do business with Bosnia, Serbia, the rest of them?"

"I went to Belgrade when I was a kid. My mother had cousins, they got me some gig at a summer camp, two weeks, the only two decent weeks in my fucking life."

"You held onto that?"

"What?"

"Maybe you had a thing for the Serbs?"

"You think I'm a warlord, check out the gold chains." He burst out laughing, that rolling merry laugh, then poured himself another drink.

"Maybe you were doing funny money in the early nineties, maybe you wanted to keep some of it in different accounts, maybe you put some in Levesque's account, then decided it was a pain in the ass, it wouldn't look kosher, a good guy like you with a wife who wanted you to clean up your act."

"Very smart."

"It got screwed up because you decided to let it lie but someone tried to forge a check on it."

"Who's that?"

"Martha Burnham."

He finished the drink. "You spin a good little tale, Artemy Maximovich Ostalsky, but you don't believe it." He used my Russian name ironically. There was a pale wood desk opposite one of the green sofas and he went towards it.

I said, "Sit down."

Fallon sat on a chair. "I'll tell you what, Art, give me your gun and I'll tell you everything."

"What?"

"I'll trade you. Information for the gun." He bunched his shoulders as if they ached. "You said Lily could recover if she had the information. Her memory, I mean. Didn't you say that?"

I waited.

"I'll trade you Lily's memory for your gun. Fair trade?"

"It depends."

"What on? You don't think I killed Levesque, do you?"

"What?"

"Christ, you don't think I'm that good, do you? I mean I couldn't crash a plane with 167 people on it, could I? I mean I'm not such a big bastard."

"You could get Levesque's name on the list. That's what I'd do. I'd find someone who could fix the passenger list. He didn't have any family, the bodies were trapped in the fuselage, so who knew or saw?"

"Go on."

"So Levesque, who maybe knew something about you, who you did business with in Russia, women, models, whores, has this account. Someone writes their name on a check but doesn't wait for the teller to confirm the signature. It's maybe a forgery, so people start paying attention. The bank looks into it and discovers Levesque is dead, otherwise the account could lie around, the bank wouldn't even know he's dead necessarily. This stirs up attention. People pay attention to Levesque. Is he dead? Isn't he? Who's writing his name? You're connected to this, you feel maybe you're unclean."

"Yes?"

"Someone who isn't the bank hires Keyes to look into this weird little detail, and I'm looking for a job in Europe, and I'm good at paper trails and there was maybe a Russian connection and I can do the language, so they put me on the job."

Glass in his hand, face compressed with tension, he listened carefully. "OK."

"You found out it was me." I glanced around the room. The skylights were high up, there were no other windows, the door was at the end of the space that was fifty, sixty feet long. I paced up and down, watching him.

He said, "There's no one else, just us, man. You're eating yourself up with paranoia."

"You were freaked out I was on this job."

"No, glad."

"What?"

"I was glad."

"The meeting in the bookstore wasn't an accident."

"What do you call an accident? Two Americans in an English bookstore in Paris? So read Henry James. Happens all the time."

"You wanted to clean up your life."

"For Dede's sake," he said.

"And I come along and I find stuff out and you can't really climb out, you need to dump it all, meaning me."

"You were always my past."

I said, "What about the trade? The gun for the information, the weapon for Lily's memory."

There were no other witnesses. Momo Gourad was dead. Martha Burnham was dead. The only person who knew what had really happened was Lily, and she couldn't remember. They did that to her. They hurt her and they took her. I tossed the gun onto the sofa.

Fallon didn't touch it. He settled onto the red chair where he could reach it, but he didn't touch it, just crossed one foot over his knee and massaged his bare foot.

"What do you want, Artie?"

"You know what I want."

"At least sit down and stop wandering around, will you?"

I said, "Let's start all over again. Let's cancel the bullshit and start over."

I pulled over a chair, sat near Fallon, found a cigarette, looked around the room again, kept my peripheral vision on the weapon.

He sipped his drink. "Where do you want to start?"

I gulped mine. "With the fact that you were Eric Levesque."

34

"You ever been to Denver Airport, Artie? They got these crazy announcements on a loop that keeps calling out names: Mr Cheese, Dick Cheese, Mrs Hard, Hillary Hard, I swear to God, like that, it goes on and on and I was stuck there once on my way to Aspen, for hours, and they keep calling for a Levesque, Leo, or Leon, I don't know, maybe it was Herman. I added the Eric." Fallon was consumed with the details.

"Go on."

"You're right, it got to be a pain in the ass, all those accounts and names I couldn't remember. I would have let it be, I wasn't greedy, there was only a few hundred thou in the Levesque account." He found some cigarettes and played with the cellophane, peeling it, twisting it. "Then someone forged the check. I had someone at the bank who knew someone who kept an eye on those things for me."

"You figured out it was Martha Burnham."

"Not right away."

"You hired Keyes?"

"Yes. Sure. Someone forges my check, does a real sloppy job, the bank finds out Levesque's dead. Whoever's forging a dead man's check must be doing it to call attention to the whole deal. I figure someone's pissed off with me. Someone wants to stir things up a little with me in the middle. Maybe the tax guys found out. I do what everyone else does. I have a good accountant, I don't see why I should give all that money to the government, you know? I'm a Republican."

"I was an accident?"

"Sure."

"When did you find out Keyes put me on the job?"

He laughed, the throaty laugh. "I couldn't believe it. It made me laugh so hard I thought I'd bust a gut. Artie Cohen was chasing my other self for a bad check, and I thought, what should I do? I decided I'd let you do the job, then tell you about it and we could have some laughs together."

"What about Lily?"

"I had no idea you two were connected. Someone heard Lily was nosing around in London. Then I find out you're on the case for Keyes. Then I hear she's your lady. I figured maybe you put your girlfriend to work on it."

"You weren't so sure I'd stop when I found out who forged the check?"

"Something like that."

"But you thought you could fix everything like you always did?"

"I thought we could fix it together like we used to."

"You're a real sick guy."

He said, "I'm the guy the system invented."

"Oh please. Can the clichés. Your people beat her up. Raped her."

"You're nuts. I wouldn't hurt her. I didn't even know who she was at first."

I was silent.

"Lily must have heard something from you that made her suspicious," he went on. "She calls a million people looking for information about Levesque and the whores, she gets in touch with Marti Burnham who's some kind of expert on prostitution who cranks it all up, and some cretinous enforcer who knows about the Visno thing shows up."

"Your guy."

He didn't answer.

"Lily led you back to Martha," I said.

"Tell you the truth, I'd forgotten all about Marti Burnham, but Lily seeing her, and then you catching on, wised me up, and I remembered. A wallet of mine had disappeared years ago, credit cards, everything. I didn't even know there were blank checks in it. I thought I lost it at some kind of benefit for Marti's shelter, there were hundreds of people, it could have been anyone. I never thought about it again. She must have found it."

"You killed Martha."

"I don't kill people, Artie."

"So he was your creep, the toad, Zhaba."

He pulled out a cigarette and lit it.

"I bet you never even had to tell him. You just mentioned someone was getting in your way," I said.

He was silent.

354

"Who will rid me of this turbulent priest?"

"Something like that."

"But you knew who he was, you saw he got paid, this monster who killed and raped Katya Slobodkin, Lily, Martha Burnham, the girl behind the billboard. He was the bastard who pimped for the women from Visno."

"I didn't know about any girls getting beaten up when Lily first called Martha," he said.

"You don't bother with the details."

Fallon said, "Martha was a very nice woman, but she was a pain in the ass, she was crazy about me, she had these fantasies after Dede died that I'd marry her. I didn't mean for Marti to get hurt or Lily."

We sat and talked, two civilized guys in a nice house in New York; in his bare feet, Fallon sipped the whiskey.

What proof did I have? How could I make the case? Where was Sonny? All the time I was listening for Sonny, a taxi, a car. No one came.

"He got off easy," I remembered Eva saying after Zhaba died. He got off easy. I didn't want Fallon off easy, I wanted it public, I wanted his past to destroy him because it was the only thing that scared him.

"I'm a businessman," he said. "I make money, sometimes I help other people make money."

From outside I could hear the scrape of snowplows. Otherwise it was quiet.

"We're really the same guy, Artie. We both made it out of Russia. Did OK in New York. Both Americans. What's the difference between us, really? I mean, honest to God?" He grinned. "Except maybe I can play the sax a little."

I kept my mouth shut and the silence made him uncomfortable. He said, "Lily should keep her causes simple, you know. What's the point of saving the world when it doesn't want to be saved?"

"What about the women?"

"They're not going to medical school, Art. They're not Americans. What the hell else can they do? You think I'm any different from your friend Sverdloff with his fancy whorehouse? You think we're any different, you and me, or me and any other corporation? You take jobs from people you've never met. You're not a real cop anymore. You take security jobs, you do investigations, who are you working for? You think firms like Keyes don't take jobs from guys like me? They work for anyone who pays them. They protect creeps you can't even imagine. Long as the money flows."

"Bullshit."

"Those women, you saw the places they come from, there are millions of them."

I thought of something: Billy. Fallon's son, Billy, who gave up time to work with refugees. "You had your kid in it too?"

"My kid does what he does. What do you want? You want a big finale with strings? You want an apocalyptic episode? What? Don't be such a Russian. Let's listen to some music," he said and got up and went to the stereo. "Anything special you want to hear?" He put on a CD, then turned back to me.

"What about the roller-coaster?" I said.

"What roller-coaster?" He laughed. "We could have settled it all in New York, here at home, over dinner. I told you when we met in Paris. You wouldn't let me help. You didn't believe me. I didn't attack your Lily," he said. "It was an accident. The Serb prick who did it is bottom of that pond."

"You knew."

He laughed. "More than that."

"You wanted him dead."

"I let you have him. You did me a favor. Zhaba was getting crazy. He was selling the dolls on the side."

"Dolls?"

"The Natashas. The whores."

I could feel the other gun in my waistband under my sweater.

"You wanted me to kill him."

"It was only fair. You got your revenge. I let you have it. So now it's over."

"Tell me something."

"What?"

"How did you connect me and Lily? I didn't tell you about her until we met at the bookstore."

Joe Fallon got up and went to the desk. I followed him.

"Take it easy. I'm just going to show you something." He pulled open a drawer, took out a picture and tossed it on the desk. "Go on, take a look."

I picked it up. On New Year's Eve, before we got on the London wheel, we had had our picture taken along with everyone else. In the chaos afterwards, I forgot about it. In the picture were Lily and me and, behind us, another couple. At the edge of the frame, wearing a wig and a New Year's party hat, was Zhaba.

I couldn't tell what time it was when Sonny arrived; my watch had stopped. When I heard the car pull up outside Fallon's place, I was ready to turn Fallon over, let the system take him, make it hard for him. Let his kids see him for what he was.

Fallon heard the car too. He was watching me, his eye on the gun. I didn't move. *People Time* played on the stereo.

Fallon said, "I think it's the most sublime album, you know, and Getz was dead a few months later. What would you trade to make a sound like that, Artie?"

I didn't answer.

"Another drink?"

I looked at Fallon and saw the pale handsome kid I once knew. He would always get off easy. If I turned him over to the system, there would be the lawyers, the friends, the appeals. And all the time he'd be in New York, near me, watching; he would be a few blocks away from me and Lily.

There was no hard evidence; the only person who could put Fallon in the picture was Lily, who couldn't remember. But I knew it was Fallon she'd met at the Ritz that night she was attacked, I knew.

Maybe he called her in Paris and said he was a friend of Martha's. Shall we have a drink? I'd like to help. And Lily, in love with the idea that you could help other people, would have said, sure. He was charming. Maybe they had a couple of martinis and he said, there's a woman I'd like you to meet, one of the women who got hurt. She doesn't like going out in public. Lily, already

358

obsessed with the cause, would have agreed. I'll meet you, he might have said. Lily would have gone to the empty apartment near the rue de Rivoli where Zhaba was waiting for her. He beat her up. Raped her. Hacked off her hair. Fallon made it happen. He did that to her.

"Been to the Ritz Hotel in Paris recently, Joe?"

Distracted, he looked at me and, without thinking, said, "Sure. All the time. Why?"

35

Fallon was dead when Sonny Lippert came through the door. Enveloped in his camel-hair coat, his face withered from fatigue, Sonny hurried in, looked at Fallon, then me, went over to the stereo and turned off the music.

"So he went for you. The son-of-a-bitch came after you. Art? Isn't that right? Look at me, man, look at me."

He shook me, put his hand on my shoulder where I was sitting on the floor, back to Fallon, head down. "Come on," he said and helped me up. "Isn't that right?"

I nodded.

"Say it. He pulled a gun and he was going to fire, he threatened you, and you had to do it. It was self-defense, no question. Isn't that right?"

Already Sonny was rummaging in Fallon's desk drawer, shuffling papers, looking for a weapon. He found a gun and tossed it on top of the table.

"Say it." He poured out a big drink, shoved it in my hand, watched me drink it.

"Yes. Self-defense. He pulled a gun on me," I said.

Without missing a beat, Sonny said "son-of-a-bitch" again, then told me he had the information I wanted.

One of his cronies had traced the Paris apartment where Lily was attacked to a real-estate agent who, when the cops finally got to him and leaned on him hard, revealed he managed it for Eric Levesque.

Sonny picked up the phone on Fallon's desk now and called 911, called his office, talked to guys he knew, guys which, as he said, owed him plenty. His voice was hard and certain; he cut through the bureaucratic bullshit. I sat on the edge of Fallon's green silk sofa which seemed like the edge of the world, and waited for the cops to come.

They took Fallon's body away. Sonny went down to his office in the Special Prosecutor's division to fix the paperwork, I went home, slept a few hours and got cleaned up. Then I went back to Lily's clinic and waited in the hallway until she woke up.

I sat on the side of her bed and told her everything as best I could. London, Paris, the Czech border, Vienna, Bosnia. I told her all of it: how I started on the Levesque case and it caught her up, and how they hurt her because of it. I told her about the women.

I told her nobody was pushed from the glass pod on the big wheel in London on New Year's Eve. As gently as I could, I told her it was a hallucination. Not knowing if she was taking it all in, I held her hand. She kept her eyes shut and listened to me.

When I was done, she opened her eyes, raised a hand to her head and felt her hair where it stuck out around the bandages.

"It's too short," she said.

"I'm so sorry, sweetheart."

Slowly, she said, "It's OK, you can stop now Artie."

"I'm sorry."

"Artie?"

"What's that, sweetheart?"

"You smell nice."

"Good."

"I think I know who you are."

So I shut up. I wasn't sure if she was faking it or someone had told her or she really knew who I was, but I wasn't in this for the philosophy, I didn't care so long as I was with her. I put my arms around Lily and said, "I know you do."